REQUIEM FOR
NOAH

A SUPERNATURAL MYSTERY

DOUGLAS COCKELL

For Fraser, artist and musician,
And
For Dylan, whose gift for story-telling
enriches these pages.

Published in Ontario, Canada

Hardcover ISBN: 978-1-989733-62-2

Paperback ISBN: 978-1-989733-63-9

Ebook mobi version ISBN: 978-1-989733-64-6

Ebook epub version ISBN: 978-1-989733-65-3

Library and Archives Canada Cataloguing in Publications

Requiem For Noah is the 2nd book in the Requiem Series.

Book One is titled *Requiem For Thursday.*

CHAPTER ONE

"So where am I exactly?" Weiss asked.

A voice called out from the darkness, "Well, you're on the lakebed under Hamilton Harbour."

"You mean right under the shipping lanes?"

"Well, yeah, sure. Leading into a couple of the industrial loading docks. If you watch for it, you'll see a couple of shadows passing overhead—lake freighters coming in through the lift bridge. Hamilton's the busiest port on Lake Ontario."

Detective Eilert Weiss of the Halton District Police Services stared into the encircling gloom. Across his field of vision was a steady drift of tiny particles—of what, he had no idea—but they streamed like gentle snow until a current in the water shifted, and the flakes pulsed this way or that in the lights of the submersible rover.

"Okay, so I'm here. What do I do?"

"You don't actually have to *do* anything; just watch. The movements of the cameras are those of the original operator of the rover—a scientist from Canada Inland Waters. What you're watching is a recording, remember."

"Yeah, I get it. So this scientist is looking around on the lakebed. What's he looking for?"

"It was *she* actually. Obstructions, pollutants…guidance for dredgers, for water treatment plants. Anything useful, really. There are two overlapping cameras on the rover, so you're getting a stereoscopic 3D image. Oh, here…"

The voice behind Weiss went on, an unseen hand touching his shoulder. "Watch for a momentary jump in the image. It's barely noticeable. That's where we think the actual tampering began." The voice had a pleasant east coast cadence.

Behind bulky virtual reality goggles, Weiss blinked. "There. Was that it? Just a little shift in the picture?"

"Yes, that was probably it." McNeil, the first officer of the *Cormorant*, sounded a little miffed. He didn't like the stereoscopic high definition image Weiss was enjoying being referred to as a "picture," as though he were watching a seventies rerun. "Me, I'm just following along on the flatscreen monitor. You have a much better view on that VR headset."

Weiss sat upright in his chair, his topcoat still draped over his knees. "Man, you're not kidding about the view. These goggle things are incredible. It's like I'm standing on the silt, looking around from side to side like I was there. It's eerie." He gave a little palm-down wave. "Hey, Prem, you wouldn't believe this. It's so real."

Detective Prem Joshi, a comfortably squat figure with large hooded eyes, was sprawled at a booth-like table behind Weiss, holding a mug of instant coffee. "Plodding around under forty feet of polluted scum? Enjoy yourself, Eilert." Joshi crossed his feet on the opposite bench and tipped his hat forward to block his view of the monitor.

The *M.V. Cormorant's* small cabin with its computer desk and printer might have been someone's office, except that the portholes had brass fittings and the light switch was on a conduit that ran up the wall and across the ceiling to a caged bulb.

McNeil cast a disapproving glance at Joshi. "There's no 'plodding' going on. In fact, at this point, the rover would be floating about shoulder height above the mud to avoid clouding. It's murky enough down there. Oh, and you're at twenty-two metres, not forty feet."

He leaned over Weiss's shoulder and adjusted the flatscreen that allowed him to follow the detective's point of view, albeit in a degraded 2D form.

Weiss nodded, a movement that had no effect whatsoever on the steady panorama he was seeing. "Still, I can see a ways. It's like peering through heavy sleet, though. Great, so what am I supposed to observe?"

"Okay, watch here." A few seconds winked by on the tiny green readout. "There. Do you see it? It caught the attention of the rover operator and she's turned towards it. Do you see? She's rotating the cameras slightly."

At first, Weiss didn't catch what it was that made the original operator of the rover swivel its cameras to the right. Weiss had the uncanny sensation of his eyes turning to one side, as though he himself had turned his head. And then: "Yeah, okay. It looks like...like..."

McNeil sniffed. "Say it, Detective."

The implication was, 'I told you so.'

Behind the heavy VR headpiece, Weiss's eyes were wide. "It's a goddamn railroad track."

"Exactly."

Joshi pushed his hat back on his head and put down his coffee.

"On the bottom of the harbour?" Weiss continued, "What... I don't understand. Is the harbour bottom around here settled land that's submerged—like some sort of old locomotive spur servicing the docks or something like that?"

"Well, now," said McNeil, "that's exactly what we all started speculating, of course—how could this be? That's before we caught on to what we were *really* seeing. Suffice it to say, don't waste your time thinking about how there could be a railway track on the bottom of Lake Ontario."

Weiss felt himself moving forward and intercepting the line of steel rails and wooden sleepers. "She's following it. Lining the rover up over it. The operator, I mean."

Joshi sat up and put his rubber-soled shoes down on the decking. McNeil took a step back so Joshi could see better. "Yeah. Just what anybody would do, right?"

As though he were walking slowly along a deserted country railway line, Weiss drifted ahead, plowing through the angled hail of particles. The lights mounted on the remote rover made the closest particles glow like flies near a lamp. It was as though Weiss were moving within a luminous bubble, but the beams had little penetration and the near distance was a grey void lit only by shafts of weak sunlight from above.

A shadowy armature emerged from the distance, developing like a Polaroid photo. Weiss narrowed his eyes, which didn't help. At last, the shape entered the rover's glowing bubble.

"My God, is that a track signal? One of those warning light things?"

The wooden post held a little metal flag out at a right angle. The flag was a washed-out red with two white stripes. Its inward end encased a couple of coloured lights, barely recognizable as red and green.

"Yup. Just what you'd expect along a rail line. Right?" McNeil tapped his flat screen with a fingernail. "It's all there: crushed stone on the roadbed, creosoted ties, iron cleats, track signals…"

Weiss marvelled at the sensation of actually standing there within touching distance of the post, frustrated that he couldn't turn his head to look around. Only the rover operator could have done that earlier that morning when she was making this recording.

"How long does the line go on for?"

"Well, we don't actually know, but, again, as you'll see, it doesn't really matter."

The rover surprised Weiss by surging ahead, and he was drawn further into the illusion of plodding along a railway through slow-motion billows of sand. After two or three minutes, the grey distance took on a darkening solidity.

"What's that?" Weiss shouted, his voice too loud for the little cabin. "Up ahead! It's hard to make out through all this drifting stuff—what the hell is that, anyway?"

"The drifting is normal," McNeil said. "Silt, waterborne plant life, particulate matter. The lake water is a real soup near a big industrial city like Hamilton. As for the shape coming up? Well, I told you on the phone what we found."

"Yeah, okay, but, Jesus! A station? A railway station?" Weiss turned toward McNeil's voice, but oddly the image on his headset remained steady. "It was hard for me to take you literally on the phone. But… Holy shit, it's a real country railway station. Are you seeing this, Prem?"

Joshi, not buying into the illusion, grumbled and returned to his coffee. "Find out if they sell sandwiches."

Detachment was more difficult for Weiss. His eyes were fixed on the three-dimensional space he was moving through. It was utterly convincing. A microphone on the rover picked up the steady booming of freshwater currents and the intermittent whirr of the rover vehicle's electric screws.

"Circa 1920, wouldn't you say? Cute. A Hollywood designer's idea of a country railway station. Oh, come on… I don't believe this. All you need is Judy Garland singing Atchison, Topeka…"

"And Santa Fe." McNeil groused, "Right. Except that you're standing on the bottom of Lake fucking Ontario."

"Does the rover operator move right up to it?" Weiss said in wonder.

"Of course. Wouldn't you? Believe me, the best is yet to come."

Weiss moved in his wooden armchair, his right hand groping out into non-existent water. "I don't know. This thing is so realistic, 3D and all. I might not have had the nerve to step up on that platform. The rover operator—she must have been a brave woman. I'd have called in the Marines at his point."

"Huh, to do what?"

Weiss ignored that, dealing with the uncanny sensation of mounting a set of wooden stairs. "Okay, so I'm walking up onto the train platform."

"You're actually floating, but fine," the first officer said patiently.

"It *feels* like walking. Well, now, look at this. There's a poster on the wall: 'Day Trips to Port Dover.' And there's a painted sign above the windows... What does that say? 'Ridgeway Heights?' And there's one of those old-fashioned baggage carts with a built-in weigh scale; I think I see another one down at the end of the platform. My God, that one's got baggage on it—suitcases, a trunk. Window to my right. Jesus! Is she going to look *in?* Oh, there she goes, rotating the cameras. I'm looking in the window of the station..." Weiss leaned forward, gripping the chair arms.

"So, it's a...waiting room in there." He gestured blindly towards McNeil. "The rover's lights are pointing the wrong way —down the platform. It should be dark in there, inside the station. Pitch black, but it's not. There's some kind of illumination. How can that be? How deep are we anyway?"

"Not very. Six fathoms now according to the pressure gauge on the rover which corresponds to our topographic chart of the harbour. We checked. All of the readouts from the rover are normal and accurate."

"God, Prem, I hope you're seeing this. Benches, a ticket

wicket—you know, with the little bars? More posters. Nice old-fashioned woodwork. Vertical board and batten panelling."

Weiss heard McNeil's voice near his ear. "Don't get too caught up in the details, Detective. Remember, in the real world, it should be dark inside the station. There's nothing normal about that illumination."

"Right, so…damn. Is that an electric light fixture? Up there on the ceiling inside?"

"That's what someone wanted you to see. So, what does that tell you?"

"That this is impossible. I'm on the bottom of the harbour." Weiss half lifted out of his chair. "Oh, no. The rover operator's going inside, through the door of the station building."

Joshi got up, his voice calm. "Relax, Eilert. It's a remote rover; you're wearing a damn headset."

Weiss sagged back. "The researcher—how did she even open the door? It's just swinging aside. The rover's dragging cables, right? Control tethers back to the surface?"

"Yup. All the way to the *Cormorant*. Again, Detective, don't get too caught up in the details. It'll drive you crazy. Like it did us."

Weiss swivelled his head in a fruitless attempt to look around. It was a large room with a row of bench seats along the walls and down the centre of the floor. He could make out the yellowish varnish colour of the seatbacks, although strangely enough, the drifting murk of waterborne particles was as thick in here as it had been out on the tracks. Weiss was puzzled to see that none of the drifting silt had settled on the benches, and he could easily make out the long slats and grooves of the carpentry.

"It's gloomy even with the overhead light, but I can make out a rack of newspapers." The recording Weiss was watching showed that the woman operating the rover was attempting to get a closer look at the papers. Maybe she was trying to see a date on the publications, but the billowing movement of the lake water wouldn't allow for that kind of detail. "Huh. Okay, now this is crazy; the newspapers don't even look wet."

There was a humming sound as the stereoscopic cameras rotated again, giving Weiss the eerie feeling that he was turning his head involuntarily. The rover operator was following the curve of the bench as it met the far corner of the room. The lights on the rover seemed to have no effect in here, and the feeble illumination from the single ceiling fixture allowed only an oppressive gloominess.

The image wobbled a little, as though the operator accidentally goosed one of the drive screws, and Weiss jumped out of his chair. He stood straight, pressing the VR goggles tight against his face. The cable that ran down into the computer tugged at his temple.

"What is *this*? Omigod!"

McNeil, who had rerun this part of the recording a dozen times, sighed. "Yeah, I know. It took the operator a few minutes to recover, too. In a minute, she'll approach the body."

Weiss sagged back into his chair and his voice took on a matter-of-fact air as though he was reading into his small digital recorder. "The body: male, balding, grey hair, below average height, slight build. Distinctive narrow features. He's wearing… What is that? An old-fashioned suit? Edwardian looking. Pale complexion, but no sign of trauma or decomposition. Head lolling back against the bench."

The first officer laid his hand on Weiss's shoulder and gripped him tightly. "Brace yourself, Detective."

Weiss frowned beneath the heavy headset. "What? Why?" Then suddenly, he bucked under McNeil's hand. "Holy sh…"

The figure on the bench remained sagged in the posture of a splayed corpse, but the eyelids popped open and the three-dimensional high definition eyes stared directly at the cameras of the rover. Directly at Weiss.

Joshi staggered, his cynical pose momentarily shaken.

Only McNeil was amused. "Nice effect, huh? The rover operator peed herself. Remember, at this point, we didn't realize what we were *really* seeing. The data team wasted ten minutes trying to imagine how all of this could be. The operator was so shaken that I sent her home. It was in the middle of all that confusion, with the crew running about, that we got the police involved."

Weiss tightened his grip on the wooden arms of his chair. "When in fact all this…couldn't be. Couldn't be real."

"Exactly." McNeil's voice was calm. "Eventually, cooler heads prevailed and we knew we'd been played. Still, this is unprecedented, so I figured a detective might bring perspective to it. Couldn't hurt, right?"

The image in front of Weiss's face had frozen—the staring eyes fixed, the swirling particles in the water stopped dead still. The playback paused.

"That's fine. You did the right thing. So, sum it up for me. All this—it was what…"

McNeil shrugged. "Call it hacking. All of the software for the rover—the cameras, the processors, the VR headset—you're basically looking at a computer system. And that's what the whole bloody railway scenario is: a simulation, seamless; inserted into real-time video by a sophisticated hacker."

"The body, the posters, all of that are what? Animation?"

"CGI, whatever you want to call it. Of course. The only thing that's real is the currents and the silt—the background in general. All the rest is an incredibly elaborate stunt by a damn clever programmer with talent and money."

Weiss peeled off the VR headset and turned in the chair. "But the eyes—opening up like that at just the right moment."

"When you think of it as a glorified video game, it's not quite so miraculous, but still, the sophistication of the hack is astounding. When I told my daughter about it, she knew what it was right away. Not VR, but AR: augmented reality. It's the big thing in online computer gaming, it seems."

"Then the rover's remote viewing must be wired into the web somehow. That's how a hacker would get into the rover's system."

McNeil gestured at the desktop and its computer. "Our connection is wireless to a router, but we have to be able to share our findings with government labs and scientists, so we need the connectivity. It's standard practice with all government labs, even floating ones like the *Cormorant*. All the same, only a brilliant hacker would have been able to find his way into our camera feed. It's scary that he could. Makes me wonder if anything is safe these days."

Weiss got up, shaking out his coat. "I suppose you can print out a few frames of the video for me, Mr. McNeil. I want a close-up of the face, the full body, the room…and some kind of long shot for reference."

"Sure, still frames are easy, but do you mind telling me why? What are you going to do with them? You sound like you're treating this like a real crime scene. You do understand none of this is real."

"Yes, I get it. But my partner and I are here, and I'm intrigued. Not so much by 'how' it was done. I'm wondering why this brilliant individual went to all this fucking trouble just to scare a cabin full of government scientists. And there's another thing: the face. There was nothing generic or stereotyped about it. It looked to me like a portrait—digital, but full of character, and plausibly ill-favoured."

Joshi nodded. "Ugly, you mean."

"It looked real." Weiss started to put his overcoat on. "Your still images will be fairly high resolution, I hope. As soon as we get your outtakes, I'd like to run the face through some facial recognition software."

McNeil blinked. "Seriously?"

"Something like this—this cyber attack—it was an act of supreme ego. Maybe the culprit signed his work with his likeness. It's worth a shot."

McNeil leaned back against the computer desk and scratched his ear. "What's the crime, exactly?"

"I'm not sure. Public mischief, maybe. Take away all the theatricality and you've got someone screwing with scientific data. That's not in the public good."

———

Leaving the boat, Weiss and Joshi walked down the gangplank to the concrete government wharf. Weiss turned and paused to look back at the red funnel and white superstructure of the *Motor Vessel Cormorant*. The little submersible rover hung on a winch near the stern, its claw-like appendages drooping below a boxy orange shell. The lights and double camera arrangement seemed to stare back at him. Everything was backlit by a threatening storm cloud that cast a blue gloom over the docklands.

"That was different," Joshi offered.

"Yes. A lot more interesting than routine street violence. I'm kind of intrigued." He glanced over his shoulder at Joshi. "Is that okay, Prem? I know we should hand it off to another department, but let's wait a bit."

"Knock yourself out, Eilert, but be careful. Time is taxpayer money as the superintendent is always reminding us."

"I know. You're right. But what we saw—that whole illusion —it must have cost a fortune to pull off. The expertise, the facilities you'd need, the artistry. It's a big deal. I don't want to write it off as a fancy prank."

"But that's what it was."

"Think about the context, Prem. To justify that kind of investment, it either has to *mean* something, or it's part of something much bigger."

Joshi laid his hand on Weiss's back. "Ah, the search for a larger meaning. You're such an optimist."

Weiss laughed. "So, how about the search for where we left the car? You up for that?"

CHAPTER TWO

It was a fairly long drive from the narrow end of Lake Ontario up the gradual slope to North Burlington. When they got back to the District Three Station, Joshi headed for the washroom.

Weiss walked through the reception area and into the corridor leading to the main office. He had one foot on the stairs up to his office when his phone chirped; he pulled it out of his jacket. Lapsing against a glass partition, he looked at the screen and read the text from Detective Toni Beal. He narrowed his eyes, his mind drifting for a moment.

A woman from accounting walked by glancing at him, and he straightened his back. She smiled and walked on.

Still lost in thought, he forgot about the stairs and wandered on until he became vaguely aware that he was standing in the centre of the main office. He stopped, staring at the floor, the strange little face with its digital stare replaying in his mind.

It was less than a minute, but when his head came up slowly, he looked around at the six computer desks, becoming aware of people looking back at him.

He pocketed his phone, catching a smile here and a conspiracy of suppressed laughter there. What was going on?

A uniform with a phone to her ear grinned. "Heading down to archives again, Eilert? I hear it's quiet down there."

Weiss stared her down. "I'm serving..." He straightened his tie. "...and protecting." He turned and resumed his walk back to the stairwell, timing it so that Joshi was ready and just arriving at the stairs.

Joshi waved his own phone at Weiss. "I got the text, too. Heddy is waiting." His eyes grew wistful. "She *needs* you, Eilert."

Weiss gave him a patient look before heading down to the evidence and storage section.

Heddy Nesbit, neat and business-like but with an angelic face, was writing on a clipboard when she saw Weiss. A look of pain passed over her pale, unblemished features, and she swept a wave of silver-grey hair behind her left ear. "Jesus. Eilert Weiss. Why'd it have to be you?"

Weiss was taken aback. "Nice to see you again, too, Heddy." His tone was hurt, shading off into indignation.

Heddy looked at Weiss's partner who, grinning now, kept glancing from her to Weiss. "Hello, Prem. Well, here we all are." She made a defeated gesture with her clipboard. "This way, gentlemen."

They walked between open-faced shelves loaded with boxes and wire baskets and beneath narrow windows high on the walls.

Weiss frowned. "Why have you got a problem with *me* coming down, Heddy? We got a message from Toni Beal that you needed help."

She stopped at an open doorway, looked at him, and stared. "Because I *like* you, Eilert, and I don't want to make your life difficult. I didn't know Toni would send you." She looked at him, her eyes hooded, shaded in pink. She remembered where she was and looked away. "It's in here. A box marked Esc. 119."

Weiss followed, confused. Heddy pulled a cardboard box with a pre-printed label off an upper shelf and laid it on a long sorting table. She pulled the lid, laid it aside, and began displaying yellowish bone fragments on the surface.

Weiss titled his head as he leaned in to look. "Okay, human remains. No surprise there. I figured it was something like that. They've been through forensics testing, I assume."

"Of course."

"A partial skull, vertebrae, ribs. How old?" Weiss asked.

"About a year, they said. Animals scattered the skeleton so we don't have much of it. Bears, foxes—who knows? None of the long bones were left at all."

"Have you got any context for me?"

Heddy pulled up a folding chair and sat down. With her crisp white blouse, she wore black slacks that made her look professional and poised. Her shoes were flats but looked too expensive for browsing cardboard boxes and file folders.

"Kind of interesting. They were found on wooded land up on the edge of the escarpment off Appleby Line, mixed in with fragments of a second, older skeleton. Degraded clothing frag-ments all over the place. Most useful thing—a removable dental bridge with three front teeth."

Joshi was leaning back with his elbow on a shelf. "I heard about this. I thought Toni Beal was following this up herself."

"Oh, she is. It's her case, but she has nothing yet." Heddy gave the two detectives a moment to lift and turn the fragments, then she got up and pulled another box out, sliding it onto the other end of the table.

"What's this?"

Weiss watched her arrange a second grouping of bone frag-ments, being careful to keep the two sets apart: digits, another skull fragment, a scapula. These were darker, abraded, and fragile looking.

"This is box Esc. 120," she said. "Also from the Appleby Line site."

Weiss moved down the table. "The older skeleton. Just how

much older *is* the second set of remains?"

Heddy picked up a darkly stained skull fragment. "These? At least ten years old, although they could be twice that. But like I said, they were found in more or less the same location."

Joshi moved towards the darker fragments. "Hmm. Appleby Line? Is there much development nearby? Houses, apartments?"

Heddy shook her head. "No. Up there is where rich people build their mansions on the slopes and cliffs so they can see for miles right down to the lake. There's a lot of untouched woodland around the houses. We're talking about people with large properties and plenty of privacy."

Weiss smiled. "Toni loves those Dalton Abbey cases. Did we do the forensic testing on these in-house?"

Heddy crossed her arms. "Toni sent all the remains over to the OPP in Orillia for sorting and testing, then they came back here to Halton this week. Toni wanted to see if either set of remains matched a missing person cold case from anywhere in Halton. She hoped the OPP lab would give her something to go on."

"And did they?" Joshi asked, turning a small bone in his fingers.

"The dental trace is promising, but nothing certain yet."

Joshi put the bone down and leaned back against a shelf. "Are you getting to the part where *we* are sent down? This is still Toni and Tom's case."

Heddy gave him a patient look. "You following this, Prem? There were actually two sets of fragmentary remains found mingled at the same site. Okay, the second set is obviously much older, and since the pile of fragments were apparently from two different skeletons, the OPP folks sorted the remains into two separate boxes for labelling before they sent them back —and here they are." She made a gesture that encompassed the whole table.

Weiss looked at Joshi. "The possibility of two sets of bone

fragments ten years apart being related in some way? That *is* interesting."

Joshi scratched his ear. "Buried at the same site? It would mean one less location to be discovered, I suppose. But ten years apart..."

"That's another odd feature," Heddy said. "They weren't actually buried at all. The remains were found in the under-brush by a dog walker."

Weiss had been turning the dental bridge in his hand, the metallic framework still bright. He put it down and shifted his attention back to the older bones. "So, just a couple of body dumps. That's remarkable in itself, that there was no real attempt to conceal the bodies. Appleby Line above the escarpment isn't that remote."

He picked up the older skull, a right side only partial. The weight of the older fragment surprised him; it felt lighter, ready to crumble to dust at the slightest pressure. "Is Toni considering that angle, that this might be a killer who dropped off two bodies in the same location ten years apart?"

"I'm not a detective, but you'd think so, wouldn't you?" Heddy sat gracefully on the metal chair and her arms, bare from her elbows, again folded. Oval nails, a light pink, drummed against her left arm. "It's the easiest way to account for the coincidence of two sets of bones in the same general location. Unusual, but not *Twilight Zone*."

Weiss caught her eye. "Okay, so what's the matter, Heddy? What's bothering you?"

Heddy got up slowly, as though tired, and stood opposite Weiss looking into his pale Nordic eyes before dropping her own gaze to the older fragments. "I just want you to be clear on this. This is Esc. 120, bones sorted out by age from the site. Even a layman can see they're a different colour and texture."

"Yeah, sure. The older set from the same location."

"Exactly. So fragmentary remains again, apparently disarticulated by animals."

Joshi sighed, impatient now. "We *got* it, Heddy. They look totally different."

"Not less than ten years old, judging from the fragility and deterioration. Look at the pitting, the staining."

Weiss shrugged, wondering why Heddy was belabouring the obvious. "Okay," she said at last. "Toni might find something in the missing persons database using the dental prosthesis that will give her an identity for the newer fragments. The bridge looks fairly modern to me. But we've got nothing on this older set except the location. Still, if Toni can identify the new set from the dental records, she'll try to make a connection to the older set from the missing persons database—a family, a workplace, a common location. I mean, that's the way these things go, right?"

Joshi, looking skeptical, scratched his ribs. "But ten years apart? I don't envy her."

Weiss didn't take his eyes off Heddy. "Why do you need us?"

"Well, you see, Eilert, Toni would be wasting her time trying to connect the two sets. I know it's weird that I would be the one to notice this, but even forensics people can miss things if all the evidence points them in another direction. Anyway, I thought somebody should see what I found, so I'm not the only person in the building going nuts."

With that, Heddy took the older skull fragment and stepped along the table to the newer fragments, her movements measured and deliberate.

"Now watch this," she said. "The skull fragment from box 119. About a year old, okay? And now here we have the skull fragment from box 120, the older remains. Ready? Prem, how about a drum roll?"

Prem's smirk did a slow dissolve to surprise as he watched Heddy's hands. "The skull fragments fit together."

"Perfectly."

Weiss dropped his gaze from Heddy's face to the tabletop. "Wait, what? We've got *one* skull? I don't understand. Who screwed up on the dating?"

"We all did, but you can see how it would happen. This older set doesn't look anything like the newer fragments. It's like comparing an archaeology dig to last night's dinner. Of course, when I noticed this, I had to tell someone. It's a miracle I spotted it. I just got curious when I noticed that some of the fragments complemented each other: two skull fragments, similar vertebrae."

Weiss was glancing back and forth. "Let me get this straight. You *are* saying that with all of these bones, there's only *one* skeleton?"

"Unquestionably. Once I started looking, I found another fitting pair in the rib fragments. I'm telling you, Eilert; this is the same individual. This is one body. I figure the reason the fragments crumbled apart in the first place is the difference in strength and texture of the different bits. See? This part of the skull is solid bone still—this other part is almost granular; you could crush it with your fingers."

Weiss stared. "Have you got any scientific precedent that would account for this effect?"

"Well, I suppose if the skeleton was partially immersed in polluted water...but there was no evidence of that. No, I really can't explain this."

Joshi brightened. "Well, at least now we know why they sent *you* down here, Eilert."

Heddy looked at Joshi. "What? What do you mean?"

Weiss closed his eyes. "*Don't* Prem."

Joshi grinned at Heddy. "Eilert's got a rep, you know."

Weiss gave him a warning look. "Prem."

Joshi ignored him. "'Give Eilert the weird shit.' That's what they say upstairs. You have no idea what a joy it is being his partner."

CHAPTER THREE

The photos from McNeil arrived on Weiss's laptop the first thing the next morning. The close-up of the little man in the railway station waiting room stared back at Weiss with the same startling intensity he remembered from the bizarre augmented reality prank.

It was a little less disturbing seeing the face on the flat surface of his laptop, but Weiss was still intrigued. Reduced to two dimensions, the face seemed marginally less real. It occupied that zone techies called the uncanny valley, in which images were completely realistic until you took a second look.

Weiss realized that he might be wasting his time on a fictional individual, but the face was so...particularized. Who would invent that mousy chin, that dipping upper lip that looked like the grill of a BMW? Who would think to inscribe that unsettling lack of symmetry about the eyes?

No—the artist, digital or otherwise, had worked from a willing model, a model who had patiently rehearsed that look of resentful challenge: "Boo," writ large with a side of "fuck you."

Weiss thought about trying to run the image through the database of felons and murderers right from his own computer.

Once again, he nearly gave up. This little gnome of a man wasn't likely to have a history of violence. Corporate fraud, perhaps. Besides, Weiss hated the unfriendly software. With quiet satisfaction, he realized he'd get away with delegating the task.

He saved the single close-up to an SD card and headed down to the main office. He stopped briefly in the doorway to survey the desks full of busy people. Who to bother? To his surprise, a woman near the back looked up at him and smiled. Weiss surged forward to exploit this fleeting moment of vulnerability.

"Hi, Gail."

Gail, a uniformed officer with long straight hair draped over her white blouse, leaned back from her computer screen, put her hands behind her head, and went on smiling. She was ready to talk.

"Eilert."

Weiss held up the SD card. "Do you think you could run this face through a facial recognition database?"

"Sure," she said. "Have a seat."

But she didn't offer a chair. Apparently, she wanted Weiss to sit on the corner of her desk.

"Oh, ah…"

"Relax. It won't be more than ten minutes."

Weiss thought about what it would be like to be perched on the woman's desk for ten minutes like a torch singer on a piano, then chose to lean over and rest his hand there instead. Gail didn't seem to mind, plugging in the card and clicking on its icon.

"It's that file there," Weiss said, pointing at her screen.

Gail double-tapped the folder. The little gnome leapt up to the full size of her screen and she jumped in her seat.

"Omigod!"

A couple of people at nearby desks looked up at them and smiled at Weiss.

Weiss straightened and stroked his moustache in embarrassment. "Sorry. I should have warned you. It's sort of a Halloween picture, isn't it?"

Gail leaned back in her chair with one hand over her heart. She took a deep breath and then peered at the screen again. "I heard you got the strange ones. Hmm. Wait a minute."

She got up, touched Weiss's arm, and walked out to the reception area. Weiss could see her rifling through some of the old flyers on the coffee table and then in the upright magazine rack by the coffee machine. He tried to look casual, straightening the half Windsor knot of his necktie, but it only encouraged the nearby peepers.

At last, Gail found what she was looking for and returned. As she sat back down, she handed Weiss a large-format slick magazine.

It was well worn, but the glossy layout still looked stylish and sophisticated. Weiss studied the cover for a moment. It took him a few seconds to reconcile the dapper tech entrepreneur on the cover with the gnome on Gail's screen, but she was right—it was him.

In the cover spread, the little man had his arms crossed and he looked self-satisfied; a typical pro power pose. He was wearing blue jeans and a black Steve Jobs turtleneck, which was about as formal as tech guys got. It would have been hard to make the odd, mismatched features elegant, but he managed to look affluent.

"I thought I recognized the face," Gail said. "It's what's-his-name, the tech wizard. He's local."

Weiss read the subscript: *Noah Goodwyn Wins the Cyber Wars.* "Noah Goodwyn? Never heard of him."

"I couldn't have told you his name, but you don't forget a face like that."

"Just how famous is he?"

Gail raised an eyebrow, considering the question. "Oh, he's

not Justin Bieber famous. Just one of those names Gen Xers like to drop. Somewhere below Brian Gluckstein."

"I've never heard of him either."

"There you go, then," she said as though her point was made.

"Thanks," Weiss said, rubbing his cheek. "Well, I should…" He gestured towards the stairs.

Gail raised her eyebrow and smiled quizzically. She ejected the card and handed it to him with exaggerated elegance. The SD card in hand, Weiss backed away, leaving Gail with her fingers entwined on her lap, looking amused. He appropriated the magazine.

Back in his office, he began leafing through the slick pages filled with fashionable ads.

Joshi came in, thudded down a stack of file folders and sat at his own desk. "We have time for magazines?" he said. "Looking for a new spring ensemble, perhaps? You could use a new coat."

"My coat is fine, and it's not just any old magazine, Prem. This is *Escarpment*. Ring a bell?"

Joshi gave a skewed smirk. "Carly Rouhl's glossy celebrity magazine. Sort of a coffee table thing, right?"

"And, guess what? Our Carly has written the lead profile for this particular edition."

He held up the front cover with the magazine's elegant red title across the top, disappearing behind Noah Goodwin's balding head. Joshi looked at it for a moment without catching on.

Weiss gave him a quizzical glance, urging him on. "Think, Prem."

Joshi got the message and looked again, squinting. "Noah Goodwyn. That's not… Looks kind of like… You think that's our soggy stiff from the harbour?"

"It makes perfect sense, Prem. Goodwyn's a tech entrepreneur with scads of money and access to the best graphic designers in town."

Joshi shrugged. "Okay. You think anybody's going to prosecute this guy for screwing about with the government?"

"Oh, I suppose there might be a lawsuit in it if we were to show the harbour photos to a lawyer, but I'm more interested in finding out what else this guy is doing with his money. There's something going on here, Prem."

Joshi looked morosely at the folders on his desk. "Fine. Dig away at your prankster if you like, but I think you're being quixotic again, and you know how *that* goes over with the superintendent. What are we going to do?"

"Well, we're going to try and find Noah, I guess. Talk to him. Confront him with the stills from the harbour. See where it leads." Weiss opened the magazine. "But right now, I'm going to finish reading what Carly Rouhl says about him."

CHAPTER FOUR

The wind was buffeting the windows and rattling winter-bleached leaves against the row of upscale houses facing Lake Ontario.

At a bit after seven p.m. on a Tuesday, Carly Rouhl, wearing a pair of ivory-coloured slacks that belied the name, answered the doorbell—and there was Eilert Weiss on her porch, touching the brim of his tweed hat. She gave him a quick, uncertain smile and ushered the detective into the front hall of her father's house. Now *hers*. Weiss was accompanied by a brief swirl of damp leaves.

Weiss removed his hat. "Hello, Ms. Rouhl."

The early evening meeting felt awkward to Carly. Her last dealings with Weiss had been tense and peculiar. A couple of months ago, she stood with him out there besides the lake, and somehow the two of them managed to make sense out of her father's suicide and the shooting death of Marcella Cole. The report Weiss had then written spared her a lot of questions, for which she would have had no answers, anyway.

"So, Detective Weiss, I don't see Detective Joshi. I expected he'd be with you." In fact, she didn't, but it seemed like the Victorian thing to say.

"No, Prem is home with his family," Weiss apologized. "Very sensible, too, on a night like this. Sadly, I don't have family in Canada, so here I am bothering you. Thank you for agreeing to see me. I hope my phone call didn't bring back too many memories."

Carly didn't need help remembering. The death of her famous father, a much-loved author, changed her life and she had been struggling each day since to redefine herself.

"No," she said. "I'm fine. I still haven't figured out how you managed to sell our interpretation of my father's suicide to your superiors, but I'm pretty sure that at the end of the day, I'm in your debt."

"For threatening you and coercing you into perjury?"

"For giving me closure after Dad's death, and a way out of a legal mess. Have you come to claim your glass of whiskey?"

Weiss's smiles tended to be lost beneath his full moustache, but somehow they enlivened every other part of his face, especially his eyes which wrinkled in an endearing way.

"Ah, yes. I said I'd love to hear what you would say about the Cole business when I wasn't threatening to lock you up. Tempting, but no. That conversation would make me forget why I'm really here." He turned to the deep window seat that fronted the house. "Hello, Indy."

The handsome Labrador, who was apt to do a loud and crazy dance around the legs of strangers, stepped down languidly from the cushions to the carpet and padded over to Weiss. The detective stooped and vigorously rubbed the dog's ear. It earned Weiss a contented yawn, after which Indy curled up at his feet. No hard feelings there.

Carly watched the performance. "You must be lonely, Detective Weiss, coming out in the evening to talk to me, buttering up old Indy like that."

Indy wasn't particularly old, but he was her father's dog and he'd picked up some of the old man's sedentary ways.

Weiss looked up in surprise. "Lonely? It must be obvious. Some of the staff at the station are trying to 'fix me up.' I'm hoping I won't always be such a loner. But since I'm not really on duty—not officially, that is—I wonder if you could call me Eilert. It's a German name. My partner, Prem, tells me I have a slight German accent, too, but I've never even been there. It's a long story."

"Eilert. Sure. Come and have a seat by the fireplace. I promise we won't go near my father's office."

Weiss looked down the hall; it was short, with a room let off to the right and the front of the house. The office door of the late A.L. Rouhl formed the end of the passage. He couldn't forestall the picture of the old man's sprawled body and the small pistol on the rug developing in his mind.

"*Your* office now, I suppose?"

"I haven't used it yet. I sometimes think I should just leave it as it is, as a national shrine. Mind you, my father would be horrified by that." Carly turned a high-backed armchair towards the fireplace, inviting him to sit.

"I can see why you'd consider keeping it as a memorial," Weiss said. "They'll be teaching his books for years to come."

He accepted the armchair and settled, turning to the fireplace as it suddenly popped into life. Carly smiled at his surprise and brandished the remote control.

"I think this gas fireplace amazes me more than my smart TV. Watch this."

She pointed the remote and the colour of the flames changed to a warmer red and threw shifting shadows behind the imitation logs. Weiss nodded, his moustache bristling with a smile.

"Ah, well—speaking of the wonders of technology: I had occasion to do a web search on the subject of Noah Goodwyn." He watched her face and noted the fleeting look of concern that crossed her brow. "I wasn't surprised that your profile of him was listed prominently. I had already read the piece in your magazine. Your take on Mr. Goodwyn's life was a pleasure to read. You did a fine job of presenting him as a successful and influential tech superstar. The 'genius in our midst,' I think you wrote."

Carly seemed relieved. "Just another puff piece for the magazine, I'm afraid, but I don't think 'genius' is far off. I grew up with a genius for a father, so I know what I'm talking about."

"So you think your portrayal might have been a bit…sunny, then? I mean, there were less flattering listings online. Goodwyn was a known drug user, and from what I've been able to find out, he was almost always being sued by some corporation or celebrity for mischief, defamation, or the like."

"Oh, I know about all that. Well, some of it anyway. I did my research, too, but it's the nature of my magazine; we're a booster for local business and the arts. We have to stay friendly with the community and, well, the advertisers who keep us in the black. I didn't set out to be even-handed in my treatment of the man."

Carly was beginning to relax. Weiss was the police, and although a mere two months ago she'd found herself under suspicion for murder, somewhere along the line, she'd sensed that Weiss trusted her. She wasn't quite sure why. She took the opposite chair and looked at the imitation logs aglow with a designer shade of red.

"Okay, so, the profile… To be honest, it's an aspect of journalism that bothers me a lot. My father was ruthless and insightful, and it made his writing famous. He was interested in the dark secrets people try to hide. I've always recognized that *my* skill as a writer is…of a different sort." She sat forward miming a sort of no-nonsense authority.

"On the other hand, I've taken pride in my ability to keep my magazine afloat, and one of the ways I've done that is to write and commission the kind of glossy showpieces the public wants to read. Human interest? Sure. Exposé? Not bloody likely."

Weiss bowed to the seasoned editor she conjured up in his mind, and asked, "What was he like to talk to? Noah Goodwyn, I mean. He's what, fifty? Fifty-five now?"

"Fifty-five, yes. He's a funny little man, really. Not at all well-looking: pale and with a visible tremble in his hands. I figured it was the drugs he was on. I remember he was witty in a cynical way. Very polite, though; I think he got his manners from reading fantasy novels. You know, heroic knights, genteel ladies. He told me he grew up as a gamer. In fact, he said that his various computers and game systems had given him more parenting than his mother, and he barely knew his father."

Carly looked up at her mantle and indicated a small carving sitting there surrounded by candlesticks and platinum framed photos of her father with Margaret Trudeau and Leonard Cohen. "He actually gave me a gift after our last interview. Seems he was a big fan of my father's work. Noah's quite a cultured man in his own right. A lot of those people who grew up on Dungeons and Dragons and *The Hobbit* are, you know, because they tend to be readers and role players."

Weiss stood to examine the dark green piece of shaped stone. "May I?" He moved his palm, testing its unexpected weight. "Two figures intertwined. With…drums? Noah gave you this?"

"Yeah. Funny, huh? It's a soapstone carving, Cape Dorset Inuit. He said it was from his collection. I wondered about that; the way he's moved about, where would he keep a collection of anything?"

"Yes, I've yet to find his current address."

"He told me his home was wherever his best computer happened to be—which as often as not was in some luxury hotel where the weather was warm." She indicated the little carving. "I think it's probably quite valuable. I protested, of course, and tried to refuse the gift. I told him it wasn't ethical for a journalist to accept gifts."

Weiss's brow went up. "Isn't it?"

"I haven't a clue. I made that up, but he was persuasive to the point of bullying, so there it is."

"Lovely little thing. Quite heavy. What are the two figures doing? Drumming, I suppose."

"Noah called it 'The Song Duel.' I looked up the phrase online. Seems it was a tradition for two Inuit men to insult one another in song while beating a sort of sealskin drumhead. Anthropologists love that kind of thing."

"I don't know about anthropology, but I can see how he'd enjoy the idea of trading insults. Noah's got a reputation for pranks."

"His hacking, you mean?" Carly put the fireplace remote aside, looking thoughtful. "Still, the carving was a hell of a gesture. I wonder if he has a reputation for giving gifts, too."

Weiss watched her, wondering what kind of impact the little golem made on her. She used Noah's first name without thinking about it; it must have been an informal interview.

"Unlike his so-called pranks, gifts don't show up in the legal records," he said. "I was wondering if there was anything else you remember. For example, in the course of talking to him, did you learn where he was currently living?"

"Actually, no. I made contact with him through his local software company. When I finally got a call back from him and explained who I was, he seemed enthusiastic about giving me an interview—to 'set the record straight,' as he put it. He recognized my name, and it turns out he's an A.L. Rouhl fan. I think he chose to come to my house because he wanted to see it. My Dad's house, I mean."

Weiss looked around at the comfortable room with its mid-century furniture and pinch-pleated drapes. It wasn't the home of a career publisher who still had the fresh look of youth about her.

"Are you living here now?"

"I'm in the process of moving my stuff over from my condo. Yes, I'm going to *try* living here. I was here practically every night when Dad was ill."

"It's a lovely house with a view of the lake."

"And it's within walking distance of the magazine office, so..."

"Goodwyn never gave you an address or phone number?"

"Oh, I got both, but save yourself the trouble. I tried the number; the phone always goes to messages which he never returns. As for the address—someone else is living there now."

"You mean he gave you a false address?"

"No, he'd just moved out. Honestly? I bet he's in a hospital or rehab or something. As I said, he didn't look well. He would be bright and clever, and then he would just...drift. Defocus for a moment or two. I found it unsettling, but he was so talkative the rest of the time that I had plenty of material for my profile."

"In your article, you never said if he was married. There's no mention of a wife on the web either, but it seems he has a daughter."

"I think he's got a common-law wife. The daughter's from a youthful affair, though. The daughter must be twenty or so by now. So, what's a detective doing looking for Noah Goodwyn? Has he finally done something criminal?"

"Ah, well, we're not the first to be taken in by Noah, but he led us a merry chase just this morning. Staged his own corpse for us, but it turned out to be a remarkably sophisticated computer prank. I should have handed the business off to the courts—it's not really our kind of case—but I can't help wondering about the mentality that would go to such lengths."

Weiss told the story of Hamilton Harbour, and they laughed,

imagining the poor woman from Inland Waters who first stumbled onto the bogus railway. There was no whiskey, but Carly made some tea and enjoyed watching Weiss relax. He was a raconteur in a dry, amusing way, and the time went quickly. When he finally pulled his coat on, he drew out a small leather case and opened it.

"I expect you've still got one of these." He handed her one of his cards. "I hand these to people all the time, but I'd actually enjoy it if you'd give me a call sometime." She smiled at him, and embarrassed by his own familiarity, Weiss reverted to cliché, "… if you think of anything else." An awkward pause. "About Goodwyn."

Indy followed them to the front door, getting underfoot in the enclosed space. Weiss pulled his hat low against the damp breeze and thanked Carly before stepping out into the night.

Carly was left idly stroking Indy and wondering: Weiss had come to her to talk. He could have asked his questions on the phone. She couldn't entirely forget that as an authority figure, he had some lingering power over her, but something in the language of his lanky body and laugh-lined eyes told her that he liked her, and that made all the difference.

She walked back into the living room, a smile lingering on her lips, and she found herself facing the mantle. The olive green Inuit pair still banged their silent drums at one another. With exaggerated care, she took Weiss's card and leaned it against the drummers.

CHAPTER FIVE

Carly stood at the mantle for a moment, ignoring Indy's flank against her leg. As her thoughts drifted back over her conversation with Weiss, her father's office came naturally to mind. It was Weiss, after all, who examined the scene of her father's suicide while she'd wept in the dark behind the wheel of her car.

Carly had been embarrassed to admit to Weiss she'd not been in the little room since Marcella Cole had forced her way in and died there over two months ago. And of course, the office was where her father had taken his own life with a pistol. He'd probably drawn the little handgun from the cluttered shelves and bookcases that housed the remnants of his colourful life.

In the weeks that passed since then, the uncanny tension that built up in the room's atmosphere seemed an unreal memory—a dream, almost. But the questions the office posed about her father's gifts as a writer still obsessed Carly. So much of A.L.'s time, especially in his later years, had been spent sitting at that oak desk, staring at his wall of books and keepsakes. That was her father's life: he'd make a leisurely trip through the southern states or the lowlands of Scotland—it didn't seem to matter where—and then he'd come home and sit in that office and slowly begin to write.

"Travel writing" his publisher had called it, but the rich stories of love, betrayal, and ambition that he wrote were so much more—compelling in their intimacy and humanity. It had made him one of the nation's foremost men of letters and Carly, growing to maturity in the old house, wondered at the ease with which her father pulled the stories out of the air.

Sighing and reaching to rub Indy's ear, she turned to face the living room. She made her way to a side table, took up the remote and killed the fire with the push of a button. After the fire winked out and the artificial embers disappeared, her eyes drifted up and she found herself staring at Weiss's business card.

Carly picked it up and quickly glanced at both sides. From there, her gaze continued to the sculpture. Laying the card flat on the mantle, she picked up the little Inuit carving where Weiss had replaced it. The weight, the heft of it, amazed her.

She went to place it back on the mantle, but the olive sheen caught her eye and she found herself rolling the sculpture in her palm. She knew that the soft grey soapstone turned that rich green colour when you oiled it, disclosing its dense grain.

Her earlier embarrassment still weighed on her mind. She was a strong woman—people kept telling her that—and yet, when it came to her father's office, she had allowed Weiss to see her inner child.

She straightened, instantly self-conscious about the way she was staring into an empty corridor as if it held some unname-able threat. This was her home now, or at least it could be if she could make herself comfortable here. Carly set her jaw and walked down the hall to A.L. Rouhl's office...and opened the door.

The small room was quiet and gloomy, the street lights

projecting the window panes over the mocha coloured desk pad where her father's laptop once rested. She turned on the overhead light and the shadows retreated into the deep bookshelves.

Carly approached the black leather desk chair. This would be the test. She hadn't actually seen the old man's body slouched in this chair, his cheeks discoloured by the mouth shot. They'd taken him away before she'd been allowed back in the house, but the final escape act of A.L.'s suicide—the decision that would free him from a withering decline—was imbued in every bit of bric-a-brac throughout the room.

Summoning her courage, Carly took the upholstered arm and slowly eased herself into the chair. The leather creaked as it always had through her adolescent years. She'd sat there before, playing author like her dad, but this was different. Could she ever make the chair her own, or would she have to admit defeat and send it to the new Joseph Brant museum beside the hospital?

Face your fears, the homily went. Reclaim the little office for the living. Sure, A.L. Rouhl's office was a national landmark—they'd put a plaque on the front porch someday—but it was her house now. That was the way her father had wanted it. She was sure of that.

Carly sighed, her eyes half-closed, and she listened to the sounds of the night; the wind raked the bushes and cars sped by on Lakeshore Road, sizzling over streets wet with spring rain.

She tried to quiet her mind; it seemed to be filled still with thoughts of Noah Goodwyn, that funny little man in his expensive polo-necked shirt and jeans. She closed her eyes, rubbing her temples to get the buzz of journalistic curiosity out of her mind, but the unfamiliar weight in her other hand snagged her attention. She didn't have to look; her thumb conjured up the shape: the two rounded hunters locked in a twirling match of drumbeat and invective, their mouths roundly open. She still had the sculpture in her palm.

Carly smiled to herself, letting her imagination embrace the scenario—a scatter of pelts, the family gathered round, grinning in the gloom of a snow block house, the two figures dancing...

And oddly enough, that's when she saw the pineapple.

Its incongruity caught her by surprise and her eyes popped open. Carly blinked and looked about the room. Where on earth had she seen such a thing—among the tins and medallions and baskets that crowded the shelves? Amid the pocket watches and postcards hung on the walls?

No. She'd imagined it. Must have. It was just a random flash of synapses in her mind. But why a pineapple? Where did *that* come from?

She couldn't help it; she found herself trying to grasp the logic of the image. After all, it wasn't *just* a pineapple. It was wooden and polished, the kind of thing you'd see carved into antique furniture. The image seemed to hang in the air, breeding its own context: stairs, arched ceiling beams buttressed by carved lintels, the lintels fashioned by a skilled craftsman into...pineapples.

Out loud she said, "Come on, Carly. What are you doing?" It was a rebuke, her voice low lest the books and bric-a-brac might hear. "Get it together. Be sensible."

Annoyed at herself, she put the soapstone carving down on her father's desktop—could she ever think of the desk as her own?

The room came back into focus, and the pictures in her mind were gone. The chair back rocked her upright and she put her elbows on its arms. There was the little sculpture tipped on its side, a tiny authentication label visible on its base.

She gave a small, forced laugh. "Geez, Carly. Get a grip."

But even as she said the words, she realized that everything that had happened to her in the terrible winter of her father's death had taught her just the opposite: let yourself go. Let it come. That's what her father would have done with his fingers poised over the keyboard of his laptop.

And did it make him happy?

No. Not really.

Did it make him a great writer?

Yes, unquestionably, it had.

She sat there for a long moment, uncertain. Surely the choice wasn't so stark—between mediocrity and genius? Surely there was a middle way.

She became aware of the faint ticking of a clock lost somewhere in the chaos of the shelves. Then she picked up the carving again and let the creaking chair back ease her down. She closed her eyes and allowed herself to think...about pineapples.

CHAPTER SIX

It was one of the two massive blocks of high rise and retail that loomed over the Burlington GO station, and as such, it was a prized location for people on the move. The GO station was the anteroom of Toronto and the expensive pleasures of the megacity: galleries, the Distillery District, Massey Hall, and the Eaton Centre. There was plenty of parking at the buildings if you owned it, otherwise, there was the Walmart lot, which was also within walking distance.

And that's where you would have found the unmarked cruiser assigned to Eilert Weiss and Prem Joshi.

They searched out the main lobby which was a trick if you were walking and a stranger, and once inside, they found the choices bewildering. There were signs for the sauna and the pool and the meeting rooms and two banks of elevators which ascended in different towers. It took five minutes with the concierge to find the Goodwyn suite, which was in the west tower, and the uniformed concierge insisted on announcing that they were on their way up.

In answer, Alicia Goodwyn's voice said, "Send them up" as clearly as if she was standing there.

There were some people in Burlington who would have happily made a home in the big mirrored elevator—a few throw pillows, a sleeping bag, some beer. It took them up to dizzying heights that were rare in Burlington with its bylaws and suburban zoning.

The suite they were invited into smelled of flavoured smoke, vanilla perhaps, and Weiss noticed an e-cigarette hanging off the side of a huge television by its charge cord. The TV screen, which dominated the long wall, was vast, flat black, and seemed to swallow half the light in the room, allowing no reflections from the pole lamps with their conical shades.

It was a sprawling space, the equivalent of an upscale house, with the addition of floor to ceiling vistas of midtown. From here, you could see a few narrow gaps onto the lake to the south, and bits of the escarpment to the northwest.

"Have a seat, Detective. Just move that stuff." Alicia Goodwyn, who they would learn went by Sammy, moved and spoke with a languid purr.

She was young; too young to be living on her own in such splendour, but nothing, even a formal visit by two Halton detectives, seemed to bother her. She was protected by a force field of money and privilege. If she was "on" anything, it wasn't food; she was skinny and long-limbed. No one would mistake her for a runway model, though. With her short, dark mop and shredded jeans, she looked ready for the revolution and the overthrow of her own privileged class. There wasn't much of her father to mar her features, except perhaps that praying mantis V-shape in her lower lip. On Sammy, it only looked sensuous.

"I have Mountain Dew or Red Bull," she said. "This is Bonnie. She lives here, too."

They noticed Bonnie as she orbited in a chair that looked like an egg. Bonnie was wide-eyed and wary and wore a white t-shirt that dropped to her chubby knees.

"Oh, nothing, thank you," Weiss said, eying the cushioned basket chairs on offer.

"How about coffee? I have this really fantastic machine. Obscenely expensive. I had it shipped from Texas. You can have espresso, Columbian, dark roast, or pretty much anything you could get at Starbucks. All I have to do is pop in a pod and press a button. It came with a whole chest full of pods."

Weiss found himself wondering what Sammy would do when the chest was used up.

Joshi's eyes, however, widened slightly. "An espresso would be nice."

Weiss looked at Joshi accusingly as their interview shuffled off behind the kitchen island. Weiss turned back to watch Sammy work the magic coffee maker. He noted that she was actually quite beautiful and wondered at the way she had deliberately begun to deface her beauty with tattoos, piercings, and her dark, shapeless clothes. She had Noah's oddly shaped eyes, but hers were pleasingly symmetrical, and Noah's weak chin looked nicely feminine on her small face.

Weiss tried to get on track. "As I explained on the phone, we've been trying to get a handle on where your father might be, Ms. Goodwyn. He seems to have dropped off the map."

"Call me Sammy. I'm not a Mzzz Goodwyn." She gave him a sleepy smile. "You have no idea how funny that is, you asking me where my father is. You know, as if *I* was responsible for *him*." She gave a mirthless laugh.

"He was supposed to be responsible for me when I was growing up, but he didn't *have* to be, you see. Because he had money—lots of it—born into it and stacking up more every year with his patents and shit." The smile was gone. "Whoa. Sorry. Guess I'm a little bitter, huh?"

In the elegant finish of this suite, her bitterness sounded unseemly. "You seem to be doing well," Weiss sniffed.

Sammy shuffled back, holding an orange mug with the

symbol for woman on the side. She gave it to Prem, who had been expecting a demitasse. He stared at it and then sniffed. A look of bliss suffused his face.

"Oh, the condo, you mean?" Sammy looked around as though she took such things for granted. "Yeah. I'm a Goodwyn, so I get sprinkled with cash on a regular basis. It's true: the place is actually pretty exclusive; view of the lake, concierge, media theatre. You can tell that…" She indicated the exotic clutter of fabrics and rolls of vinyl thrown everywhere. "…despite my, uh, lifestyle."

Her lifestyle appeared to demand clutter and chaos.

"So, your father hasn't contacted you recently?"

Sammy flopped into a hanging basket chair that swung gently. "Well, yeah. There was this phone call about four months ago. Craziest damn call."

"Could you tell me about it?"

"It was like, you know, 'Hi, Sam. How are you? You gonna be okay?' Like he was suddenly worried about me." She laughed, a not unpleasant tinkle. "I might have been touched, but there were these awkward silences. I figured, yup, he's drugged up again. It's hard to take a guy seriously when he's obviously not all there."

"You were well aware of his drug use, then. The cocaine habit? The hallucinogens?"

"Yeah, coke and whatever else he took a fancy to. I remember Special K because I thought it was a cereal then. Ha! In our family, it wasn't even a dirty little secret. My dad was proud of his 'altered realities,' as he called them."

"How did he manage to be so successful if he was using?"

"Oh, he was brilliant. He had a gift for coding and it aligned nicely with his love of gaming and media. He had a wildness about him that passed for imagination. Most of his innovations were sold or licensed when he was still in his twenties and early thirties. Since then…"

Weiss leaned forward, quite a feat in the deep chair. "Since then, what?"

Sammy shrugged, the cynicism resurfacing. "Well, how motivated can you be when you've already got more money than you know what to do with?"

"What *did* he do with his wealth? He seems to have taken care of you financially."

She pouted, conceding the point. "Yeah. My mother, too, wherever the hell she is. Last I heard, she was killing herself with prescription drugs down in Vegas. When they were together, they just enabled one another—drugs, expensive liquor—and IMAX sex, of course." Sammy grinned at Bonnie, who laughed. "It's a wonder," Sammy said, "that I'm not fucked up more than I am."

Weiss picked up on that. "Are you...unhealthy?"

"Hmm?" She knew what he meant. "What, drugs? Nah. I saw too much of that up close. Caffeine's my hit. I'm high on living my own way. I'm an artist. The kind of artist you can be when you don't give a shit who buys your stuff. I figure, why not take this money for a ride, right?"

Weiss nodded his understanding. "Getting back to his, uh, affluence. Did he travel, invest...? What was his pleasure?"

"I don't know about his business dealings. We all have people who do that stuff for us. Pleasure? Well, he had his Italian cars, his crazy friends, and he still loved his games, of course."

"What sort of games?"

"Well, he'd get hold of the hottest computer games of the day, and, I don't know, try to subvert them somehow? He'd break into the coding of a single off-the-shelf shooter, and before you knew it, he'd deconstruct it and be online screwing with their whole game culture worldwide. I have no idea how he did it. I remember he got in trouble for crashing into video conferencing, chat rooms. I've no idea how he did that either, but he had the resources. He would get bored and raise hell for the fun of it."

"I don't understand how you could, uh, screw with a commercial video game. I don't mean technically. I mean, how would the prank play out?"

"Oh, in different ways. Easter egging, for one thing. You know, he'd work himself into the game, wandering into the middle of the action. You'd be delivering a package of drugs in Grand Theft Auto, and the damn door would open and there he'd be, telling you to get the fuck of his porch. Part of the joke for him was that it actually *looked* like him. You know, a digital portrait. And of course, he had a following. You know, fans? Some of the creeps from the dark web would try and catalogue his trolling."

Weiss was having trouble understanding, and he telegraphed his confusion to Joshi, who made an unhelpful grimace in return. Sammy saw the exchange and asked, "Wanna see?"

Weiss nodded. "Sure."

"Bonnie? Fire up Undergrowth, will you?"

For her part, Sammy touched a wall plaque and shadow curtains purred into place on two walls.

Bonnie reached for a controller and the TV came alive instantly with moving boxes and pop up logos. With a speed that made Weiss blink, Bonnie selected a game and had them standing in the blue ruins of a neo-gothic mansion, complete with ragged drapery and soaring flagstone hearth. Faint stars winked through the sundered vault above them.

Sammy had her own controller now, and their viewpoint shifted as though they were collectively turning their heads.

"Watch. I saved this bit."

The wide, crystal clear screen of the television changed the ambience of the whole room, bathing them in shifting shades of indigo and purple. With practiced ease, Sammy walked them through the gloom of the mansion until they were on the landing of a descending spiral of stairs. Their avatar walked down, following the blue curve of the stone walls until the screen was filled with the image of a dungeon-like chamber.

The ugly stone arches of the ceiling were almost completely obscured with hanging pods woven of spider silk and strewn with cobwebs, and each pod revealed the partially covered faces of men and women whose hair dangled down in matted strands. Their eyes were dead, their faces a bluish-white.

One of the shadowy pods separated itself from the others and began to descend as though on a thread, and its own furred web broke as great bat-like wings uncurled. The shape revolved until slender black legs tore free and made contact with the stone floor. A loathsome figure, half man half creature, shrugged into a standing pose, its head the last thing to disentangle from its webbing. The brow rose and beneath a ragged cowl, the eyes flared open, the pink orbs emerging from the gloom in a beautifully rendered chiaroscuro.

"The figure reveals itself," said Sammy, enunciating clearly, apparently for the benefit of the game console.

A tiny icon flashed red, and the words she had spoken appeared to scroll across the bottom of the screen. The hunched figure straightened slowly, reaching up with bony claws to draw back its threadbare cowl.

Joshi reacted first, capping his mug to stop it from splashing. "Jesus."

Bonnie, her wonder untinged with bitterness, said, "Cool, huh?"

It took Weiss a moment to recognize the sardonic, utterly realistic leer. His mind was taken back to the watery shadows at the bottom of Hamilton Harbour. It was the same pallid face that had opened its eyes and stared back at him then—the face that he now recognized as Noah Goodwyn.

Weiss shook his head. Other kids had photos of Dad on their mantle. Sammy had this.

"Speak!" Sammy's voice was once again clear, but even that one word, as it scrolled along the bottom of the screen, carried scorn.

A voice boomed out of the TV, dripping with the hollow echo of the stone chamber: "Welcome, traveller," it sneered, the words dripping with menace.

Weiss turned to her. "Is that your father's voice?"

"Oh, yeah. That's my loving father, the Banksy of the internet. Unmistakeable."

Sammy turned off the TV, leaving only her sarcasm hanging in the air. The room lights came up, apparently of their own volition.

Weiss settled back in his chair, a feeling of horror in his gut, not from the sneering figure in the chamber, but from the idea that his daughter was seeing it. Noah Goodwyn had played his little trick on the gaming community without thought that his daughter might someday come down those blue stairs.

"Was your father a violent man, abusive?" Weiss asked.

"No, not like that. Neglectful, but he never hit me or anyone else, and God knows my mother provoked him enough. No, he was just...bitter. Mostly about his body—his appearance. You know, what he looked like. It bothered him much more than it bothered us."

"But he had so much. Born to wealth, successful in business."

"It was much more personal than that. Being small, misshapen, self-conscious, he overcompensated like hell, but he resented his limitations. Maybe..." She became thoughtful, withdrawn.

"Maybe he was trying to...escape. You know? Get outside himself? My mother was beautiful. At least back then she was. Dad wanted her and was jealous of her at the same time. He was into masks, dressing up. He got that from his cosplay. He played monsters and Gollums and shit like that because he couldn't carry off the heroic characters."

"If you wanted to track down your father, where would you look?"

"Try the local hospitals. He's *so* burned out."

"All right. Thank you," Weiss sighed.

Sammy reconsidered. "You might try his sister, Ruth, though. She's got money of her own from her late husband's family, except she's into God and stuff. Dad used to go there a lot in the summer."

"Is your aunt in the GTA?"

"Oh, yeah. Old money, mansion on the hill."

"Where would this 'hill' be?"

"Well, you know, the Niagara Escarpment up towards Milton. I've been there plenty of times, but I can't remember the address or anything. I just go, drop in, you know. By the way, don't go up Appleby Line. There's a scary switchback up the slope. Try Bell School Road. And don't take the first entrance. That leads you to the lower gardens. Go up the hill to the house."

———

Weiss and Joshi left the apartment and walked along a corridor that was floor to ceiling glass on one side until they reached the elevators. Weiss pressed an unyielding touchscreen button which lit up with an animated down arrow. He slouched against the wall, doing up his coat.

"What do you think, Prem?"

Joshi stood with his legs apart, holding his hat in both hands. "I think Noah went from computer games to hacking corporate computer systems. Is that why we're here? Computer fraud? I'm still not clear on that."

Weiss's eyes crinkled. "Sorry, Prem. I think it's my obsession with the paperwork again. I like things to make sense, fit into categories so they can be written up neatly. It's like that A.L.

Rouhl suicide—a suicide and murder all rolled up into one. Bizarre, but at least it made sense when you typed it down on a computer form."

"Not so much in the real world."

Weiss's smile faded and his eyes focussed on somewhere down the corridor. In the Rouhl case, he hadn't exactly deceived his partner; not really. After all, the guilty had been punished and the innocent spared—he was sure enough of that. All the same, the truth about Marcella Cole's death lay in some murky world of possibilities best left unspoken. Weiss still had his sanity, and there were times over the last few years when he had reason to question that.

"I think," he said at last, deliberately changing the subject, "that Noah Goodwyn is a spider, sitting at the centre of a great big web, and I'm wondering how big the web is."

"And who's stuck in it?" Joshi smirked. "Oh, geez, Eilert. You've got *me* talking in metaphors now. I'm a simple cop and I'm standing here with nothing but a fancy mischief case."

The elevator door opened on the large space made luxurious with mirrors and polished nickel fixtures.

"Do you think Noah's using his tech skills for stealing?" Joshi said, sounding almost hopeful as he touched the screen for the lobby.

"Why would he? He's rich." Weiss pulled his Harris tweed hat on, ready for the rain. "No, I think the daughter's got it right; Noah's got some fixation on escaping. Escaping his own stunted body, escaping his nomadic life, busting into other people's orderly, comfortable spaces."

The two detectives got to their car through the busy midtown crowds and got inside, Weiss taking the wheel. Weiss tossed his hat in the back seat and ran his hand over his long crew cut. When it came time to turn the key and pull away from Walmart and the great colonnade of Sammy's condo tower, he hesitated.

"Prem, you've never pushed me on the A.L. Rouhl case. I appreciate that."

"I could tell you didn't want to be pushed. The superintendent accepted your interpretation of the events and that got us off the hook."

"But you understand, it was just an interpretation."

"The only one possible under the circumstances."

"Yeah." Weiss sounded defeated, bitter.

"What's the matter, Eilert? Not thinking of reopening the case, are you?"

"God, no. We gave the only reasonable explanation for the facts of the case. We accounted for the evidence."

"Why don't you stop right there and screw the rest?"

Weiss held the steering wheel in both hands and watched the raindrops merge and dash. "You know, I can live with the outcome, I can live with the belief that I used the evidence selectively to protect innocent people. But I'm having a hard time being dishonest with you. You deserve better from a partner and a friend."

"What, you think I'm some sort of white knight of the mean streets or something? I know that business about Marcella Cole's body being moved doesn't hold up."

Weiss turned to stare at his partner. "You know?"

Joshi shifted uncomfortably, wishing this conversation could end quickly. "I saw you come at that shooting from every reasonable angle. I did, too. At a certain point, you just have to call it. It's what the taxpayers want, it's what the superintendent wants, and it's what every cop that worked on the Marcella Cole murders wanted. Somehow, you did it without anybody being hurt. So, for God's sake, stop tearing yourself up. Move on with your life. Ask Heddy out and go eat shawarma somewhere."

Weiss turned back to the windscreen and thought for a moment. "Which one is shawarma again? I get all that Middle Eastern stuff mixed up."

CHAPTER SEVEN

Driving away from the lake and up towards the District Three station on Constable Henshaw Boulevard, Weiss and Joshi detoured into the Longo's plaza long enough for Weiss to get his brewed tea from Tim Hortons. Joshi stayed in the car, not wanting to brave the pissing rain. He'd get something in the station cafeteria.

When they at last parked in the station lot, Weiss made for the stairs, tapping the rain off his hat, and Joshi sidled through the office to the large room full of tables that served as a cafeteria. He got himself a muffin from a glass-doored case as a woman in a catering company uniform was stocking it. The coffee came from a machine that had cute graphics of pouring coffee on a small screen. He finished both, relishing the chocolate chips, the quiet, and the warmth while the parking lot outside the windows glistened in a brief respite of watery sunlight.

He was getting up to leave when Detective Antonia Beal, tall and graceful in her navy pantsuit, walked past him carrying a lidded coffee cup. Without stopping, she slapped a single piece of paper on Joshi's chest with her open palm. Joshi grasped at the page to keep it from falling and managed to stop it at his groin. By the time he turned around, Toni was gone.

A couple of uniforms holding their own cups chuckled at him from their table, but he shut them down with his best chain of command frown.

He didn't look at the sheet right away because that would have been uncool. Instead, he feigned dignity and ambled towards the staircase, holding it in his hand. It wasn't until he was alone on the upper landing that he took the time to examine the page. It looked like a photocopy made at the front office machine because the text was greyish. He skimmed it, got the gist, and resumed his amble to the office he shared with Eilert Weiss.

Weiss was inside, fingering his reusable Tim Hortons mug, filled—Joshi had no doubt whatsoever—with the inevitable brewed tea.

"Hey, Eilert. Toni gave me something from her file search. It's about Heddy's bones from the escarpment. Toni traced the thingamajig—the dental bridge."

Weiss stopped his unfocused gaze out the window and turned his chair in a stately half circle. "Okay, my good man. You find me at leisure. You may proceed. Speak."

Prem lidded his eyes. "Or I could just put the print-out on a velvet cushion and lay it on your dick. Maybe I should come back when your pinky isn't raised."

Weiss grinned. "You're a good soul, Prem, but don't knock tea breaks. They're the backbone of civilized policing."

Joshi tapped the page. "Here's our peculiar two-tone skeleton: James Emile Krauss. I.T. manager at MorwynBIO. Not a missing person, at least not technically. He was never reported missing after he was suspended from his job. Everybody figured he was in hiding or on the run. But it seems legal affairs has had inquiries from a legal firm trying to track him down so they could sue his ass. There's also a note formally withdrawing the request."

"Aha, so a fugitive from justice, then. Sue him for what?"

"'Theft of intellectual property,' it says."

"That's what I like," Weiss muttered with patient irony. "A nice, clear-cut felony. What the hell does that mean?"

"Don't know," Joshi answered, "but if we found out who was pissed off at him, maybe we'd be able to figure out what he stole. Toni's got the name of the legal firm making the inquiries. It's here in the print-out. I could phone them up."

"Good man, Prem." Weiss sagged back in his chair, brandished his Tim Hortons cup, raised his little finger and sipped. "But aren't we forgetting something? This is Toni's case."

Joshi sat down at his desk opposite Weiss. "Damn. This could get complicated."

"How is it complicated? We could just forget about the whole bones thing until Toni and Tom do the legwork. That would clarify things. We could worry about the condition of the remains with some background to work with. You know, motive and guilt and so on—none of that is our case, see? Technically, we're just being asked to explain the state of the remains." Weiss drummed the fingers of his free hand on the plastic cup and frowned, tipping his head from side to side slowly as though weighing options. "But then again, it *is* our case. Sort of."

"Jesus. Eilert. Just when you were on to something."

"The remains, Prem. The two-tone bones. Heddy doesn't know how that could happen. Her collection isn't neatly shelved by date, and I can sympathize with that. Everything needs to be in its place, neat and tidy. We were asked to consult."

"Yeah, because we're, like, 'open-minded.' Eye roll."

Weiss ignored that. "So, ours is, what? A parallel investigation? Gotta keep things in perspective. It's a question of paperwork, Prem. Somebody has to write something down about those bones—an explanation. Think of it as a scientific thesis." He held his cup up in a formal toast. "'An Explanation for Anomalous Skeletal Fragments, by Joshi, Prem et al.' In learned journals, they list the names alphabetically, you know."

Joshi closed one eye. "Well, I'd gracefully accept top billing, if there *was* an actual explanation. Does anybody really care why the bones are two…why they're different?"

Weiss sniffed. "Apparently, Heddy and I care. Aren't you curious?"

"Maybe in a 'gee-whiz, what'd ya know' sort of way."

"Well, I'm interested in a 'what actually happened to James Krauss's body on the escarpment' focused kind of way." Weiss put his cup down. "So, Prem, would you see what the legal firm will tell us about Krauss? And while you're at it, let me have a closer look at that print-out, will you?"

Joshi turned to his laptop and Weiss started to read through Toni Beal's research. As he skimmed, he muttered to himself, "Krauss, Information Technology Manager. Does *everybody* work on computers now?" And then, peering at the fine print, he thumbed the MorwynBIO company number into his phone.

An admin assistant transferred him to a different department. He got someone with access to the boss's calendar and was put on hold. Eventually, he got a voice that rang with the resonance of command.

"The manager's not working this morning," she informed him. "I could make an appointment for you. Say tomorrow at two?"

"Can't I speak to him on the phone?"

"That would be his personal mobile number. I can't give that out without his permission."

"Can you get him and tell him that a Halton detective wants to talk to him about James Krauss?"

The female voice on the other end sounded conflicted, making the phrase "one moment please" sound like a question.

She was back in less than a minute. "The manager wonders if he could avoid discussing this on the phone. Are you at the station on Constable Henshaw? If so, he's near you."

Weiss scribbled the location down. "We'll meet him there."

Joshi turned with his own phone in hand. "I got the law firm. They won't say anything, about anything, period. Wouldn't tell me if it was raining there. Not without a court order."

"Let's bypass them. The manager of MorwynBIO is over at that driving range at Guelph Line and Number Five."

"Christ, who hits golf balls in this weather?"

Weiss looked out the window at the overcast sky. "Gotta get ready for sunnier times, I guess." He stood. "It's still cold out. We'll need our coats. You've heard the theory that golf was invented by the Scots as a joke? The rest of the world just never caught on."

CHAPTER EIGHT

It was a miserable day, but if you had the money and the inclination, you could whack golf balls out onto the wet grass all day from under a taut canvas roof. And if you cared about such things, you might occasionally plonk a target marked with the distance in yards. Apparently, golf addicts didn't bother with the metric system. If you were terrible, you could dribble your bucket of balls into the catch net below your little green mat.

While Joshi took in the row of enthusiasts with their carbon fibre drivers and baseball caps, Weiss approached the MorwynBIO manager. He was a regular around this time of year and the attendant selling balls had no difficulty pointing him out.

"Your secretary told me I'd find you here," Weiss said, touching the brim of his hat.

The manager, a tall greying eminence in a windproof Raptors jacket, reluctantly took his eye off the ball he had perched on a rubber tee. "God, don't call her a secretary," he said. "She'd poleaxe you with her paperweight. Yes, my *managerial assistant* called me, and I knew I was close to your headquarters. I live over in Headon Forest, you see. Anyway, I suggested you meet me here—save us both a lot of trouble. So, what can I do for you, Detective?"

"I'm following up on a Mr. James Krauss. His remains were found recently, and we're treating it as a suspicious death. We believe he was killed about a year ago."

"Or ten," Joshi muttered under his breath.

Weiss ignored him. "At that time, Krauss was being sought by lawyers for suspected copyright theft or something of that nature."

"That's correct. We found out he'd been accessing secure files that he had no business with. Mr. Krauss was an I.T. specialist responsible for servicing everyone's work stations and there was no legitimate reason he needed to subvert passwords to view our test files. He was responsible for maintaining our system, but he wasn't a chemist or even a marketer. His activity was discovered by one of our researchers. Mr. Krauss was put on immediate suspension pending court action. He subsequently went missing, which I think speaks to his guilt."

"You think he was stealing valuable research with a view to selling it?"

"Almost certainly. There are competitors who would pay a great deal for the results of our hard work. The pharmaceutical world is very competitive."

"I noticed that the inquiry about Krauss was terminated. If he was about to sell your research to a rival, why would your board do an about-face and stop the legal action against him?"

The manager stared off into the rain-swept distance, his expression pained. "I'm not comfortable talking about this, Detective."

Weiss looked around at the neatly spaced row of golfers with their whistling arcs and meaty thwacks. "Prem, give us a minute, will you?"

Joshi looked weary but he was happy enough finding a

folding chair under the porch of the sales stall where he could watch a neon Coors Light sign flicker.

Weiss waited, then said, "It's just us now. What do you think happened?"

The manager wore fingerless golf gloves; he crossed his hands on the grip of his driver and made an eyes to heaven expression. "It got back to me that Mr. Krauss was a friend of the Moreland family who are major shareholders in our company. He was a long-time companion of Ruth Moreland's brother in particular. In fact, James Krauss and Noah Goodwyn were childhood friends."

Weiss, who had been standing casually with his hands in his coat pockets, suddenly straightened. "Wait, what? Noah Goodwyn? Noah Goodwyn is Ruth Moreland's *brother*?"

"Yes, of course. Between the two of them, they hold a controlling interest in MorwynBIO. Mr. Goodwyn isn't actively involved, of course. Word has it he's one of those oddball technogeeks, but I think Mrs. Moreland knows she can count on her brother's proxy. My guess is that the two of them came to some kind of arrangement with Krauss to save him from jail. Out of a misplaced sense of loyalty, I suppose. I just hope to God they got him to hand over any digital copies he may have made. A successful formulation can be worth millions to the first company to register a patent."

"Do you know what specific drugs were compromised?"

"It's not that simple. There would have been at least twelve promising patents among the files. I can't think of a drug that would have been *especially* promising—they were all potentially valuable, or would be on the market if their clinical trials were successful."

"The drugs Krauss was after are untested?"

"We do bio testing and some animal trials in-house, but the actual clinical testing goes on at the McMaster Medical Centre. We have a licensing agreement with them."

"Whatever it was that Krauss was after, it would be illegal and unsafe as is. You believe Krauss broke into the protected files using his position as the system administrator; is it likely he was looking for something in particular?"

The manager scratched the back of his head. "Presumably whatever he thought he could get the most money for. Mr. Krauss isn't…uh…wasn't a chemist, but he would have known which drug does what in a general way. More importantly, he would know which drugs had promising results so far. Those would be the most valuable ones to a competitor. All that information would be in the files he accessed."

Weiss thought for a moment. He found himself visualizing the manic Halloween face on Gail's computer screen.

"What if Krauss wanted to actually get hold of one of the drugs—I mean, the real thing. Could he do that?"

"He wouldn't need a sample of the actual drug to sell the formulation."

"Yes, I get that. But what if he *did* need the drug itself? How would he get it?"

The manager looked confused. "Well, naturally we have specimens of the drugs in our labs for experimental work. That's what we do. But there are protections at all levels. The drugs are shelved without labels—with nothing but a digital code to identify them. The thief would need to use a handheld barcode reader to identify the specific drug he was looking for."

"A code reader. Huh? That would be easy enough to manage if you were an I.T. specialist, wouldn't you say? Like James Krauss?"

The manager's face visibly blanched. He laid his driver on his shoulder and affected a casual stance, not quite carrying it off. "I suppose it would."

"And he would be free to move about within the lab area? They must have computer stations there that need servicing, I would think."

"Ye…s."

"Would you have any way of knowing if a particular drug was missing from your inventory?"

The manager looked down the row of swinging clubs for a moment and gave an apologetic smile. "You know what, Detective? I don't feel at liberty to say more without an attorney present. Perhaps you'd like to meet with our legal department. You know our number." Between whacks, an awkward silence allowed in the steady dripping of rain from the canvas. When Weiss didn't say anything, the manager bent down to his bucket of golf balls. "Now if you'll excuse me."

———

Weiss and Joshi got back into the cruiser, doing their best to leave some of the beaded raindrops outside. Joshi shook his hat out the window and put it on his knees.

"What was that last bit—the bit about Krauss getting his hands on the actual drug? Why would he need to do that?"

"So what, you heard everything from your folding chair?"

"I judged the distance discreetly."

Weiss snuffed in amusement and arranged his keys. "Just a long shot, Prem. We know Noah is a drug abuser. I found myself wondering if James Krauss was helping out his friend."

"Oh, you mean like *drug* drugs. Psychedelics or mood-altering stuff."

"Or fentanyls, or uppers. Hell, I don't know. The drug spectrum is vast these days. But Noah would have been a real connoisseur of highs. The more I think about it, though…it seems pretty far-fetched. Those drugs would be potentially dangerous, maybe even fatal. It seems far more likely Krauss was fishing randomly for something to sell." Weiss started the car and the wipers swept away the beaded rain.

"Still…" he said. "We're missing something here, Prem."

CHAPTER NINE

It was a short run back along Number Five, down Walkers Line to the parking lot off Constable Henshaw Boulevard. When they pulled in, Prem started to make a phone call to his wife who worked as an optician in a nearby plaza, so Weiss left him in the car and headed for the entrance. Once through the sliding doors of the vestibule, Weiss made his way alone to the first-floor office shared by Toni Beal and Tom Krosnow.

He knocked on the open door and stepped in. Toni Beal was by herself, ball-point in hand.

"Jesus Christ, Toni. *Noah Goodwyn.*"

Toni, at a loss, clicked her pen and looked up. "Does this have something to do with the flood?"

"Flood? What flood? Oh. 'Noah—flood,' right." Weiss wasn't about to be distracted. "Did you happen to notice Ruth More-land's maiden name?"

Toni sat up straight, looked wary. "Uh, oh."

"She was Ruth *Goodwyn.*"

Toni nodded slowly. "Ye-ah. And I should be ashamed because...?"

"Her brother is Noah Goodwyn."

Looking blank, Toni narrowed her eyes. "Sorry, I'm still thinking 'flood.'"

Weiss's excitement ebbed. "Ah, yeah. I don't know why I assumed everybody would know who Noah Goodwyn is. After all, he's not dating a Kardashian." He slumped against the doorjamb. "He's a big wheel in tech. Kind of a local hero. He owns dozens of patents and exclusive rights."

"Anything to do with drugs?" Toni said hopefully.

"Not directly. Think animation at Sheridan College, computer games, CGI effects and like that. He's as rich as Croesus."

"Do I need to know who Croesus is?"

"It's an expression."

Waving her pen in surrender, Toni said, "Okay. I screwed up, but you're not going to tell anyone, right?"

Weiss couldn't help a weak smile. He owed Toni a great deal. Following his wife's suicide, Toni helped him through the darkest days of his life and there was a lingering bond there.

"It's *my* screw up," he said.

"I'm listening."

"Prem and I have been following up on a nuisance report from Inland Waters. It led me right to Noah Goodwyn."

Toni raised a skeptical brow. "Goodwyn screwed with Inland Waters? How do you even *do* that, and why bother?"

"Forget that. The point is, this just got a hell of a lot more interesting. MorwynBIO, for instance. 'More' plus 'wyn,' get it? It's family money. All part of the same pot, although Ruth got a lot more from her husband's estate.

"Prem and I talked to the manager of the drug company that was taking action against James Krauss. MorwynBIO was accusing Krauss of accessing their proprietary drug research. Krauss was a techie, not a chemist or medical researcher. He had no business dealing with the drug research side, and he got caught using his knowledge of the system to break in.

"The company suspects him of selling patented information to the competition or the Chinese or someone. But here's the interesting part: the lawsuit against Krauss got shut down by the company's own board of directors."

Toni nodded, back on familiar ground. "The board of MorwynBIO is mostly Ruth Moreland. I know that."

"And Noah Goodwyn. I love it when the pieces fit together."

"Whoa. Big pieces missing. What was Krauss after? And why did Ruth get him off the hook after he got caught?"

"I'm just saying, that's what you have to find out, Toni."

Toni waved her hands, gesturing at the futility of the matter. "But...there's no case there, Eilert. Krauss is dead, and Ruth doesn't want the theft pursued, anyway."

"But you're investigating a murder, right—the murder of James Krauss?"

Toni narrowed her eyes. "Probably. So who wanted Krauss dead?"

"Well, what if Ruth—or Noah—got what they wanted from Krauss and decided to silence him afterwards?"

"Holy shit, Eilert." She picked up a file folder and tapped it on her desk like a deck of cards. "There's a whole lot of supposition in there. But, okay. Say that's a motive for murder; Krauss may have been stealing the drug information for Ruth or Noah, but I don't get why they had to steal from their own company. Ruth would be entitled to look at MorwynBIO's files any time she wanted. I'm simplifying a bit, but it's her patents we're talking about."

"Yes, but what if Krauss wasn't stealing computer files? What if he was after the drug itself?"

Toni blinked. "He could do that? Get his hands on the product?"

"The manager obviously thinks so, and remember these drugs are not approved for use. That makes them illegal."

"So, what drug are we talking about?"

"I have no idea."

Toni deflated. "I thought you were onto something there. The point remains, why steal something that they technically already own? And why kill Kruss? Even if the theft is traced back to Ruth or Noah, they're still not in trouble. Not really. It's their company, for God's sake. So there's no reason to silence Krauss."

Weiss eased himself into Tom Krosnow's chair and twined his fingers. "I have no idea what they might have been after. I'm just saying…" He shrugged. "…if they were planning on using a drug, one that was technically still illegal…"

The train of thought petered out as though Weiss had no idea where he was going with this. There was potential wrongdoing here, but it didn't seem serious enough to drive a prominent citizen to murder.

Toni watched Weiss's face—the way it lapsed from excitement to sadness. "Say, how are you, Eilert? This is just work, right? No emotional irons in the fire this time?"

Weiss cringed. For some reason, Noah's daughter came to mind. He remembered Sammy Goodwyn's disgust at seeing her father in the video game; the bat creature and his sardonic giggle. Weiss always had to do inventory on his emotions these days.

You needed to be able to detach yourself in this job, and he was still in recovery from his own personal tragedy—his wife's cruel and pointedly hurtful suicide.

Weiss masked his discomfort with bluster. "Mm? Oh, no. Just another day at the office. Thanks, Toni, I don't need rescuing this time." He gazed out the window to the northeast, towards the distant line of the escarpment. He couldn't help adding. "But maybe Noah Goodwyn does."

He got up and walked to the door.

Toni, wide-eyed, watched him go. "What the *hell* does that mean?"

"Oh, uh. Somebody told me Noah isn't well."

It wasn't an adequate explanation, but Weiss was out the door and down the hall before Toni could question it.

C H A P T E R   T E N

An hour passed, Weiss turning his mind to clearing some paperwork off his "in" tray, transferring dates to the calendar on his
phone, while Joshi tapped away at his laptop. At last, Weiss put
his phone away and glanced out at the overcast sky. He got to
his feet and was looking out their second-floor window when
he noticed movement below.

There were two figures on the tarmac heading for a parked
cruiser. In her heels, Toni Beal was as tall as Weiss and leggy,
even in her car coat; Tom Krosnow was a square-shouldered
tough guy with a scarf around his thick neck. Under the overcast, they didn't cast shadows on the puddled lot.

Acting quickly, Weiss picked up his phone again and touched
Toni Beal's cell number. There was a commotion on the other
end for a second, then Toni's voice: "I'm in the parking lot.
What's up?"

"Where are you off to?"

Weiss could see her look up in his direction. She knew
exactly where his office was. "Moreland House up Appleby
Line," she said. "I'll wait by the car for a few minutes if it's
important. Hurry up. It'll be raining again in a minute."

"Thanks. Be right down."

Weiss and Joshi grabbed their coats, chugged down the stairs, and out the sliding glass doors. The three flags in the parking lot—Canada, Ontario, and the Police Association—hung wet and still against their poles. Toni's Ford SUV cruiser was up near the building and Tom Krosnow, Toni's partner, was leaning on the roof toying with car keys and looking bored.

Weiss pulled his coat collar together against the dampness. "Hi, Toni. Tom. It's about James Krauss again."

"Yeah, you got anything more?" Toni said.

"Well, you know, we were told to look into the condition of the remains."

"You mean why the fragments appeared to be of different ages?" She smirked at some private joke. "I asked for another pair of eyes on that; I can see how it would appeal to you. You think it's worth following up?"

"It's best not to ignore evidence even if it's weird."

Weiss sounded a little preachy, and it was enough to bother Tom.

He spoke across the roof of the cruiser. "You know, Eilert, you may have closed the Marcella Cole murder, but some people think your incident report reads like *Harry Potter*."

Joshi shrugged. "At least the superintendent didn't laugh. Which is what we were going for."

"When you eliminate the impossible," Weiss grinned, "whatever remains must be the truth, Tom. However it plays in the squad room."

Toni smiled. "Leave Eilert alone, Tom. He helped us out on the biker case, remember?"

Prem coughed gently.

"Okay, so that was Prem, but Eilert got Therese Cherry's killer, and that was one of ours. What do you want, Eilert?"

"Well, I was just thinking. Krauss—our bone dump—was found on undeveloped regional property off Appleby Line, up on the escarpment. You know that, right? So, I looked it up on Google Earth. It turns out that the land is right next to the home of Ruth Moreland. I figure you know that, too."

"Yeah, we know that, Eilert."

"I remember you said that you were 'probably' investigating a murder. Is there any question in your mind that Krauss was murdered? I mean, you've got the full file. We haven't seen the whole thing yet."

"There's not a lot to see. Offhand, we can't think of any other reason that would get Krauss's body in a secluded patch of forest like that. The remains, however, could have been dumped from a car. They were about the distance from the highway that I could lug a body. Well, Tom could anyway."

Joshi brightened and said, "Ah, a suspect."

Tom ground the car keys in his fist.

Toni smiled. "Look, I heard what you said. Ruth Moreland is definitely a person of interest. If she killed Krauss, she'd want him forgotten."

"Or, more likely, if she had him killed," Weiss said. "She's rich, remember. Rich people don't generally do their own killing."

Toni crossed her arms and leaned back against the cruiser. "There is one thing that bothers me. Either way—murder or assassination—why would Ruth toss the body so close to her house? That'd be stupid."

"Most criminals are stupid. You know that."

"Anyway, Tom and I have an appointment to interview Ruth Moreland this afternoon."

"Is there a current husband?"

"No, she's still a widow. Her husband was a lot older than her—died back in 2011, but she kept the name, and the money."

Weiss began, "I don't suppose you'd let Prem and me..."

"Come on, Eilert. We can't arrive at her house on a tour bus.

Let us talk to her. If you want in on the case, try and come at it from a different angle."

Weiss gripped his coat together. He hadn't buttoned it up yet. "Right. A different angle. You wouldn't mind if we had a look at the site where the remains were found."

Toni smiled with an empathy that was never far below the surface when she was dealing with Weiss. "Enjoy yourself, Eilert. The mosquitos aren't out yet." She stepped forward and tapped his cheek affectionately. "Very pretty view from up there."

She got in the cruiser and, with Tom driving, they pulled out under the yellow lift barrier.

Joshi yawned, watching them go. "We're going to stomp around in the sticks? You know there won't be anything to see now, except..." He thought for a moment. "...sticks?"

"I want to see the soil. Maybe it had something to do with the condition of the bones."

Joshi gave in and took out his car keys. "So. Dirt, then."

CHAPTER ELEVEN

The south wing of the Moreland estate seemed designed to intimidate the common folk.

Toni Beal and Tom Krosnow followed the private road that led in off Appleby Line. The road became a gravel drive that skirted the west wing of the estate, leading them to the impressive facade of the main house. This was the period showpiece that looked out towards the lip of the escarpment and the airy vista beyond.

They parked the department SUV under an arched portico, mounting the stairs to a set of double doors flanked by windows. Tom rang the doorbell while Toni looked up and realized they were on not one but two security cameras.

After a few minutes, the door was opened by a middle-aged woman with an immaculate sweep of silver blond hair. Ruth Moreland had a long, flawless face with a pointed chin, and she was wearing makeup that Toni thought a bit overdone for daylight. Ruth made Toni think of the women on the televangelist TV programs who wore makeup and hair as emblems of righteousness. Toni put her credentials away and waited while Tom fussed with his hat.

"Kind of you to see us, Mrs. Moreland. This is my partner, Detective Krosnow. We talked on the phone; I'm Detective Beal."

Ruth's flared trousers and tucked in blouse showed off a tidy figure to best advantage as she gestured towards the entrance hall. "Yes, we can talk in the living room." Her nails looked like red jelly beans and her earrings caught the light from the hallway chandelier.

Toni glanced around, self-conscious about the film of rain on her coat. "You have a lovely house. Is it on a historic register?"

Ruth smiled with patrician patience. "It's not quite that old, and nobody really famous has lived here. Stephen Leacock visited once, but nobody outside of CanLit remembers him. The house was built in the twenties—the nineteen twenties. We have to specify the century now, don't we."

She continued to talk while she led them to the first room to the left of the hall. "There used to be a railway line from Toronto to Guelph that went behind the property. The family had its own small station back then called Ridgeway Heights. These days, we're quite remote up here, as the contractors are fond of reminding me."

"Contractors?"

"Oh, uh, we've had to do some repairs lately. Woodwork and plaster mostly, but I understand they replaced some old wiring, too." Toni thought Ruth looked unsettled by the digression. "A house this old needs a lot of upkeep. It's hardly surprising. You're here about James Krauss, I believe?"

In the corner of her eye, Toni caught a movement and turned. A tall, strikingly beautiful woman had stepped into the doorway behind them. She wasn't young, but she had one of those emaciated runway faces; all cheekbones and thin nose. Toni thought she might have had a bruised neck, but realized it was a tattoo of lilacs. Ruth followed Toni's gaze.

"Ah, Merrit, come in, will you?" Ruth smiled as though in relief. "This concerns your Mr. Krauss. You recall I told you the police were dropping by. Detectives, this is Merrit Simpson, my brother's companion."

Merrit stood beside an armchair, one hand resting on its back. "I prefer 'wife,'" she said, "but things are more complicated these days. Yes, I know James, but we haven't seen each other since last May."

Toni became wary. "Were you and Mr. Krauss close?"

A dismissive laugh. "No, of course not. What I mean is, he was in my husband's circle of friends. There were a lot of us in that group. James was one of many that we used to see now and then, mostly in the summer months when we would come here."

Toni felt a sudden sympathy for Krauss, the working guy being denied by his rich friends. "I'm sorry to have to tell you that James Krauss is dead."

She hadn't expected much of a reaction. Krauss had been missing for a year and nobody seemed to have paid much attention to the fact. But the reaction was there, all right. Not a change of expression, but Merrit shifted her stance and there was the slightest reddening of her cheeks.

Tom moved further into the room to stand behind Toni's shoulder. "His uh, remains were recovered not far from here," he explained, gesturing towards the tall westward looking windows. "In the woods."

Toni anticipated a reaction from Merrit this time, but it was Ruth who spoke.

"In the woods? You mean near the highway? That's astonishing."

"Not *especially* near the highway, or near any beaten path. There's a snow fence and a gulley along Appleby Line, which is why we're thinking he probably came from your direction. From the house. You're the closest habitation. You have no idea what he might have been doing out on regional property?

Hiking? Sightseeing? There's a lovely view down towards the cities, I believe."

"No... I haven't any idea why someone would wander into all that bush."

Once again, she deferred to Merrit, this time with an expectant glance.

Merrit's eyes darted about as though she were looking for help, but she remained still, gripping the chair back. After a second or two, she shook her head.

"Sorry."

Toni persisted. She could tell from Ruth's body language that Tom and she weren't going to be offered a seat. Ruth wanted this over with.

"The site is relatively close to your property, a ten-minute walk at most, I'd guess. It does seem likely that Mr. Krauss came from this direction."

Ruth gestured her indifference. "Since you're here, there must be some question about his death."

"Fragmentary remains in a remote woodland. We'd have to call it suspicious."

"And yet you're avoiding the word 'murder' or even 'accident.'" Ruth wasn't about to be intimidated. "I get the impression you don't know what you're dealing with. Were there no indications?"

Toni sought for the standard cliché: "The remains are..."

Tom rescued her: "We don't have a lot to work with."

"Well, I knew James to say hello," Ruth said. "He was a frequent visitor once, but we haven't heard from him since—what did you say, Merrit? May?"

"Wasn't he an employee of yours, Mrs. Moreland?"

Ruth seemed momentarily uncertain. "A friend of the family, but yes, I think you're right. Merrit had to remind me that James, in fact, worked for MorwynBIO, in which I hold a sizable interest. That makes him an employee of sorts, I suppose, though I never thought of him that way."

"Do either of you recall the last time he was here? The circumstances, that is."

Ruth shrugged. "I'm sorry to tell you that I don't. I barely noticed James's comings and goings because he wasn't here to see me. He would have joined my brother down on the terrace level. I seldom went down there." Once again, Ruth tried to hand the inquiry off to the slender figure clinging to a high-backed armchair. "Merrit, darling?"

"There was nothing special happening in May," Merrit added. "Noah and I entertained down below on the terrace, so it would have been social. Drinks and lunch maybe. Cards in the games room. Lots of other people. Not card cards, mind you. Magic: The Gathering, maybe."

Toni picked up on Merrit's use of the past tense. Did they no longer entertain?

She looked back at Ruth. "Could your brother help us clarify the relationship and the circumstances?"

There was a pause—a sudden sense of discomfort in the room. Merrit stared at the carpet and Ruth wrung her hands slowly.

At last, Ruth said, "I'm sad to say, that's impossible. My brother has been unable to communicate for some time now."

Toni glanced at Tom, genuinely confused. "I'm so sorry. What happened to him?"

"There isn't a simple answer to that," Ruth said. "And believe me, we've spared no expense trying to find out. I'll just say that his condition is related to his long-term use of drugs. You'll forgive me if I don't go into it further. He had nothing to do with James's disappearance." She too lowered her eyes to the carpet for a moment.

"And even if he had, my brother's beyond punishment now. Dr. Hudson here will confirm everything I've said."

The sudden reference puzzled Toni, but she glanced to her

left as a tall man in a grey suit unfolded himself out of a wing-back chair. He'd been listening silently, turned away towards the great fireplace with its towering blue-tiled mantle. Hudson's features were strong and unlined, but his hair was thin, like a silver sheen on his scalp. His eyes looked enormous behind black-framed glasses.

He nodded solemnly, then began speaking without being prompted. "Catatonia, triggered by withdrawal from cocaine and opioids. Probably induced by drug interactions, but it's a condition that was developing over months. He's at the point now where he's confined to a wheelchair, unable to speak."

"I see. I'm sorry. He's in a care facility then?"

Ruth shook her head. "There's no need for that. We have plenty of room and resources here, and Eric sees to it that Noah has the attention and medications he needs. I don't want Noah forgotten in some seniors' residence, especially with all this talk on the news of substandard care."

"Noah…is *here*?"

Toni glanced up at the top of the grand staircase, her mind racing. Eilert was right. The business of James Krauss's death had become more focussed, and this house appeared to be at the epicentre.

Tom punched at his hat—a sign they should go. Toni would have tried another tack, but the news about Ruth's brother had thrown her, and she blanked. In the short term, it felt like a brick wall had been placed in their way.

"Well, uh. Thank you. If we have more questions…"

The rest of her sentence was lost in a mutter of pleasantries and a clatter of shoes on the marble tiles of the entry hall.

CHAPTER TWELVE

Just above the hair-raising switchback that climbs Appleby Line up onto the escarpment, Prem Joshi stared at the ground, kicking at weeds. A torn piece of old yellow police tape was knotted around a nearby bush.

"Toni knew we wouldn't find anything out here," he grumbled. "The site team picked up all the useful fragments a year ago."

"Not quite." Weiss squatted close to the tangle of spring weeds and matted pine needles. "You can still see where they raked the ground to extract the remains, and they haven't bothered with these scraps of fabric. Look at that, that little piece of material."

Joshi bent over. "It's a belt loop."

"Good for you, Prem. The way you said that, I could practically see Krauss standing there fully clothed."

"You're easily pleased."

"It is pretty out here though, isn't it, even without the leaves? This time of year, you can see the cities down through the bare branches—Oakville, Burlington—all the way to the lake." He pointed to the west where Lake Ontario seemed to dwindle to nothing. "That's Hamilton over there."

Joshi was unimpressed by the view. Instead, he was facing east along the rim of the escarpment. "A lot of dead trees over that way."

"Trees without leaves, you mean."

"No, I mean, *dead*."

Weiss stood, rubbing his hands to get the leaf meal off his fingers. "Yes, I see what you mean. No buds, broken branches. That's the direction towards the house over there."

Joshi smiled, knowing what was coming. "We're going to just mosey on over to Moreland House, aren't we?"

"Approaching the case from a different angle, Prem."

"Yeah, from the west," Joshi smirked.

The two detectives began hiking through the trees, a mix of spiky conifers and budding maples, the dead leaves crunching loudly beneath their feet. There appeared to be a rough path, defined mostly by dead ground cover. It was as if some natural blight had run its course along the lip of the steep slope.

Joshi was watching his feet on the uneven ground, but Weiss kept looking up.

"Odd. Healthy trees with brittle branches. On Google Earth, you can see all this area. Just north of where we left our car? That's the private access road to the house. It runs right to the gates of the Moreland property." He pointed towards the lake. "You can enter Ruth Moreland's estate on a lower road, too, down below the escarpment. That road leads to the gardens, pond, and terrace. There's some sort of lift between the two levels."

Joshi looked back over his shoulder. "They have to take an elevator down to their front yard?"

"'Front yard' doesn't do it justice, Prem. Judging from the aerial images, they could sell tickets to their gardens."

The only sound in the early spring air was the steady

crunching of sticks and leaves beneath their feet. They walked with a constant craning of their necks, taking in a phenomenon neither one of them could put into words. It was as if a large beast had smashed its way through the lower branches.

They broke through the last thatch of withered branches and the western aspect of the Moreland mansion presented itself in a sweep of colonnades and turrets.

"And there's the house," Weiss said.

Joshi reared back, wide-eyed and nodding. "Chateau, you mean. Looks old. Early twentieth-century maybe?" He looked around at the expanse of lawn leading up to the house and sniffed. "You couldn't sell tickets to *these* gardens. Not the way the grass is all gray and matted down."

Weiss slitted his eyelids, which allowed him to get an impression of the vista. It was obvious to what Joshi was referring. The wet grass was long and its narrow leaves shone in the afternoon light, but the velvet sweep of unmown grass was bisected by an avenue of grey about the width of a car. The bleached grass here seemed to run in an erratic, meandering path to their feet. Weiss stopped following it with his eyes and turned slowly until he was looking back at the woods.

"Hmm. Something's killed that swathe of grass...and a number of tree branches all the way back towards the crime scene. It's obvious once you notice the pattern."

They crossed the lawn, avoiding the parched growth that marred the grass, until they were standing beneath a grand two-storey structure supported by columns. The surfaces of the columns were engraved with sinuous Art Nouveau reeds that spread into an arrangement of plaster leaves at the capital. Overhead, a tracery of painted wood had partially collapsed, sagging a raw tangle of broken moulding just above their heads.

Joshi ducked his way under. "This entrance way's in pretty bad shape. I thought Moreland had money."

"This is the old porte-cochère where limousines could pull

up out of the elements," Weiss said. "You wouldn't want to get your derby or your silk cravat wet, now would you? The modern driveway and portico are round the front—on the southern facade.

"And here, see? You see these sliding glass doors? They were for admitting carriages or limousines right into the interior of the house."

The glass doors were partially open—again about the width of a car—but their black wrought iron frames were misshapen and the glass had an irregular pattern of opaque blotches like leeched concrete.

The wooden beam that allowed the doors to slide open on suspended metal tracks looked ready to collapse. Even the surrounding stonework was crumbling in places; the mortar had turned to powder which bleached the gravel drive with a grey bloom of lime. Joshi looked at the dust on his fingertips with distaste.

"I can't believe Mrs. Moreland would let things get so bad. Maybe she's not as rich as we think."

Weiss raised one brow and stated the obvious: "It seems the doorway to the interior is open."

The door frames weren't rusty. Instead, it almost looked like the iron had been corroded with acid. Weiss entered the house, cautiously, careful not to scrape his coat on the rough metal.

Joshi followed, wary, his neck craned. "Hey, this is B and E. Think about it, Eilert; you're breaking and entering a house that already has cops in it. Why do you have to be so damn colourful?"

But Weiss was lost in wonder at the enclosed space. The crushed gravel floor was clearly intended for loading and unloading vehicles, but the broad skylight high above their heads was etched in Art Deco fans and framed in geometrical lines of applied gold. The ground level trappings—the stained glass screen in repeating rosettes of purple and Parrish blue, the green copper wall sconces with their crystalline bulbs—had an aura of decay and disuse.

About the length of a carriage and two horses inside the house, there was an entranceway designed to lead visitors even further into the interior and the guest reception rooms beyond. Its flattened arch was flanked on either side with figurative peacock tail tapestries. Weiss couldn't resist running his fingers across the faded fabric.

"They must've shut down this wing completely. Look at this weaving, Prem. My God. The material is unravelling from its own weight. It looks a hundred years old and completely neglected." He looked around at the decrepitude that seemed to have bleached the life out of everything. "It doesn't even look *safe* in here."

Joshi sneaked a wary look at the elegant skylight, imagining its weight crashing down to complete the scene of ruin. He laid a hand softly on Weiss's back.

Weiss turned, nodded, and they began working their way back, heading out through the iron doors, towards the woods.

When they had reached the fringe of trees at the edge of the formal lawn, Weiss slowed and looked up.

"What are you thinking?" Joshi said.

"I'm seeing that tree—the healthy one with the withered branches?"

"So?"

"So? So, I'm thinking about James Krauss's skull—his two-tone remains?"

Joshi closed one eye. "Oh…kay."

"Fuck, I don't know, Prem. It's just interesting, isn't it? A pattern." He gestured to his right. "I mean, here you've got wood that's dead but still solid…" His pointing finger followed the branch outward. "…and here, you've got wood that's punky and ready to drop off. Same branch. Now, what if Heddy had that branch on her table, broken in two. What would she say?"

Joshi thought for a minute, then caught on. "She'd say, 'Oh, this wood is a year old. And *this* wood over here is ten years old. And then she'd bat her sexy lashes and say, 'I think you're cute, Eilert—in a decrepit sort of way.'"

"Keep your eye on the ball, Prem."

"Hey, you brought her up."

CHAPTER THIRTEEN

Weiss thought long and hard about asking Heddy Nesbit out. James Krauss's poor brittle bones gave him an excuse to drop by the evidence archive, but the conversation about the bones had nowhere to go. That Friday Weiss had prepared, however.

"Have you ever been to The Greenhouse Café?" he said, leaning in the doorway of the corner office where she catalogued the lower level holdings. "They've got this wooden trellis on the wall where they hang potted plants. Their spring display should be nice..."

"Sounds lovely."

She sat swinging demurely from side to side in her swivel chair. When he asked her out, her answer had been brief, but her lips were tightly pursed as she tried to control a grin that threatened to light up the gloom of her office.

The next day was a Saturday, and Heddy looked surprised when he came for her at her townhome opposite the Mapleview Mall. The surprise was directed at his car, a generic but new-looking Chevrolet.

"I thought you had an older car."

"It's being appraised by the Smithsonian. This is a rental."

It was late afternoon and the overcast skies had persisted over the GTA. Weiss parked at the Royal Botanical Gardens and they walked on towards the main building. They lingered in the gift shop, Heddy admiring the floral design plates and hanging glass orbs until their conversation led them down a level into the café.

And so there she was with her vegetarian chilli, and he with his seafood pie.

"This is nice," she said, "but I'm curious why you wanted to come halfway to Hamilton."

"To the botanical gardens? I brought you here because I wanted to show you something."

"The trellis? It's lovely."

"No. That's not it. You brought me in to consult on your mysterious skull fragments, so I'm bringing you in to consult on my Noah Goodwyn file."

She smiled her skepticism. "The Noah Goodwyn file doesn't officially exist yet. I have a computer in my office, too, you know."

"And you've been checking my caseload?"

"I worry about you. Is that okay?"

Weiss gave a little bow. "Well, I don't want you worrying, but thanks. I'm already a universal object of pity in the department."

"Don't say that. You're not the only person in the division to have personal tragedy in their lives. Take me—widowed at thirty."

The comment wasn't meant as a rebuke, but Weiss saw the truth in it. He couldn't help the self-pity that would come to the surface from time to time. He would brood like some Byronic loner until someone spoke to him, and then brighten and become affable.

If you make enough mistakes, it becomes your style, and gloom had become his style of late.

"What happened?" he said.

She touched his fingertips, thanking him for his concern. "He was military. Killed in a training accident at Camp Borden. He wasn't even overseas, and I got this phone call..."

"My God. I'm sorry."

Her hand went to her neck and she absently fingered the gold chain that hung there. Weiss noticed for the first time that it was a cross. Some part of him recoiled. His wife had been religious and she'd used her beliefs like a flamethrower to curse him. In the process, she'd reamed out any vestige of belief he had inherited from his Scottish mother.

"That was many years ago now," Heddy was saying. "And yes, we're the same age, you and I. I checked. Give or take."

"That computer in your office again?"

"It can get slow down in evidence."

"Does it bother you, being below street level like that?"

"I've got windows."

"Yes, but they're above your head."

"Have you ever heard of anyone working their way *down* in the world? That's me. I was perfectly happy to get assigned to archives. In fact, I lobbied for it."

"Are you hiding from something? It strikes me as lonely and quiet down there."

"No, not hiding. I just like the idea of being someplace safe and controlled."

"Controlled?" Weiss raised an eyebrow.

Heddy blushed and laughed. "I suppose I *meant* controllable. What's the opposite of claustrophobia?"

"Agoraphobia. Fear of open spaces."

"No, that's not me either. I just find comfort in being..."

"Confined?"

"Cut that out."

"Cosseted, then."

"I don't even know that word." She looked at him accusingly. "I've heard you're something of a renaissance man."

"I'm not sure what that is these days. I think it means old-fashioned. But, I do like art. Sort of."

"How can you like art 'sort of?'"

"I love illustrations, particularly the great works of the early twentieth century: Maxfield Parrish, Coles Phillips, J. C. Leyendecker."

"Norman Rockwell?"

Weiss nodded. "I've been to his studio in Stockbridge. Met his son, Jarvis."

"I'm sorry I don't know more. I'd like to talk to you about art."

"What about you?"

"I was a hairdresser when I was young. Went back to college when my husband passed and got into police services as a second career. I wanted to be able to say I'd served, too. By the way, I was a great hairdresser."

"It explains why you're so... Would it be harassment if I told you you're attractive?"

Heddy primped happily. "I don't feel patronized at all. Maybe it's because you're looking at me over a glass of white wine in a lovely café."

Weiss folded his hands on the white tablecloth. "That's a relief. I really wanted the 'attractive' thing read into the record. I felt it was something that needed to be acknowledged."

"It's duly noted. Thank you. So, what did you want to show me?"

"When we're done, I'd like to take you down to Cootes Paradise. That's the wetland just off the harbour. It's near here."

"What's there?"

"Do you like balloons?" he asked.

***

It was a short drive from the lot of the Royal Botanical Gardens, off the highway and down onto the wetland path.

It was still relatively early, but the cloud layer had deepened and dropped low over the marsh. Herons, bitterns, and egrets skimmed and alighted across the broken vastness of shallow water. Even the open waterways were green with water plants that here and there broke the surface.

Weiss cruised the roadway slowly, letting Heddy enjoy the view until they came to a lay-by. He pulled off and parked facing the rushes and shallows.

"Look, out there," Weiss said, rolling down her window using the button on his side. The rich humidity of the swamp filled the car with the smell of mellow growth and pond water.

"What is it?"

Heddy looked out across the thick thatch of green, scattered with open water. In the early twilight, she could make out a looming shape that didn't belong there. Floating on a nearby stretch of grassy marsh was a soft plastic bubble the size of a panel van.

"It's a big balloon thing," Weiss explained. "Semi inflated—kind of a weather balloon, I guess."

"What's it doing out there on the water?" she said.

"There are five of them spread along the walkways down here. It's an art installation. The artist moored those balloons out there using a small boat and inflated them with a hairdryer, so I read. The idea is they're supposed to be like lungs. She's trying to make the point that the wetlands are the lungs of the planet. You know, like the rain forests?"

Heddy looked at the pearlescent bubble nestled in weedy water and nodded. "It's strangely beautiful in this half-light, but what an odd idea. I think of art as something that you can buy and set up in your yard or on your estate. I can't see how anyone could *buy* such a thing. I mean, where would you put it? How would you maintain it?"

Weiss laughed. "I know. Kind of crazy, isn't it? But I think that's part of the point. The artist who did these installations is independently wealthy, you see. She put her own money into organizing and deploying all of this. The installations will get a little coverage in the press, and then they'll be gone. Maybe the artist will build a sort of reputation with time."

"I hope she's got a *lot* of money, otherwise she's going to have a short career. You could go broke saving the planet."

Weiss turned to look at Heddy's heart-breaking profile against the pale light of the window. "As a matter of fact, she does have a whole lot of money, and one day she'll have a whole lot more. She could be an entrepreneur or a big-time investor if she wanted, but she chooses to do…" Weiss gestured. "…this. To make little statements about her world."

Heddy sensed he'd grown thoughtful, so she turned and looked at him in the darkness of the car. They made eye contact and he said, "So, that's my question for you, Heddy. What do you think? Is it healthy, what this young woman is doing? Is she an artist, or is she a flake?"

Heddy knitted her brow. "I think…she's an artist." Weiss nodded. Then Heddy smiled and said, "Not an illustrator, though. So why are you interested?"

"Ah, because the artist's name is Sammy, and she happens to be the daughter of Noah Goodwyn."

CHAPTER FOURTEEN

Evan Favaro was seated at a glass coffee table with a television host, a woman almost as photogenic as he was. Evan wore a light grey suit with a baby blue shirt open at the neck. The host was a beautiful Black woman who carried herself like a model, blooming under the glare.

Shrinking under the same hot studio lights was a member of the studio audience, a full-figured woman with a pretty round face. She was wearing a well-fitting pantsuit in a patterned satin material. In anyone's living room, she would have been the object of admiring glances, but in the fashion hyped world of daytime talk shows, she couldn't hope to compete and she winced at her own clumsiness.

At the same time, she was thrilled to be the object of Evan's attention, however briefly.

"Now, Mischa," Evan smiled at her, "you've been warned not to take our little talk too seriously—we're just having a little fun here. By giving me this little sample of your handwriting, you're granting me permission to read what I can into it? Right?"

Mischa grinned and nodded, touching her cheek with on-camera embarrassment.

"So, you understand that I'm just guessing when I say that you're a care provider...that you carry a lot of responsibility in your daily life. But you find ways to relax, don't you? Music makes you feel good." Evan pointed to his clipboard and appeared to trace something with an elegant pinky.

"The way you terminate your descenders here—and here." Evan's eyebrows went up as though he saw something floating just in front of Mischa's eyes. "A guitar. Yes...an acoustic guitar. Country...folk. You're learning; you already make people happy with your songs."

It went on like this, the studio audience, composed mostly of well-dressed women, young and old, glancing from the fashionably decorated set to the flat monitors above their heads. On both, Evan Favaro looked good. His clothes were provided by designers who were credited at the end of the show, and subtle makeup chiselled his features to a fine edge, but there was more there: the personality that jumped off the TV screen and made love to women seated on their couches at home while they sipped diet soda was real enough.

The audience listened to Evan's "guesses" and imbued them with wonder as though the careful generalities that Evan delivered were magic utterances.

Carly Rouhl was seated near the back of the audience, perched on the upper level of an aluminum bleacher. It was the first time she had attended a live taping of Evan's work. Watching Evan on her home TV, she'd been a bit embarrassed for him. A victim herself of Evan's charm, Carly nevertheless thought what he did amounted to a silly magic show masquerading as lifestyle programming.

Being in the studio audience, watching the fawning smiles of the women around her, she hadn't changed her mind. Still, there was something different this time, something about the fine line between fun and charlatanism that fascinated her.

When Evan's workday was over and the last adoring fan

walked out into the streets of downtown Toronto, Carly drove him to a quiet coffee bar in Port Credit. A place anywhere near the studio was out of the question—that's where the fans went.

Of course, Evan had brought his megawatt charm with him, but Carly was beginning to develop a sort of antibody that allowed her to tune out his gentle touch and adoring smile.

"You were great, as usual," Carly said, wanting to get the formalities out of the way.

"Don't," he said, looking away in embarrassment. "I know you don't approve of my show biz nonsense."

"No, I mean that you're genuinely good at what you do. Not the easy, ingratiating manner and all that. I mean the way you draw people out using their handwriting as a sort of prop."

Evan stared at her over his coffee cup, skeptical and wary. "What's this about? You *hate* daytime TV, and what I do makes you squirm."

Carly couldn't help it. She squirmed, conceding the point. "I want to ask you about 'cold reading.'"

"Oh, my God…"

"Look, don't get all defensive about it. I know all that stuff about how it's entertainment, not deception. I'm not judging you. I have a reason for being interested."

Evan raised his eyes to the ceiling fan, pleading for deliverance.

"Please, Evan."

There was something heartfelt about Carly's tone that made him frown in concern. "What's this really about?"

Carly thought about being coy, but she realized that if she wanted Evan to be square with her, she had to do the same. "It's about these…imaginings I'm having."

"Visions, you mean."

"Now, see, that's where I want to draw the line. I believe that I'm using my imagination, piecing together bits of information, maybe even at a subconscious level. What I wind up with is a sort of intuitive leap. I see things in my mind's eye and sometimes I get it right."

"We talked about this before. You said that your father was inventing his stories using that kind of intuition."

"Yes, and we literary types call it 'the creative process.' Dad was a genius at it in his own way."

"And now you think *you're* doing it?"

Carly winced and sat back to sip her tea. After a pained second, she said, "Maybe."

"What does this have to do with me interpreting handwriting?"

"Well, I've been thinking about what you do; you use your knowledge of graphology to make broad inferences about a person, but the rest…"

"Go on."

"Take that stuff about the woman playing country music on her acoustic guitar…" She waited while Evan sighed and stared out the window.

Carly was insistent. "Go on, tell me."

Evan put his cup down and hung his head. "She has calluses on her fingertips. Nails shorter on the chording hand, long on the picking hand—except for the little finger which rests on the pickguard. If she's fingerpicking, she's probably fairly good. Most women her age don't buy electric guitars, and if she's picking on an acoustic, she probably goes for simple country or folk tunes. Just guesses."

Carly nodded. "Skilled guesses."

"Cold reading."

Carly became thoughtful, staring at the tabletop. "I've been reading about Peter Hurkos."

"Who's that?"

"He was a famous psychic. They brought him in to consult on the Boston Strangler case and the Sharon Tate murder. He was the most famous psychic of his day—maybe one of the most famous ever—but the article on Wikipedia says that he did cold readings, taking in all sorts of little clues and weaving together clever guesses."

"Look, Carly, I never pretend to be a psychic."

"No, it's not that. What I'm wondering is… Can someone be cold reading and not *know* she's doing it?"

Evan shook his head. "I know exactly what I'm doing, and there's no ESP about it."

"And when you were speaking to that Mischa woman, did you ever find a picture developing in your mind? Did you begin to see her with her guitar?"

Evan's eyebrows rose. "Well…I…I suppose. Maybe. But that's just the thinking process."

"Yes, it's true. Some of us think visually—which means we conjure up images in our minds." She sat back, her cup in both hands. Her head bobbed gently as though she was congratulating herself on an insight. "So, when I experience a so-called vision, I could be just putting together some remembered observations and drawing some conclusions. Thanks, Evan."

Evan looked defeated. Would he ever get used to the way this fabulous woman thought?

CHAPTER FIFTEEN

Harriet Blain, a bespectacled blond with red lips and green shell earrings, tapped her cheekbone with a yellow highlighter. "And he's coming here to your office?"

"I called, and he offered to drop by. He should be here any minute."

"A detective? Doesn't that kind of give you the creeps? Like everything you say to him could become a…a dossier or an affidavit or something. Why do you want to talk to him? You have me."

"You're sweet to listen, but you're also way too credulous. I need someone to tell me I'm fucked up and need to see a specialist."

"Okay, but you're going too far. He's the police; he might get you committed."

Carly smiled. "He's nice police. He doesn't get you committed. He takes you out to a child's playground covered in snow and tells you what the authorities might actually believe. That's what happened when my father died. He's like a…" She thought for a moment. "…a go-between."

"Between what?"

"Between what's wacko and what's 'huh, really?' Between—I don't know—madness and reality?"

Harriet moved to the window and looked out over the plaza's rain-soaked parking lot. She pretended to be arranging the potted plants on the windowsill. A tall, thin man with a long greying brush cut was closing the door of an unmarked police cruiser. He put on a tweed hat against the rain.

"Is this him? This guy is way too old for you, by the way."

Carly grinned. "It's not like that." She looked around the offices of *Escarpment Magazine*. "Tell the others to give us some space, will you? This shouldn't take too long."

Harriet looked at Carly's white blouse. "Fine, but put your sweater on. You're showing way too much skin for a police interrogation."

"This isn't an interrogation. It's…civic involvement."

"I thought you were involved with Evan."

"Harriet. Be good, will you? Sit at your desk and act casual. *Please.*"

Weiss stepped in through the glass door, turning his coat inside out to trap the raindrops. He took his hat off and gave a little bow before hooking it on the coat rack.

"Detective." Carly took the coat and found an empty hook.

"Ms. Rouhl." Weiss smiled, giving a polite nod.

"Thank you for dropping by. I wanted to tell you…" Carly looked across the open-plan office where Harriet was dutifully telling the staff not to stare. Harriet caught Weiss's eye and sparkled, but Weiss rubbed his chin and turned back to watching Carly fuss with the furniture.

"I…uh…started writing a story last night." She offered Weiss a chair. "Sorry about the chair. It wobbles a bit. So does mine. I guess they all do." She was babbling and knew it.

Weiss settled. "Another profile piece?"

"No, this story I'm writing is…fiction."

Weiss squinted at her. "The expression on your face says,

'Fiction, nod, nod, wink, wink.' I see that look a lot in my line of work." He reached into his jacket and waved his little digital recorder. "Relax. You're not being recorded."

"That's good. After that murder-suicide business at my father's house, they must already think I'm a flake."

"They, meaning my superiors?" Weiss thought for a moment. "They think you're a…woman of mystery. My friend, Heddy, down in Evidence coined that phrase."

Carly glanced out at the office where reporters and layout people worked at their flat screens. "Oh, great. Carly Rouhl, woman of mystery works here. The advertisers will be thrilled."

"Your magazine sells perfume and cosmetics. 'Mystery woman' works for you."

Carly's brow went up. "Huh. Hadn't thought of it that way. That's good."

"So—'fiction.' I didn't know you wrote fiction."

"I wrote some short stories when I was in university, but the truth is I gave that up years ago. I couldn't stand the contrast between my lame efforts and my father's gift for truth."

"Literary truth. It's helpful to keep that separate from the Truth with a capital T. Anyway, what possessed you to start again, writing fiction?"

"'Possessed.'" She shook her finger at him. "Nice. Nice way of putting it. I don't know what got into me. These thoughts were just buzzing around in my head and I thought maybe if I could put something down on paper…well, on a screen anyway."

"And you want to tell me about it?" A softness came into his voice and his eyes radiated smile lines. It was like watching cracks form on pond ice. "What's on your mind, Carly? I mean, Ms. Rouhl…"

She noticed the formality. "Oh, that's right. I've caught you on duty, haven't I? Call me Carly anyway. I won't tell anyone— and you're not recording."

"Then maybe you won't tell anyone if I ask you for a cup of

tea." He nodded towards the hot water dispenser nearby where two staffers were lingering over instant coffee. "I've had a rough morning."

"Oh, sorry. Sure. That will be nice. I'll just be a moment. Earl Grey okay?"

"Perfect. Black, please."

"Lemon?"

"I'm a policeman."

"Oh," Carly said, not sure what that meant.

Weiss looked around, returning a few curious glances with little nods.

When Carly returned with hot mugs flagged with Twinings labels and no lemon, he said, "I want to hear your story."

"I warn you. This isn't the story I owe you either—the one where we drink scotch and talk about my father."

"Okay, that story can wait. What's this one about?"

Having settled in her chair, she immediately popped up again and returned with a saucer. "For our tea bags. I always forget that."

Weiss noted the avoidance and her nervousness. Carly took a deep breath. "So, this story is about…a pineapple. Well, it started with a pineapple, anyway. A wooden pineapple on a staircase bannister. Beautifully carved and finished, and worn with decades of use." She closed her eyes for a second. "Or maybe it was on a wall. Anyway, some kind of carved decoration." She went on. "Carpet runners, oak panels. Very classy."

This wasn't going well. Carly had to stop and blink her eyes as if to stem the flow of images.

Weiss watched, nodding encouragement. "So, a story about a staircase?"

"See, that's the thing—it's not just the staircase. They're everywhere, like a motif. On the furniture above the doorway arches, even in the carpet. Pineapples…"

"Sounds a bit…gaudy."

"Oh, no, it's not like that. It's all very tasteful, actually. Rich and mellow. Of course, we literary types are very keen on symbolism, so I looked it up online. Seems the pineapple is a traditional symbol of hospitality. It originated in the eighteenth century in New England." Carly was excited now.

"It started with the horrors of the slave trade, you see. There used to be a triangular trade route: slaves from Africa to Jamaica and the islands where the ships would pick up rum, sugar…and pineapples. The pineapples wound up along with the rum, among the rich landowners of Newport, Rhode Island, and then the ships would sail off back to Africa for more slaves. Pineapples were pretty exotic back then, and only the rich people in their great panelled mansions could afford to serve pineapple to guests. It's a complex symbol, tainted by its association, not just with the inhumanity of slavery, but with the extravagance of the upper class."

"I see. The pineapple became a symbol of lavish hospitality."

"Among the well to do, yes. Exactly."

Weiss smiled. "What can I say, Carly? I'm no critic, but your story may need a bit more plot."

Carly's attempt at a light mood failed her. She had to make him understand. She looked Weiss straight in the eye and grew still.

"They're killing him, Eilert."

"What?"

"Torturing him, over and over. He's going slowly mad with the pain."

"Carly, what are you telling me? I'm just a simple policeman."

"Not so simple. That's what I'm counting on. After all, I've seen your…what shall I call it? Your open-mindedness?"

Weiss leaned forward in concern. "You seem genuinely upset."

Carly pinched the bridge of her nose, letting her glossy hair fall forward. "I'm not used to this. I write softball profiles of celebrities and local entrepreneurs because I've led a peaceful, privileged life in the home of a great writer. What do I know of torture and murder? Right?"

"You made the acquaintance of Marcella Cole."

"Well, there is that. But that kind of violence is alien to me." She sat back, crossing her arms defensively. "But then, what did my *father* know? Everyone's heard stories about A.L. Rouhl's so-called adventures through Ireland, Louisiana, or wherever; how he would set himself up with a bourbon in a noisy roadhouse, pass the time of day with strangers, and jot down the odd note on a yellow pad. Then he'd come home to Burlington and sit in his desk chair and write—wonderful and terrifying stories of hatred and conspiracy."

"Yes. The creative process."

"Yeah, sure," she said bitterly. "The creative process. I've had occasion to think a lot about the creative process lately. You can't win a Governor General's Award making up stories out of whole cloth. I can't really understand it, but A.L. Rouhl is the one who was *possessed*."

"Are you being metaphorical here? I can see this is frightening you, but I don't know how to reassure you. You're a very clever, very strong woman. I've seen how you handled the death of that Cole woman in your father's house."

Carly looked around wildly. She wasn't explaining this well because she couldn't. At last, she said, "Do you want to know who the hero of my story is?"

"I..."

"Well, of course, I'd have to *change* the name if I wanted to get my story published, wouldn't I? I don't want any actions for libel. After all, that's what my father did. Then, I could call my story 'fiction.'" She grew thoughtful. "Or I could get a little closer to the Truth with a capital T, and call it 'nonfiction'—travel writing, you might say, being careful once again to change the names."

"Yes, I see what you're getting at. That's what your father wrote: travel books about real people. At least, that's what he called them."

"That label was actually his publisher's idea. They needed a way of marketing his stuff. It didn't matter to my father; he somehow managed to compartmentalize it all in his mind. He wrote his stories and didn't lose any sleep over the real people who inspired him, even when he wove their lives into disturbing melodramas. Until Marcella Cole decided to murder him in revenge, that is, because he had written about her."

Weiss strained to understand. They were back to the evil woman who had tracked Carly down to her father's house and threatened her with a gun.

"Your father believed that he was, in effect, murdered by one of his characters—Marcella Cole. But what about you, Carly? Are you losing sleep over real people?"

Carly had lost the aura of calm assumed for the benefit of her staff. Anyone in the office could have heard her say, "I'm talking about Noah Goodwyn, Eilert. The man you were asking me about. You came to me wanting to know about him and where he was—the funny little man who gave me a piece of carved soapstone from his personal collection."

"And you think he's in some kind of distress?"

"Please don't ask me what I *think*. I'm writing a story, okay? I haven't got any more to tell you. Yet."

"Carly..."

Weiss rocked back in the chair, testing its wobble. Who was he to press her? He had come to her at her father's house with the vaguest of suspicions of his own about Goodwyn, and now Carly was venting her own suspicions about Noah back at him.

That's what it came down to. Unsubstantiated suspicions. What Weiss couldn't explain away was that, just as he trusted his own instincts, he trusted hers. It was as if, at some level, they were in sync.

Weiss finished his tea and stood. "Are you alone in that house? Your father's house?"

Uh oh, thought Carly. *He's about to patronize me.* "I've thought about hiring a housekeeper. I can certainly afford it now. I lost my father, and I lost Peggy here at work. Peggy was a good friend."

"What about Mr. Favaro? Have you been able to confide in him?"

"Evan?" She blinked in surprise. "Yes, I should give him a call. It's not fair to leave our relationship up to him, is it? I can't seem to forgive him for being so uncritical of me."

Weiss got his coat and started to put it on. "You haven't actually *heard* from Noah, have you?"

Suddenly irritated, she followed him to the door and, leaning close, she said in a fierce whisper, "No, and—listen to me, Eilert—neither will anyone else. He's far past that now."

Weiss nodded slowly, puzzled by her certainty. "And you still can't suggest where I might look for him?"

She held his gaze. "I think I just did."

He thought for a moment. "Pineapples?"

"That's all I've got."

CHAPTER SIXTEEN

That evening was perfect for Carly. Evan called—she had always waited for him to call—and Carly suggested a reading of *Under Milk Wood* at the Performing Arts Centre which was within walking distance of her father's house. The Welsh actors, each taking several parts, wandered from blue spotlights to fishing net webbed risers, intoning Dylan Thomas's word drunk lines. Carly was in her element, but Evan Favaro shifted uncomfortably in his seat as Captain Cat incanted and Molly Garter mewed across the footlights.

For Carly, this was the old story in their relationship: they were a mismatched pair. What was she doing here with a man who only read scientific abstracts and liked movies about the Marvel Universe?

Okay, so he looked more debonair and striking than any of the actors up on the stage, his boyish features aglow from the reflected stage lighting. But there would be no animated discussion in the lobby at intermission about the merits of Thomas's villanelles. Instead, Evan would buy her a glass of chilled white wine and look at her adoringly with those almond eyes, and annoyingly, it would be enough for her.

So, why was she with him again?

There was the sex, of course. She'd spent more time choosing her panties and bra than the rest of her wardrobe. Goddamit, she'd even put on eye makeup. Evan made her feel shallow and superficial, but something in her that she'd rather not acknowledge bloomed in his company.

Then there was the walk along the lakeside park to the public pier which curved snake-like into Burlington Bay. The sinuous light posts gave a warm glow to the night, but it was early spring and the light breeze from the bay was cool. Carly turned back and took in the waterfront park and the city beyond.

"Guess who I've been seeing behind your back," she said.

"Making me jealous is beneath you, Car."

"Our nemesis, Eilert Weiss."

"The detective? Christ, is he still harassing you? I thought he had his nice tidy report filed and shelved."

"I'd hardly describe Dad's so-called murder of Marcella Cole as 'tidy,' but no, it wasn't harassment. In fact, it never really was. You can *talk* to Weiss. He's actually a gentle, lonely soul. If he was a lot younger, you just might have something to worry about."

"What did he want?"

"He was asking about Noah Goodwyn. Remember I told you I interviewed him for that local entrepreneur profile?"

"I don't like where this is going. You did a profile on *me* and I fell hopelessly in love with you."

Carly buried her face in the warmth of his shoulder as much to hide the bloom in her cheeks as in affection. "Don't worry," she said. "You're going to get laid tonight. You don't have to be charming."

"Well, that's a relief. So, what about Goodwyn?"

"The police are after Goodwyn for some public mischief thing, but that's not what I wanted to talk to you about."

"Mischief? I thought Weiss was a homicide cop."

"This is Burlington, not Chicago. A homicide cop in Burlington would spend half his time doing Sudoku. Shut up and listen. I started to write a story last night."

"Are we still talking about Noah Goodwyn?"

"Strangely enough, I think we are. I sit down at the dining room table and I just start to write, okay? Normally, I'd have reams of research beside me, but this kind of writing—well, you just write what's in your head. So, all that comes to me is this interesting character, and I know right away that the character is based on Noah Goodwyn. That's reasonable enough; Noah is the most remarkable person I've come across in a while. He has all these quirky qualities that translate to the page easily.

"I'm planning to make this a work of fiction so I need some drama, some tension. I've already written the public profile, now I'm free to use my imagination."

"And how did it go?"

Carly twisted her wide Rouhl lips into a pout. "I don't know how to explain this. I think I'm going to have to use an analogy. Brace yourself."

He grinned and took hold of the guardrail. "Okay, I'm ready."

"Well, it's as though I try to think something up and someone grabs the wheel."

"Wait, so you're driving a car, and someone else turns you in an unexpected direction? This would be easier if I had a chalkboard."

"Yeah, it's like that, like my imagination is being hijacked off in a direction I hadn't anticipated."

"Stop. Stop. You're only allowed one analogy. God, you literary people."

"Okay. You can unclench."

"What does it matter what direction your imagination takes anyway, as long as it's interesting?"

"It matters because the direction scares the shit out of me.

I'm a nice person, right? I don't have hidden neuroses in my life. I was never abandoned or abused. Sure, it was tough when Mum died, and Dad was lost in his work a lot of the time, but I was an introvert anyway. I had all the comforts and distractions that money could buy. I was never exposed to the seamy side of life. Dad never shared that stuff with me. Given his terminal illness, even his suicide struck me as a reasonable choice. Not defensible, mind you, but understandable."

"But your imaginings are dark?"

"Whoa, yeah. Noah seems to be moving through surroundings that are familiar to him. He's in places he's loved, sometimes with people he knows. There are happy, laughing parties around a swimming pool on long summer nights, charming corridors lined with tapestries and art."

"That doesn't sound so bad."

"Yes, but Noah's cut off from it all as though he's a ghost haunting his own life, and even as his favourite memories are coming to life, unfolding around him, he's being goaded, tormented, and he's so exhausted that every movement is agony. He just wants to...to die, and they won't let him, so he rears up and claws at the darkness and the memories. Is that screwed up or what?"

"Who won't let him die? Who's goading him?"

"That's the sickest part. He's being tortured by his loved ones and by people who think they're helping him. I can't actually picture their faces, and strangely enough, he can't see them either because a ghost's eyes don't work that way."

Carly waited, half expecting ridicule, but Evan watched her, prepared to listen.

"Okay, I know this is my imagination running wild, but... what if..." She faltered. "What if Noah Goodwyn really *is* in pain? Imprisoned, dying. Maybe the hands I feel on the wheel are worry. Hell, I don't know. I know this is none of my business, but I feel like I'm getting drawn into it somehow."

Evan watched the anxiety ripple across her brow in waves, feeling helpless. "I know a nice sports bar," he said. "I could get you drunk."

Carly flared at Evan's dismissive suggestion, but as she frowned at him, eyes narrowed, she realized it was the best anyone could do. Distraction was probably what she needed.

She turned her back to the lake and crossed her arms. Her hands were getting cold. "I even shared my paranoia about this stuff with Weiss."

"Jesus, Car, you could get into a lot of trouble talking to the police about Goodwyn. The Goodwyns have tons of money and they might resent someone interfering with their lives."

"You're right. Funny, I never thought about that. I must really trust Weiss. He's got that father figure thing going for him, I guess."

Evan held her by the shoulders at arm's length. "Ah, here we go. You just lost your father."

"God, I didn't drag you out onto a romantic pier under the stars—"

"It's overcast."

"Under the stars, I said—just so you could psychoanalyze me." Then Carly turned her head and blinked out at the darkness of the lake. "Omigod. Maybe I *did*!"

Evan shook his head. "Okay, I'm lost."

Carly returned to face the railing and peer down at the onshore waves of Lake Ontario as they rippled beneath the pier. "I can't explain this, Evan, but I think I'm right about Goodwyn. I believe he's dying."

Evan knew about Carly's father and his odd gift for insight. "You're not having one of those episodes that your father wrote about in his memoir, are you? The ones where he envisioned things he couldn't possibly know about?"

She turned to him in alarm. "No. That can't be. I'm educated,

I'm rational, I'm not even religious. How could I have…episodes?"

"You were always frustrated that A.L. could spin stories out of nothing but a shelf full of trophies. Now you're telling me you've started to write a story about some guy you spoke to for a couple of hours. It sounds familiar to me."

She stared at him for a minute, studying his eyes, then looked down at his chest. "Well, gee, thanks. You've identified the problem. You wouldn't happen to have a solution, would you? I mean, other than hard liquor."

"A therapy for obsession? How about this?"

And he kissed her, his lips driving her back against the big oval piping of the guardrail.

"Evan," she gasped at last from the warm curve of his cheek. "There are *people* out here."

"Why do you think *they* are out here under the stars?"

"It's overcast…" she corrected him.

Evan's therapy was surprisingly effective. They made love in his downtown condo with the lights of the pier partly visible between the high rises. The creeping anxiety that had gripped her the last couple of days was a million miles away as she arched her back and squeezed her thighs against Evan's hips.

How did this guy get so buff? she wondered.

He was a cream puff who looked great on daytime television wearing makeup, and he had turned the study of graphology into a carnival show. Why couldn't he be a tweedy philosopher or even a poet who needed saving? Or maybe a cultured cop like Weiss… Then they could discuss Sartre and romantically ruin one another.

Instead, he was—considerate, gentle, and (she moaned) seemed to know exactly where her clitoris was, damn him.

Their lips were still touching when his weight finally left her and he slid down to his knees beside the couch. For a few moments longer, she was lost in his eyes, but her common sense, which had definitely been on hiatus, returned and she wished they had made it all the way to the bedroom. Passion was all very fine, but it was an annoyingly masculine couch; the fabric irritated her rump, which, in fairness, was largely exposed.

Carly blew a strand of hair out of her eyes as she pulled some clothes back on, and when her modesty was satisfied, she sat up. She watched him do up his belt, trying to think of something to say, but Evan seemed content to return her gaze and didn't need to talk.

She waited it out, letting him settle on the rug beside her. She smoothed his hair and watched the lights outside.

In time, her thoughts began to re-engage. "I wanted to show you something," she said.

She rummaged in her purse for a moment and then handed him a card. It was a smaller version of a greeting card.

"This came to me with a gift," she said. "Would you look at the handwriting?"

Evan pulled back to a comfortable sitting position and sighed. "Not this again. Graphology isn't magic. All it can give you is some educated generalities."

"So? You're educated. Generalize already."

He smiled, got up and retrieved his reading glasses from the side table. "Fine. Let's see." He angled the card to the light of a lamp, and then he shot her a glance. "It's signed 'Noah.'"

"Go on."

Evan adjusted the half-moon glasses on his perfect nose doing a passable Cary Grant. "Florid, oversized descenders, flamboyant caps, compressed wording. I'd say…a show-off, with a side of desperation."

"Desperation? That's not a generalization. That's psycho-analysis. Where did that come from?"

He laughed. "Sorry, I'm showboating again. I just mean that there are two simple motifs here. He has a big, showy side, but you can see tension there, too. That could mean anything. The main thing is that you're impressed, and while you happen to be in awe at the cleverness of your boyfriend, I'm going to take advantage of you again."

He put down the glasses, leaned over her, and his hand cupped the back of her head. She collapsed back against the cushions.

"What, really? Now I *am* impressed, but do you mind if we…"

It wasn't a large apartment. How hard could it be to find the bedroom?

CHAPTER SEVENTEEN

The nineteenth-century brick church was lighting up the night sky, turning its own billows of smoke a yellow-orange. The bell tower, lit up like a candle, was the focal point, but the whole roof was a patchwork of blazes. A fire hose mounted on a long extension ladder added a curving torrent of water and drifting steam to the battle.

A line of Burlington Fire Department trucks pulled up along Walker's Line and crews with their iridescent striped slickers and oversized helmets were moving inside, dragging more hoses. Supporting water tankers from Milton and Halton Hills plugged the spaces between hose brigades, the whole jam strobed by flashing red vehicle lights. The blackened beams of the roof were starting to show as sections of the roof began to collapse.

Weiss and Joshi had to walk from a nearby plaza because the road was choked with crews and equipment. It wasn't hard to find Toni Beal. She was standing where Weiss would have chosen, on a slight rise at the southeast corner of the old building, far enough from the scene so as to not get in the way. Tom Krosnow wasn't with her, but he wouldn't have been far away.

"Hey, Toni."

"Eilert…"

"Arson?"

"Have a look at the east facade, near the corner."

Weiss peered through the drifting smoke. A tall gothic window dominated the corner, lit from within by the flames. Immediately below it, letters had been spray-painted on the brick. They were huge and blocky, as though the vandal had wafted his pressurized spray can up and down to thicken the lines. No subtlety here; the letters were black gloss.

"ISIS? You think it was a hate crime?"

Toni turned from the fire for the first time, looking weary. "The letters weren't there this morning. I checked, but, nah. It's a Presbyterian church. The symbolism is too vague. I think the bastard was just so filled with hate and anger he added the letters as a provocation. He wanted to stir as many people up, get as much media coverage as he could."

Prem had been trailing, but he slowly mounted the rise and stood nearby, his face flickering with reflected light.

"Evening, Prem."

"Toni."

"And how are you this sorry evening?"

"Fine. I saw a cardinal on my lawn this morning."

"They're actually pretty common this time of year."

"Not the bird. He said he was attending a synod nearby and got lost."

Toni forgot her mood for a moment and chuckled. "I believe you, Prem, but thousands wouldn't."

A movement behind them caught her attention and she indicated a small group of firefighters moving past. They were greying, exuding authority. When their backs became visible, it was easy to read "Deputy Chief" on one and "Chief" on the other. A third man carried what might have been an expensive camera or an infrared imager.

"Do you know Chief McCullough?" Toni asked.

"Never had occasion to talk to him. Do you know him?"

"Oh, yeah. Tough, humourless, but the crews respect him. Hates the press, which is unusual because the press generally paint the fire crews as heroes. He's going to hate them even more if they try and inflame public opinion with this ISIS crap."

"Did you just say 'inflame?'" Prem asked.

"I did, didn't I?"

"Who's the guy with the ray gun?" Weiss wanted to know.

"That'd be someone from the Ontario Fire Marshal's office. They'll be making the official call on the arson."

"You and Tom are on this arson thing?"

"Yeah, Tom is checking for security cameras. I'll be talking to the pastor to see if there's any history of antagonism in the community, but I doubt there's anything. The folks around here are diverse but pretty tolerant. I hear the Crossroads Centre have already offered their chapel for Sunday services, and they're an evangelical TV ministry."

"That may be the whole point. The arsonist is pissed off at everybody and just wants to vent. Have a look at local trouble makers with anger issues, road rage, fights. You might find a connection with the congregation."

"Yeah, thanks. So, how did the date go?"

Weiss turned his head. "How do you know about that?"

"Your partner takes a caring interest in your emotional welfare."

Weiss scowled at Joshi, who had taken a sudden interest in the state of the bell tower and was hastening down to street level for a better look.

From behind Weiss's shoulder, Toni said, "There are a lot of people on your side, Eilert. More than you know. People seem to think you're one of the good ones. So, how about Heddy? She seems nice."

Weiss grew thoughtful. "Of course she is. Pleasant company,

smart." He looked away at the milling personnel, but it was clear he had something more on his mind. "Did you know she's a widow?"

"No, but I figured it was something like that. A good-looking woman like Heddy has to have a past. And you happen to be a widower. I see a certain common ground there."

Weiss gave a humourless laugh. "Common ground? Heddy idolizes her late husband. In fact, her career with the police is a monument to his sacrifice."

Toni frowned. "Excuse me?"

"Heddy joined the force so she could serve like her husband —her husband who died in the military."

Toni knew Weiss's history probably better than anyone else, so she began to catch his drift right away. "You may be making too much of this."

Weiss persisted. "I, on the other hand, hung on to my career with the police by my fingernails—and your help—despite my wife's every effort to destroy me. I was lucky to survive my marriage. And I mean that literally."

The roiling clouds of smoke and steam lit by a hellish glow seemed to mirror Weiss's thoughts.

"I know you do," Toni said. "I've said this to you before, Eilert. Your wife was smarter than either one of us and her cruelty was just as refined. She almost got me, too, you know. Well, my marriage anyway."

"Yes, I know, Toni. Thank God you were stronger than I was or I probably wouldn't be here."

"That's not true. I wasn't stronger. It's just that you were the one she was out to destroy. I was just collateral damage. You and I, we were friends in a foxhole trying to keep our heads down."

Weiss faced Toni. "You know about her suicide—her last shot at me—but you have no idea the legal and financial mess she left me; bogus debts, legal suits, incriminating letters. She wanted to make sure I'd commit suicide, too. She almost succeeded."

"But she didn't." Toni could look Weiss in the eye; she was almost as tall as he was and her high blocky heels made up the difference. "We came out the other side. And every year you get through, her grip on you loosens. You'll always carry the scars, but you can be happy again. I believe that and so should you."

He read the compassion on her face through the flickering shadows, and they might have been looking at one another over a candlelit dinner, only the candle was a collapsing bell tower.

"You've been on the job since eight this morning," he said. "You must be exhausted."

"Kind of. I've been here since the fire was called in at six."

"There's a Tim Hortons back where Prem and I parked our car. Can you take fifteen minutes?"

"Sure. We've got our phones."

———

The coffee shop was busy because of the nearby commotion, but they found a table beneath a flat video screen. Weiss brought her a decaf and a plain cake donut because he knew she liked those. He slid his tea along the table and sighed noisily down beside her.

"Did you get my text?" Toni asked.

"Yeah. You found Noah. He was in Moreland House all along."

"He's been there for four months in some kind of coma. No, wait—not a coma. Catatonia. That's different, but it amounts to the same thing. He can't communicate."

"Catatonia. Sounds like a Baltic country. How did the sister wind up with him?"

"It was her or an extended care clinic. There's a doctor there at the house. Eric Hudson. I looked him up. What I found out helps us to understand the power dynamic in that house.

"Eric was a general practitioner who had his hospital privileges revoked. Seems he was promoting unscientific healing methods. He hasn't been active in his practice for over a year, but he still has patients—if you can call them that. He acts more like a psychoanalyst who does house calls on rich people now.

"Hudson found his spiritual home with The Companions of Divine Light, a group that practices something called attunement. That's a non-touch method of healing that supposedly restores the spirit by…" Toni closed her eyes, remembering. "… harmonizing the healer, the patient, and the source of all being."

Weiss sipped, looking at her over his cup. "How did Ruth fall for that?"

"We found out that Ruth's husband was an alcoholic and he eventually died of cirrhosis, but when he was in decline, Ruth joined an Al-Anon family group."

"That's a support group for families of alcoholics, right?"

"Eric Hudson was a guest lecturer at one of the meetings and that's how Ruth got drawn into The Companions. As a group, The Companions have been around since the 1930s, but they've remained small enough to avoid media attention."

Weiss made a face. "I'll say. I've never heard of them."

Toni smirked, using her donut as a monocle. "It's kind of a loose-knit cult that doesn't grow much but manages to perpetuate the influence of its leaders who stay based in Colorado. The Companions generally hold small local gatherings, and its membership tends to be older and more affluent than the usual cult types.

"Anyway, Ruth's money made her pretty important to the local gathering and Eric took her on, acting as her spiritual advisor. Looks to me like he's with her full time right now. Doesn't live in, but he's always there."

"Okay, so Ruth is needy, but how did someone like Eric get control of Noah's therapy?"

"Well, Hudson is still an accredited physician, remember. They didn't revoke his licence. And he scared Ruth off the medical establishment as being nothing but another mega corporation. Ruth is cynical about capitalism anyway because her husband was a real shark, so she took responsibility for Noah on herself."

"Funny, Ruth being part of the medical establishment herself. How'd you get all this? Is Ruth the talking type?"

"No, but her sister-in-law is, and she's pissed that she got so little out of Moreland's estate."

Weiss nodded slowly. "Your text said that Noah has a common-law wife. What about her? She should have some say in Noah's care."

"Not against Ruth's lawyers. Merrit Simpson is an addict with a spotty police record. She's scared, and at this point, she's mostly concerned about getting a living income out of Noah's money. To her credit, she's not a gold digger. All she wants is a little security and a lot of methadone."

"What about Noah's daughter? Have you spoken to her?"

"Yeah. Tracked her down to the AGB—the art gallery. Sammy is a bit self-absorbed at this point in her life. You can hardly blame her. She's grown up under a kind of benign neglect. Poor little rich girl stuff. Definitely not the take-charge type."

"I suppose not. She thought it was ironic that Prem and I were asking her about her father when her father never bothered much with her. She's got some good qualities, though. I wouldn't write her off. She might come out of this with a life of her own."

"Or she may just buy one."

Weiss's phone warbled, and he excused himself. Toni nodded and began dunking bits of her donut into her coffee.

"Hi, Prem. Sorry. Toni and I are at the Tim's by the car."

"Ah. Right," Joshi said. Then he thought for a moment. "You want me to give you some time?"

Weiss rested his forehead on his hand. Not for the first time, he wondered what his muddled life looked like to others. "No, no. That's fine, Prem. Just come on over and we'll head back to the station."

He put his phone away and looked up to see Toni watching him. There was a commotion as a crowd of young people got up to leave.

"You never got to see Noah?" Weiss asked her.

"No, the Noah angle kind of took me by surprise. I wasn't expecting to find him there, but I shouldn't have taken Ruth's word that he was incapable of communicating. I've got to go back."

"Look, Toni, I know James Krauss is your case, but I've been following the Noah trail and I'm starting to get a picture of him —his motivations and his personal demons. Let me have a look at him. Call it a different angle."

"Suits me, but I need to know more about how Krauss fit into Noah's circle, so I'll be coming back to Merrit and Ruth."

"Somehow I can't see you spending a lot of time on Krauss. You really think you can build some sort of a case against Ruth?"

Toni shrugged. "Eric Hudson is arrogant enough to have someone killed and Ruth is naive and desperate enough to fund it. But you're probably right. I've seen these daisy chains of what-ifs and maybes before, and they seldom get resolved. Let's just call it due diligence on my part."

They sat back, giving in to the hubbub around them, content for a while to exchange glances and grin at the noisy hilarity of the coffee-going civilians.

CHAPTER EIGHTEEN

The following evening was the first time Evan stayed over at Carly's father's house on Lakeshore Road. Number 24C, the right wing of an exclusive row of townhouses fronting the park and the lake, was starting to feel like Carly's home as it had been when she was a teenager, before she went off to U of T and its residences on Charles Street.

The presence of her father was everywhere in the tidy rooms—well, mostly on the main floor. He hadn't been up the stairs in the last year of his life. It felt as if his spirit had lingered, retreating in particular to the one sanctuary of clutter and disarray in the house: the great man's office.

Carly seldom looked into the little room with its window on the park and the bay, and she didn't want Evan anywhere near it. The memory of their convulsive confrontation with Marcella Cole there—Cole's dying collapse to the rug—was too fresh.

The room had been cleaned and disinfected twice. Once after her father's suicide, and then again after they removed Marcella Cole's body and the forensic team had done their work. But each time the cleanup had been done with the kind of veneration that you'd expect for a national historic site, with each book and walking stick dusted and carefully returned to its place as A.L. Rouhl had left them.

Earlier in the evening, Evan had taken her to a Raptors game in Toronto, and she'd sat there more intrigued by the antics of the fans than the interminable wobble of the ball up and down the court. The carousing in the streets afterwards and the noisy sports bar had been exciting, though well outside her comfort zone.

They'd hopped the GO train from Union to Appleby Station, retrieved Evan's car and returned happily tired to the lakefront house, and it seemed natural for Evan to stay—after he'd crammed her, laughing, into the coat cupboard and kissed her cold face and wrists. They giggled among the snow boots and sneakers until she scolded him down the hall and up the stairs to her bedroom. It seemed strange to have him here in this place of comfort and retreat, this room that had always been hers, even when she had taken her own condo nearby. But he brought life and immediacy to the fantasies she'd dreamed here in her bedroom above her father's office.

They'd slept soundly through the night until Carly woke to the weight of Evan's arm across her waist. A watery half-light from the window caught his naked leg emerging from the covers, and she smiled at the memory of the night before.

She got up, letting Evan's arm slip off onto the covers, trailing the warmth of the bed into the cool room, and pulled on her robe. Evan stirred but went on sleeping, his tabloid profile stuffed against the pillow.

Downstairs, she turned on the kitchen light and dropped a coffee pod into the machine. She got some milk for her coffee from the fridge.

When it was ready, she took her coffee into the living room and stood by the mantle. Had she wandered in here to look at the small Inuit carving, or was its presence above the fireplace incidental? She wasn't sure. But there she was on the rug before the fireplace, and the sculpture had to be lifted, hefted in her hand so she could marvel again at its weight.

Funny the way it instantly made her think of pineapples, carved wooden images, polished inlays. Marquetry and bevelled glass…

Driven by a vague sense of alarm, she backed against the wall, staring out at the rest of the house. A decorative poker clattered to the floor from its hook. She put down her coffee mug on the mantle, her hand trembling. To her left, the fluorescence of the kitchen—but everywhere else was dark: the gloom of the front hall, the shadowed corridor that led to A.L.'s office. The stairway up to the bedrooms and Evan's warmth.

She wanted to reach over with her other hand and put the sculpture back in its place above the fireplace, but a sound made her eyes dart into the shadows. Was it Evan moving, up in the bedroom? No. It was like…like something massive shifting in one of the downstairs rooms.

There it was again: creaking floors and displaced air as if some gigantic animal was rising from its belly and flexing its haunches. Couldn't Evan hear it? Shouldn't he be racing down the stairs?

Carly's eyes narrowed as she peered into the dark corridor. She couldn't see her father's office door in the profound darkness of the hallway, but she was compelled to stare anyway, her head tilting to one side with the effort. Another seismic shuffle and she swore the shadows in the corridor were swimming before her eyes, taking shape.

A face composed of black on black nuances was asserting itself against the gloom, but it wasn't human. It wasn't some horror show demon either. If it hadn't been impossibly huge, it could have been a caricature, all exaggerated mouth and eyes. A stray glint from the kitchen fixture picked out the wetness of the eyeballs, the lolling of a vast tongue, hinting at a three-dimensional, hard-edged solidity where there could be none.

She stood pressed against the wall, wanting to scream, but she was frozen, trapped between the fireplace and a corner table. For an interminable moment, time stood still in the room, Carly's trembling shoulders the only movement. At last, her hand sagged, her grip loosened and the soapstone carving she had been gripping fell to the hardwood floor with an unholy thud, to roll in a noisy circle at her feet.

There was a scrambling sound from above, and Evan came out of the bedroom and started down the stairs. He had a duvet draped over his nakedness like a quilted toga, and his expensive haircut was spiked in every direction.

"What was that?" he asked, the sleep still in his voice. "I heard something fall. Is everything okay? It sounded as though you dropped an anvil."

"Evan, don't move. Don't come down."

But he clumped down anyway until he was on the landing, his back turned to the corridor. She strained to see past him, to see the thing framed in the darkness of the corridor, a wail building in her throat.

Evan saw the alarm in her face. "Jesus, Car. What's the matter? You're white as a sheet."

He came at her and she twisted him to one side so she could see the corridor.

If anything had ever loomed out of that velvet shadow, it wasn't there now. It only took an instant for Carly to snap back to reality. Of course. She'd had a waking dream—a hallucination. What else could it possibly have been?

"I'm sorry, Evan. I feel so embarrassed." She looked down. "I dropped the sculpture—that stone thing. Here, I'll get it." Then she stopped, her eyes drawn again to the corridor. "Actually… would you get it? It goes on the mantle."

Evan hiked the duvet up against his shoulder and looked at her as though he were Cicero about to address the Roman senate. "Whoa. You scared me, Car. You're okay though, right? Just a little night fright?"

She nodded, needing time to think.

But Evan wasn't buying it. With a flourish of floral print and scalloped fringe, he knelt and then got up to put the sculpture back on the mantle. He opened the duvet and scooped her inside its warmth. His arms closed around her shoulders and he pressed her close.

Carly's eyes widened. She realized in his dash to check on her, Evan hadn't bothered to put on his underwear.

CHAPTER NINETEEN

Merrit Simpson, alluring like a faded covergirl, her eyes dark, not with eyeshadow but with a hint of dissolution, let them into the entrance hall of the Moreland house. Asking that they wait in the two-storey hallway, she left to get Ruth Moreland.

The detectives looked around. Weiss wandered over to the near wall, his hands behind his back, his tweed hat bouncing there.

"Prem, come and have a look at this."

Joshi came and stood behind him. "Nice," he said, looking bored.

"It's a barometer," Weiss said. "Do you think people even know what these *do* anymore?"

Joshi tapped his pocket. "I've got an iPhone. Would you like to know about the cold front moving in from Manitoba next Wednesday? Sixty percent chance of rain at noon."

Weiss smiled. "That's my point. Who needs an antique column of mercury anymore? Except," he said, holding a professorial finger in the air, "this thing tells us the exact air pressure, right here in this room, not at some airport weather station. It even reflects our altitude right where we're standing; think about that. We're up quite high, remember—on the escarpment —so the air pressure would be slightly lower here."

Joshi inhaled noisily. "Such a useful distinction."

"Well, you know, Prem, there's something real about that. Personal. You can't get any more local than a barometer."

"If we weren't trying to kill time, I'd tell you to quit romanticizing the thing...although..." Joshi leaned in closer, staring at the crystal dial with fresh interest. "Is it worth something? Practically everything in the house looks as though it is."

"As an antique, you mean?" Weiss angled his head, reading the small print beneath the needle. "Maybe. It's English. From the design, probably Edwardian, and it's in beautiful condition. Mahogany or something. Look at the craftsmanship. It must have cost a fortune. They called this the banjo style of barometer, because, well..." He gestured vaguely at the barometer. "Big dial, tall neck." He caught Joshi's one-eyed yawn and grinned.

"Storm coming," Weiss persisted, tapping the glass of the dial.

"Breaking news." Joshi looked away at the tall, bevelled glass windows with their velvet drapery. "Of course, you could see that from the overcast."

But Weiss was stubborn. "Twenty-nine something inches; I guess it still works after all these years."

"Give it a rest, Eilert. You sound like my old man remembering his Studebaker."

Joshi was spared a longer lecture by a couple entering from the dining room. Ruth Moreland was casually dressed, but everything from her Italian soft pocket jeans to her short embroidered kaftan suggested wealth. She didn't have to prove anything; she'd been born to privilege and she expected people to respect it.

The tall man beside her was similarly self-assured, but his power came not from his vested suit, but from his cleft chin and broad shoulders. He had the sanctimonious air of a preacher, and his perfect smile glowed with a condescending benevolence. Eric Hudson wore an open sharkskin jacket, and in the way his thumb hooked easily in his pocket, he gave the impression he was always in command of the moment. Weiss caught the glint of gold on the silk vest meant to mimic an old-fashioned watch chain, and he pictured Eric touching a patient's wrist while holding an impressive pocket watch.

Weiss introduced Joshi and himself.

"Ruth Moreland," she said, crossing her hands inside her loose sleeves. "This is my friend and advisor, Dr. Eric Hudson. Forgive me if I'm a little put out, Detective. But we spent some time talking to a couple of your colleagues just yesterday."

Ruth was a little above average height, but Eric loomed above her with an aura of righteous authority. "We got the distinct impression," Eric said, "that the detectives we spoke to were on a fishing expedition, having no idea what they were dealing with. You must know that Mrs. Moreland can call on the very best legal advisors in the province."

Eilert Weiss stood in the soaring front hall, his hat in his hand, feeling as though they hadn't even been invited into the house yet. Even under the splendour of a chandelier, he felt they were being door knobbed. Prem Joshi wasn't having any of it. From slightly behind Weiss, he spoke up, sounding combative.

"I'm thinking we could get a warrant to search your property, Mrs. Moreland. There are questions about your relationship to a murder victim."

Weiss smiled. Prem wouldn't be intimidated by a Rottweiler. "But that would be a clumsy way of going about things," he interrupted, lowering the tension a notch. "We don't want to turn out drawers or empty cupboards. We just want to have a little walk around, get the layout, meet the people informally."

Ruth looked past him at Joshi. "A warrant? How could you possibly justify such a thing? There is no crime here."

Joshi shrugged. "Well, let's look at it in the worst possible light then. Mr. James Krauss, an employee of your pharmaceutical firm—"

"I'm merely a shareholder, Detective."

"With enough clout to dictate company legal policy. Mr. Krauss breaks into data files holding the company's most confidential research and the director of the company wants to prosecute him, but you intervene."

"That was a board decision."

Weiss listened but then stepped in, conceding the point. "Detective Joshi did say he was taking the worst possible interpretation. Anyway, Mr. Krauss was found dead immediately adjacent to your property. A reasonable extrapolation is he was working on your behalf when—"

Eric cut in. "When *what*, Detective? You have no idea what happened to Krauss, do you?"

Like Weiss, Ruth was trying to avoid further unpleasantness. She said, quietly, "Stealing pharmaceutical formulations which I already own? And why? To give to my competition?"

Sensing her discomfort, Weiss turned his hat in his hand and mirrored her restraint. "You're way ahead of me, Mrs. Moreland. I'm just saying my colleagues had a right to be curious. They're thinking Mr. Krauss came from this house and walked, or ran, to the woods. It's true; he could have got there from the highway, but why on earth would he do that? There's nothing on that stretch of road. I'd like to follow up on the possibility that he was with his friends—like your brother and Ms. Merrit here at the house. I was told that your brother liked to entertain here."

Ruth was bargaining now: "I explained to your colleague, Detective Beal, that my brother can't communicate with you."

"Yes, and I could probably confirm what you and Dr. Hudson here have said with a glance. It's just a formality, but Detective Beal didn't actually see your brother when she was here, did she? What do you say?"

There was a pause as Ruth weighed the most dignified response, then she gestured to the staircase. "He's in the library upstairs. We've repurposed it as a sort of clinic."

Eric touched her arm and said simply, "Ruth."

Weiss could see that it gave her pause, but Ruth saw no graceful alternative, so she patted Eric's hand. "It will be all right, Eric. This won't take long."

"Merrit? Show Detective Weiss and his partner up to the library, would you?"

The blond who met them at the door and had obviously been listening stepped out from the dining room and nodded towards the stairs that rose in a narrowing sweep from the hallway.

Weiss laid his hat on a narrow side table. "Library?" he said to Merrit's back as she began to climb.

As Merrit led the way she explained, "There are a few shelves filled with old pulp novels and *Readers' Digest* collections. I don't think any of the family were great readers. The room wasn't used much, so we just cleared the space for Clemmie and Noah. Nice room, though. It has a balcony with a pleasant view of the woods, and it's quiet. It's also adjacent to a bedroom with an ensuite shower enclosure and toilet. My husband has all he needs in that corner of the house."

"Your husband? I understand there's a difference of opinion on that."

"I'm Noah's common-law wife. Believe me, I've studied the law on the matter and even Ruth can't change the law. But Ruth and I know her high price legal team could find a way to tie everything up in court. Enough to affect Noah's will, anyway. We just...talk around it."

"And yet I get the impression you're on reasonably good terms with her. You're actually staying here, I gather."

"With my husband, yes. I don't dislike Ruth, for all our differences."

"Does Ruth feel the same way?"

"She knows her brother loves me."

They arrived at a long corridor with doors to the rear of the house opening off to the right. The corridor was, in effect, a balcony overlooking the rooms downstairs.

"There is a will then."

Merrit led them along the broad carpeted hall. "And the will leaves the bulk of Noah's money and intellectual property rights to his daughter Sammy. However, there is a substantial annuity for me." Merrit turned to face Weiss. "I don't expect the Goodwyn fortune, Detective Weiss, but I'm going to make damn sure I'm taken care of as Noah intended. There's plenty of money to keep me comfortable."

They reached a set of double doors, each framing a lovely leaded glass panel with a stylized zodiac theme. Merrit opened one side, and they found themselves in a room that was large and a testament to fine craftsmanship. The ceiling was supported by a series of arched beams. Some of the tables and chairs had been pushed to the walls where they blocked off the bookshelves, clearing a space dominated now by a few pieces of medical equipment. The left wall was dominated by a field-stone fireplace with two brass andirons and a scuttle full of split logs.

In the centre of the room, there was an IV stand and what must have been an encephalogram with its own free-standing flat screen. A complicated headpiece hung by its wires from a chrome hook above the screen. On a large, satin-finished table, Weiss recognized a blood pressure cuff, a black vinyl case, and an infrared thermometer. There was no patient.

Merrit looked at the white smartwatch on her wrist, embarrassed. "Clemmie must be changing Noah. They'll be here in a few minutes, I expect. By the way, Clemmie is Noah's nurse; she doesn't say much. Any questions you have about Noah, I can help you with—or Eric, of course."

Weiss scanned the dark vault above them. "It's a lovely room. Do you mind if we look around?"

"Go ahead. I'll tell Clemmie you're waiting."

Joshi quickly turned his attention to the medical facilities, opening a leather case on the table and examining its contents while Weiss wandered all the way through the room to a set of doors that let out onto a narrow outdoor balcony.

Weiss opened the right-side door. Outside, the wind blew a few drops of rain on his face and he noticed the looming overcast. Weiss could smell the forest—decaying leaves and pine sap. He leaned on the railing and looked down. Because a steeply sloping roof blocked his view, he couldn't see the ground two stories down.

There was no sound except the movement of the breeze through rain-soaked branches. The balcony was a pleasant enough space. Perhaps when the warmer weather arrived, Noah Goodwyn would be able to sit here and feel the sun on his face again. The poor man could do that—surely.

Weiss was thinking about what a person in a catatonic state could actually feel when there was a sound from the room behind him.

He turned and went back in. Merrit was holding one of the doors from the hallway and a woman was backing through it, pulling a wheelchair. She was small and narrow-shouldered and wearing an apron over a white shirt and slacks. She wore the white sneakers favoured by nurses.

The nurse wheeled the chair around and Weiss got his first look at Noah Goodwyn.

Noah Goodwyn was wearing a loose turtleneck sweater and his legs were fully wrapped with a tartan blanket. Weiss put two and two together and realized he probably wasn't wearing any trousers. That would be unnecessary and inconvenient.

There it was—the gnome-like face that Carly had warned him about, but the vacancy there was now permanent. His eyes moved, but he took no interest in anything, not even his hands which lay unclasped on his lap. Carly had said he was a small man, but in that big rubber-wheeled chair, he seemed no bigger than a child. If anyone took notice of him now, it was with pity. Carly's phrase ran ironically through his head: local genius.

Weiss could see that Merrit was watching his face, reading his dismay, and he recognized real sorrow in Merrit as she saw what her husband had become in the eyes of strangers.

"Detective Weiss," she said, hurrying things along, "this is Clemmie. She helps take care of my husband's needs."

For the first time, Weiss noticed Clemmie's face. It was plain and free of makeup, with just a hint of asymmetry; her lip was uneven as though she'd suffered a stroke.

"Clementine Chessley," she said, sounding like a well-behaved ten-year-old. "I'm a registered nurse. And this…is Noah, my patient."

Clemmie made no eye contact, but there was a note of child-like pride in the way she said it.

Merrit stepped forward and rested a hand on Noah's shoulder. "As you can see, my husband is largely uncommunicative. He drifts in and out of lucidity."

Ruth came in from the hallway, followed by Eric. Weiss wondered how long they had been lingering there. "I'd hardly call it 'lucidity,' Merrit," Ruth said. "I haven't been able to get so much as hand squeeze in response to my questions. Not for months now."

There was no rancour. Just a shared sadness.

"But there are times when his eyes move from face to face," Merrit persisted.

Eric wasn't the type to indulge Merrit's weakness. "With no emotional reaction, Merrit. He doesn't even acknowledge us anymore. Not really."

Merrit straightened. It appeared she was used to standing up to Eric. "I've known him a lot longer than you, Eric. When he looks at me…well, he's *there*. Just…far away."

Weiss found himself thinking about Carly again. If Noah was being "tortured," it wasn't apparent in his face. He was slack-jawed and uninterested in the reality around him.

"Doctor, is Noah suffering?" he asked.

Eric seemed surprised by the question. "Suffering? Well, his organs are deteriorating. Not just because of a life of drug and alcohol abuse. He's been in this chair or in a bed for four months now. Clemmie does what physiotherapy she can, moving his arms and legs, helping him to stand upright for a few moments at a time, but it's a losing battle, I'm afraid. The prognosis is that he will continue to decline until his organs begin to fail. Kidneys first, most likely, though there is some cirrhosis of the liver because of a lifetime of abusing alcohol."

Weiss glanced at Ruth and controlled an irrational urge to slap Eric. Had he no sensitivity to Ruth's feelings? Apparently not.

"This could go on for a year or more," Eric went on. "Though I doubt it. All we can do is keep him comfortable."

"And is Noah comfortable?"

Merrit answered Weiss. "He's stable. I wouldn't call this comfortable. I give him what comfort I can."

There was an exchange of looks between Eric and Ruth.

"And the drug therapy you've chosen. Does that just keep him stable?" Weiss asked.

Eric laid his hand on the small black case Joshi had been examining. "I'm treating him with a drug which, in clinical trials, has had some efficacy drawing subjects out of a vegetative state. It normalizes brain cell activity. I would describe it as a faint hope, but Ruth thinks it's worth a try, and Merrit concurs."

The words "in clinical trials" lodged in Weiss's mind. Eric gave the impression that the medication he was using was approved for use on patients. If Hudson was playing God with

MorwynBIO's latest formulation, there would have been no clinical trials.

"But you said you've seen no improvement."

"It's subtle, Detective. I've recorded an increase in the electrical activity of the brain when I administer the drug."

There was a silence. Finally, Joshi said, "That's good, right?"

"It should be, yes, but the truth is, the activity doesn't seem enough to rouse poor Noah from his stupor. Difficult to explain that—why doesn't all that increased synaptic traffic translate into awareness?"

Merrit: "It might just be making his condition worse."

Eric turned on her with impatience. "Define 'worse,' will you, Merrit? He's virtually comatose. How could you deny him even a slim chance at improvement?"

Distancing himself from the tension, Weiss let his gaze wander to the ornate woodwork. The great beams overhead arched to a timber ceiling cured to a dark chocolate colour by time and cigars. The beams led his eyes down to sturdy mullions etched with decorative carvings. He moved away from the group and looked upward.

"Look, Prem. Look at the carvings here. What would you say that is—the design here at the base of the beam?"

Prem sauntered over and frowned at the embossed shape. "Huh. It's a pineapple."

"Yes. Once you take note of the design, you begin to see pineapples everywhere. See, there in the window mouldings."

Joshi nodded and then pointed to the table that supported Eric's medical case. "I see what you mean. It's even on the furniture. The carpenter must have really liked pineapples."

Weiss smiled. "I doubt whether the carpenter ever tasted one. They were expensive and hard to get when this house was being built. No, pineapples were a design convention like acanthus leaves or ivy. They were a symbol of hospitality unique to the wealthy."

"Geez, Eilert. Where do you get this stuff?"

"That little gem I got from our friend, Carly Rouhl."

Joshi shrugged. "Huh."

"Don't dismiss it, Prem. Those decorations are all poor Noah has to look at all day."

Weiss turned back to the family who was following the conversation with polite patience. "One last question. Is Noah ever left unattended?"

He directed the question at Clemmie, but it was Merrit who answered. "Clemmie is almost always nearby. Her room is just down the hall. When she needs to be away, I've sat with Noah. Occasionally, Ruth or one of the staff look in."

"Staff?"

"I have a cook and a housekeeper," Ruth said.

"Do they live in?"

"Oh no, the housekeeper's done by noon and the cook is gone after dinner."

"But Noah *sleeps* alone."

Merrit sounded worn out, dispirited. "Yes, he's generally alone in his bedroom after lights out."

"*Does* he sleep?"

It was Eric who had the last word. "Humans are hardwired to sleep in four-hour cycles. Yes, Detective, even Noah sleeps."

They began to move to the double glass-paned doors, but Weiss couldn't resist a last look at Noah, whose eyes ranged slowly about the room, seeing everything, registering nothing.

Anxious for the intrusion to end, Ruth started downstairs, leaving Eric to supervise Clemmie, and Merrit to see the two detectives out. Joshi went ahead, but Weiss sensed that Merrit was still anxious to talk, and the two of them slowed on the upper landing.

"Clemmie's a quiet soul," Weiss said.

Merrit nodded. "Thank God for that. What she does—it's a

mind deadening job. Clemmie has almost no one to talk to, and she has no social life."

"Why does she agree to do it?"

"I could say it's the money, but…that's not it. She's damaged in her own way; a simple woman. Clemmie's presence here is a form of charity."

Weiss stopped, forcing Merrit to turn. "She said she was a registered nurse."

"It's true. I've seen the papers. But when he interviewed her, Eric knew right away that Clemmie was…limited. I think he wanted someone who would do the menial work without asking a lot of questions."

"I'm sorry. When you say 'limited,' what are we talking about?"

"Of course, Eric looked into it. It seems Clemmie had an aneurism in her early forties while she was working as a nurse in Hamilton. It left her intellectually impaired, but functional. I doubt she'd get to work as a nurse anywhere else, but she's perfect for this, don't you see? Eric handles all of the assessments and medication, giving Noah his IV feed. All Clemmie has to do is sit with him and see to his functional needs. She's more of an orderly, you see."

They started down the stairs in silence, then Merrit said, "When I give her a break, do you know what Clemmie does? She goes to her room."

It was a simple statement, but it seemed to speak worlds and Weiss almost let his jaw drop. *My God,* he thought. *What a sad house this is.*

They continued down the stairs, and Weiss said, "From what you said about James Krauss, I got the impression that you've spent a lot of time here at Ruth's house—over the years."

Merrit nodded. "Noah and I were always travelling, you see —resorts, hotels, occasionally a winter condo in Florida. Noah never wanted the responsibility of owning property, not when he could be waited on hand and foot. His office was his laptop, and he could work anywhere. When we wanted to entertain our friends, we would come here. Ruth encouraged him. Ruth is quite a lonely soul, you know—has been since her husband died.

"Anyway, Noah and I, we'd have parties, mostly down on the terrace level. In a way, that was our place—Noah's place. Ruth hardly ever went down there. Just as well; the parties could get quite…uninhibited…and the noise wouldn't bother Ruth."

"Or the drugs? I'm sorry, but Noah has a reputation."

Merrit laughed. "You're the police. I'm not saying a word about that. Let's just say that Ruth wouldn't approve of anything like that. Eric's not just her physician, you know. He's her spiritual advisor."

"Ruth is religious?"

"If you could call it that. 'Companions of the Divine Light' they call themselves. They like to talk about spiritual power and energy and stuff. A lot of rich people and celebrities. Not for me —or for Noah. Noah was always a sort of cynical realist."

"Was James Krauss ever at those parties—the ones down on the terrace?"

"Almost all of them, I suppose. James was quite a close friend of Noah. I think he knew James from high school. Noah knew James's wife, Candace, too; she used to come to the parties with James, but Noah lost touch with her after James got a divorce."

As they started across the entrance hall, Weiss stopped again. "Merrit, would you do something for me? Ask Ruth if she'd let Detective Joshi and myself have a look around down there—on the lower level."

"You want to go down to the terrace, now? It's getting late."

"If you don't mind. It will save us from coming back tomorrow."

"I don't mind at all, and I can't think why Ruth would object, but I can't imagine what you'd learn about James down there now."

"Merrit, you must know that Noah had got into some trouble because of his hacking into other people's computer systems."

"That was just harmless pranking. He never did any of that ransomware stuff or stole secrets. I'm sure he could have, but Noah was a big kid who used the web as a playground."

"Was James involved in any of this pranking?"

"Well, yes. Sometimes. Noah needed someone to laugh with, and James would always go along with the craziness. They would hack into international Linux servers and disguise their attacks as adware which most people don't worry about too much."

"I've seen some of Noah's play and there's a dark side to it that worries me. Given Noah's condition, you don't have to worry about prosecution, but I'd feel better if I understood your circle better. Would you indulge me?" asked Weiss.

"Of course. I'll speak to Ruth about you going down there. You'd save time if you go down on the cable car. That's the little railway thing that goes down the escarpment. It's a long way around by road."

Merrit went ahead to where Joshi and Ruth were talking near the door. Weiss watched. Ruth looked a little surprised when Merrit asked about the terrace, but made a slight shrug and nodded. Joshi, on the other hand, shot Weiss a pained look and mimed checking a watch which he didn't wear.

CHAPTER TWENTY

With a few directions from Merrit, Weiss and Joshi stepped down to the front driveway and followed a red gravel path. They passed their cruiser and went on walking towards the cable car.

When they were away from the house Weiss said, "What do you make of it all, Prem?"

Still walking, Joshi said, "I had a look at that black case. Eric keeps the medication in there. There were two bottles. One was clearly labelled as benzodiazepine. The other bottle was unmarked."

"Unmarked?"

"Well, there's a label with a barcode. Sorry. I don't read barcode."

"James Krauss did."

Joshi looked at him. "Hmm. Damn. I should have taken a photo of the code with my phone."

"Would that work?"

"Maybe, if we got hold of a barcode reader someplace."

"Walmart?"

"Yeah, like it would be that easy."

They walked in silence for a few moments, then Joshi added, "Merrit's smart. Reminds me of Noah's daughter."

"Yes. Of course. I'll bet Merrit's a lot like Noah, too. Shared interests. That would make sense. People like her can be surprisingly learned in a new kind of way."

"What do you mean, people like her?"

"Well, you know, they live on the web, which is like a big playroom and library combined. If they're curious, the knowledge of the ages is at their fingertips. But of course, they're generally driven by the grazing principle."

Joshi frowned. "Grazing?"

"Yeah, they graze over here until they get bored and then they graze over there. You can accumulate a lot of knowledge that way. It just doesn't look like the kind of directed learning educated people used to have."

"You think Noah was like that?" Joshi asked. "A grazer?"

"Well, no. Not him. Noah wouldn't have been a grazer. He must have been focussed—an enthusiast—and by some chance, his enthusiasm for coding happened to coincide with a need in the tech economy. From what I've learned about him, Noah was what we used to call a hedonist—a pleasure seeker. He was out to have fun, and that just happened to turn him into a tech wunderkind. I mean, think about it: he wasn't motivated by money; he was born rich."

"That would explain the drugs, too," Joshi said. "He was always looking for a high. The more exotic, the better."

Weiss changed the subject. "What about Clemmie? Did you see the way she handles Noah?"

Joshi shook his head slowly. "Yeah. It's charming and sad at the same time. Noah's like a child to her. She doesn't seem to resent her servitude at all."

"That's what I thought. She's not much more than a child herself. She's like a kid with a doll."

"Ruth seems tough, though," Joshi said.

"Ah. That's just the sense of privilege. She's always had her way."

"Oh, by the way," Joshi added. "I asked Ruth how the heating and air conditioning system in the house worked. I thought it might tell us something about the crumbling draperies and woodwork."

"Ah, very good. And?"

"Not surprisingly, she doesn't give it any thought, but she did tell me she pays a Union Gas bill every month."

"So, a forced air gas furnace and ducts then." Weiss stared at his rubber-soled shoes in thought. "Although…"

"What?"

"Well, did you notice there were old-fashioned metal cabinets on a couple of the walls? They might have been some kind of gas-fired hot air registers."

They slowed, approaching a low covered platform that was cantilevered out from the edge of the cliff. Aligned with the platform was what amounted to a short railway carriage. The roof had the kind of narrow skylight windows you'd see on an old Pullman coach, but otherwise, the carriage was open like a Disney ride. Only the ends were enclosed by glazed doors and narrow vestibule balconies with elegantly wrought-iron railings.

At the inner end of the platform was a large housing which anchored the braided cables of the cable car and housed the electric motor that powered the whole affair.

"So, why do I get the feeling that Eric is running the show around here?" Joshi said, kicking the winch assembly suspiciously.

"You got that, too? It may be just his charisma."

"He's full of himself. It's ego," Joshi said.

"Something that Ruth doesn't have," Weiss muttered, half to himself.

"But you said—"

"Oh, yes, she's spoiled as hell, but that's not ego. It's just my impression, but I think Ruth is dependent on Eric."

"Emotionally, you mean?"

Weiss ran his hand over the green-painted wood of the carriage. "I've been trying to research Ruth's social standing, charity work, political involvement, and there's not much there." Weiss narrowed his eyes at Joshi. "Ask yourself why Noah is *here* and not in some expensive clinic."

"Yeah, I wondered about that."

"I think it says something about Ruth's neediness. For all her wealth, she's no society matron. Merrit thinks she's lonely. Eric and his 'Companions of Light' probably give her the human contact she needs."

Faced with actually operating the little railway, Joshi found the carriage's half-door and swung it out. He led the way inside onto the wood strip floor, and Weiss followed. Gripping the chrome handrails that ran vertically and horizontally between the wicker benches, Weiss made for the outward end which gave a clear view of the plummeting slope down to the terrace level.

Joshi closed the door and found the bronze lever that engaged the electric winch mechanism. "Pretty simple," he said. "This thing is just a glorified elevator, really."

"Yeah," Weiss agreed. "Same principle. I can just make out a counterweight down below that runs on a set of rails inside the main ones."

Joshi pointed to the handrails. "Hold on, I'm going to move the lever."

There was a slight lurch and then the carriage began to roll downward. The wood beam platform slipped away above them and then there was only the rugged sweep of the slope on both sides, tufted with bushes and weeds. Much of the cliff was exposed rock, mottled with lichen.

The ride was smooth—steel wheels on steel tracks—and

slow. The hum of the winch assembly grew fainter as they left it behind until there was only the steady grind of the wheels below them.

"Come and see this, Prem," Weiss said, looking out the glassless window frame.

Far below, the beautiful gardens were laid out in geometrical pathways and scenic arbours. A couple of magnolia trees stood out as pinkish-white accents. In the centre of the gardens was the turquoise rectangle of the swimming pool and the encompassing red tile of the terrace itself. There was a large pavilion at the nearest end of the terrace, and a dozen light standards arranged around the perimeter.

Weiss saw that they were descending in a stately fashion towards a covered platform much like the one up top. The counterweight, a dark block of iron banded wooden beams was trundling upwards towards them with the same unhurried pace as the descending carriage.

The carriage slowed, directed by some sort of automatic braking system and they drifted down into alignment with the lower platform. There was a click as the control lever popped back to the stop position all by itself, and they had arrived at the Moreland pleasure garden and pool.

Before they could leave the carriage though, Weiss's phone chirped and he drew it out of his jacket pocket. He looked at the screen and made a signal to Joshi that he should wait.

"Hello, Carly."

Carly's voice sounded soft and apologetic. "Hello, Detective...I mean, hello, Eilert. Could we talk for a few minutes? Is this a bad time? I waited until after office hours."

Weiss looked around at the wicker benches and swung down onto one. "No—actually I can't imagine a more congenial spot for a talk. I'm at the Moreland house. Ruth Moreland is Noah Goodwyn's sister."

"Have you found Noah?"

"Yes, as a matter of fact, we have. He's here at the house, but I'm afraid he's not well. In fact, he's in a sort of coma."

"Oh, my God. He's in a bed then."

"No. It's complicated. He seems to spend his days confined to a wheelchair. I don't understand the medical term, but he appears to be in some kind of persistent stupor. He just stares off into space."

Carly's voice sounded close and clear in his ear. He could hear her breath. "Is he in pain, Eilert?"

"I made a point of asking his doctor. No, he gives no indication of suffering."

A sigh of relief. "Oh. That's good. It's funny. I've spent my life being a sensible, stable person, and now here I am bothered by vivid imaginings. I'm sorry if I wasted your time the other day."

"Not at all. I hope I didn't scare your staff. Have you made any progress in writing your story?"

Carly laughed—a satin giggle. "Very diplomatic of you, Eilert. You mean have I had any more nightmares." There was a noise on the line as though she was settling back on an old sofa. "I thought my, uh, character would get up out of his chair…"

"His wheelchair?"

"No, I hadn't thought of a wheelchair. I just see him getting to his feet and, well, moving. Slowly."

"Okay. Well, you're not imagining poor Noah. I gather he can only get from chair to bed with a great deal of help. That, I'm afraid, is Noah's life these days. Very sad."

"Terrible. My character though, the one in my story? He gets around. Not much, I guess, but I see him moving around—through elegant corridors, through a beautiful garden. Is there a swimming pool there?"

Weiss turned on the bench. He could see the blue of the pool from where he sat. "A swimming pool? Yes, but then you'd expect that with the Moreland house, wouldn't you?"

"And a...I don't know what you'd call it. A bathhouse, a pavilion?"

Weiss blinked but said nothing.

"At least, I think that's what you'd call it. A sort of changing room for swimmers, but really fancy. I've been looking up images on the web, trying to match my imaginings. Research for my story, you see."

Thinking he understood, Weiss said, "Ah, of course. You have a gift for settings, but what about your character's motivations? Wandering around the swimming pool—it's a bit thin."

"Motivation?" She groaned. "That's the most vivid part. He's driven by a terrible pain. I told you. A consuming anxiety. He doesn't want revenge exactly, he's just lashing out in his agony, hurting his tormentors, blundering about destroying the places he loves, blinded by the pressure in his mind." She let out a sound that was almost a wail: "If they would just leave him alone!"

There it was again. She was crossing the line, taking all of this too seriously.

"Take it easy, Carly. It's just a story, remember?"

"Yes, of course. I think my father's death has shaken me more than a little. Anyway, it sounds like you've solved the mystery of Noah Goodwyn. Maybe my imagination will stop running wild every time I think about him now. Ever since you called about him... Well, the last couple of days have been...odd."

Weiss leaned forward in his seat, staring at the long slats of the carriage floor. "I do value your instincts, Carly. I'm sure you've inherited the best of your father."

He thought about the pineapples decorating the library, but something stopped him from mentioning them. He was worried about the edge of panic that could creep into Carly's voice when she talked about Noah. Telling her about her lucky guess would only make her more upset. He hated himself for patronizing her, but it was what a father would do, wasn't it?

"I don't know why I'm saying this," Carly said, her voice calm again, "but be careful, okay?"

"Of course. Call any time."

They bid each other a good night, and Weiss slipped his phone back in his jacket pocket, closing his overcoat over that. When he looked up, Joshi was watching him, hanging onto a chrome rail overhead.

"Okay, Prem," Weiss said cheerily. "Let's do a quick once over down here and then we can ride this jolly trolley back up to our car."

"Carly? That was the Rouhl woman?" Joshi said. "What's with that? She taken a shine to you or something?"

"She's a writer. Maybe she finds the investigation interesting. You know how civilians romanticize police work."

"And what about you? Since you lost your wife, you—Well, I mean I haven't known you that long, but sometimes you strike even me as a lonely soul."

"What do you mean, 'even you?' Who's been talking about me?"

"As a friend, I've got to tell you; you've got this kind of gothic thing going—an image. You know, tall, moody, lost in thought all the time. And then that crazy business with A. L. Rouhl. It's almost weird the way you figured out that body switch. You know, Marcella Cole being shot by A. L. and the body being hidden for a week? I mean, who the fuck would ever think of that?"

Weiss stood up and looked at his shoes in embarrassment. "Look, Prem, that case was just a jigsaw puzzle. I made the pieces fit. That's all."

He couldn't bring himself to talk to Joshi about it, spelling out the whole truth—that he'd negotiated with Carly a story that would hold water and that he himself didn't fully buy it. That he'd conveniently ignored evidence to make it work.

He gave Joshi a guilty look. "So, everyone thinks I'm gothic?"

"Hey, don't let it bother you. Women find it sexy. Go with it."

"Jesus. What women?"

"Well, Toni and Heddy for a start."

"Oh, for God's sake…"

"Look, what I'm saying is, being lonely isn't good for you. You're apt to say things to civilians that you shouldn't. Civilians like Carly Rouhl. She's the public. Worse, she's the fucking media."

Weiss didn't know what to say. Joshi was right. Feeling pathetic, he opened the half-door and walked out onto the wooden platform.

The platform ended in a red gravel path lined with cedar bushes and flowering chives. They followed it past bone-like copies of Henry Moore sculptures out onto Moreland House's splendid terrace.

CHAPTER TWENTY-ONE

From here the terrace seemed huge, despite being edged with cedar hedges and the ever-present woodlands.

The pool deck, distinguished by a smooth terra cotta tile, ran in a grand sweep right around the pool. Up close, you could see that the pool wasn't a sheet of water at all, but a large rectangle covered by a vast turquoise tarp unspooled from a long drum at one end. The pool cover was rain-soaked, and despite the overcast, it glistened under the lights. You could almost mistake it for the water itself.

Weiss found his voice. "Nice, huh? You'll have to stop calling it the front yard."

"It must be beautiful in the summer," Joshi conceded.

"Looks like it hasn't been opened yet," Weiss said, his comment seeming to apply to the whole level below the cliffs.

Joshi tugged his coat collar tight. "You know what the weather has been like."

The pool terrace was fronted on its short side by a mostly white building in the same geometric Art Deco style as the house. There appeared to be a balcony on its second level with outdoor rattan chairs and two large glass tables. The entrance to the main floor of the pavilion was an ornate double door framing beautiful stained glass panels.

"Pure Frank Lloyd Wright," Weiss said, trying the brass handle. It opened the door easily with a satisfying click as though the mechanism had been freshly oiled. "It isn't kept locked."

Joshi sniffed. "The place is remote and there's probably nothing of value inside."

They stepped over the threshold and Weiss found a light switch that dispelled the gloom of the interior with a yellow glow.

Joshi took a step back. "Christ, what happened in here?"

Weiss stared. The room was pleasantly woody, evocative of a mid-century Muskoka cottage, but the tongue-and-groove flooring sagged into rotten depressions that outlined the support beams underneath.

"I don't understand. Merrit didn't say anything about all this damage."

Joshi began picking his way around the wall where the damage hadn't reached. "Careful on the floor. Some of these wood planks wouldn't support a cat."

There was a settling sound. Joshi raised his elbows to balance as the floor he stood on subsided an inch or two.

Weiss waited a moment, then followed carefully. "When you look at it, the rotting planks are confined to a section of the floor. Mostly the middle."

"Yeah, the damage seems to follow a curving line from the front door to…to that room back there."

Weiss followed his partner's pointing finger. "Yes, I can see it. The pine boards on each side look solid. It's as if this centre portion of the floor had been subjected to…water damage? Months, maybe years of it."

Joshi sniffed loudly. "Not water though. There's no mould, no mustiness. This is dry rot."

"There's no chemical smell."

"Radiation?" Joshi offered.

Weiss looked at him. "Radiation?"

"I'm into Science Fiction."

"There *is* a smell, though," Weiss said. "What is that?"

Joshi wrinkled his nose. "Age? It reminds me of the time I toured an antebellum house in Charleston. It wasn't like the restored houses the tourists love. It had been stabilized, but not restored. Torn wallpaper, threadbare drapes; it reeked of old age. You could smell the age of the place. That's what this is like."

Weiss nodded his understanding. "Well, the buildings do date from the twenties, Ruth said."

"Sure, but if you were to look at these walls, you'd say it had been well maintained. Everything above the floor spells money. How could she let this one strip of flooring deteriorate so badly? How could they not have replaced it long ago?"

Joshi indicated the doorway ahead. The damaged floor seemed to point to it like a broad pathway of decay.

"Let's look in there."

They swung into the adjoining room, holding the door frame in both hands. The lights worked; a central fixture, resembling a ship's lamp, cast a yellow glow over the tables and chairs. There were shelves filled with board games and sports gear: lacrosse rackets, croquet clubs, and horseshoe poles.

A display cabinet caught Weiss's eye. It was glass-fronted and the shelves were filled with small figurines. He looked more closely and realized that one of the shelves was filled with soap-stone carvings—seals, bears, parka'd hunters. He had found Noah's collection.

The rest of the shelves were crammed with ceramic figures

taken from the gaming culture: squat warriors, ice queens, and the inevitable dragons of all colours and poses.

"So much for 'nothing of value,'" Weiss muttered. "I guess they relied on seclusion for security."

An oddity about the cabinet was that there were four broad strokes etched in the glass of the cabinet door. Weiss could think of no cause for the marks unless someone had daubed acid on the pane with a wide brush.

Weiss continued to look around, the sinister atmosphere of the place making him speak in an exaggerated whisper. "I don't believe this. This room is a disaster. It looks like they haven't opened it in fifty years."

Joshi made his way carefully to one of the tables and absently picked up a wooden chessboard, tipping off a clatter of knights and bishops. At first, he just held it, glancing around. "It's some kind of games room. I guess Noah's crowd wasn't always online." He nodded in the direction of a butcher block counter.

"Of course, there's a bar—glasses, fridge. No liquor on the shelves though." Only then did Joshi begin to examine the heavy wooden square in his hand. "Look at this Eilert. This chess board is like this whole pavilion in miniature."

"How do you mean?"

"Look closely—see this side of the board? It's solid. Antique, but perfect; beautiful pieces of ebony and cherry wood forming the different coloured squares. Look at this marquetry around the edges. This board probably cost a few hundred bucks new. See the corners? I think that's an ivory inlay. It may even be the real stuff."

Weiss stepped closer, noticing the workmanship. "You can't get real ivory anymore, so this must be genuine early twentieth century. It's ironic—Noah's plugged-in Gen X crowd inheriting all these antique gaming pieces."

Holding it up so Weiss could see, Joshi pressed hard on a corner of the chessboard with one thumb. Weiss jumped back in horror as a dozen squares crumbled away and fell to the floor. The broken squares of cherry and ebony looked like red ash against the grey tongue-and-groove flooring.

"See?" said Joshi. "Rotten. Just like the floor out there. Just like most of this room."

"But then the chessboard must be ancient."

"Correction. *Half* of the chessboard is ancient. The other half is fine, a cherished antique. See this part? There's still oil and polish in the wood." He sniffed. "Lemon oil."

Weiss started. "I don't understand this. Ruth Moreland's wealth is real. It isn't as though the beautiful furnishings and panelling everywhere are just a facade. Why would she keep crumbling junk like this around?"

The question hung in the air like the smell of old dust.

Weiss was the first to move. There was a set of steps that led up and back the way they had come within an enclosed stairwell. They climbed the plank stairs up a narrow passage to the outdoor balcony. The stairs were firm, the single bannister smooth and polished beneath their hands.

They emerged onto the roomy second-floor patio. It was a lovely open air space, and Weiss could imagine Noah and his friends crowding around the two glass-topped tables and lounging on the outdoor furnishings: wicker bistro chairs and cushioned chaises.

There was a curious disconnect though; like the games room, the awnings and furnishings evoked a much earlier era; mid-century perhaps, while Noah's youth embraced the nineties and the new millennium. Weiss did a quick calculation, trying to recollect the flood of new designer drugs that became available to the rich and disillusioned of Noah's generation: PCP, angel dust...

And then, of course, there would have been the alcohol. Lots of it, probably in the form of exotic mixed drinks: daiquiris and whiskey sours carried on a tray from the bar downstairs, as though the lemon slices and silver service somehow diluted the alcohol.

Joshi looked around, his eyes drawn to the brass hangings and fake portholes on the inside wall. "Hmm. Here's another barometer for you, Eilert."

Weiss appeared not to hear; he grasped the polished wooden railing and looked out at the oncoming darkness. The cloud layer was creating an early twilight, shrouding the terrace with blue gloom.

Joshi though continued to stare at the dial of the barometer. "Hey, Eilert? I can actually see the damn needle move."

Weiss, lost in thought, turned. "What? What are you talking about?"

"This barometer. I swear I saw the mercury drop a couple of lines."

Weiss gave him a dismissive laugh. "Air pressure drops a lot more gradually than that, Prem. Come and have a seat. Check out this view."

There was the sound of scraping chairs behind him, but Joshi stared at the brass-framed dial for a few more seconds, watching the needle tremble, then rubbed his chin and sighed. "Okay."

Weiss had settled himself at the nearest table where he could enjoy the panorama in comfort. There were tall light poles at the corners of the terrace which cast their warm glow on the tile surface below. With the fading light, their aura was becoming more noticeable, and the surrounding shadows more pronounced.

There would have been music, Weiss thought, picking up his fantasy. Given Noah's generation and temperament, probably folk, or folk-rock. Maybe even live music—a young woman singing intelligible lyrics about social justice while an acoustic guitar or two sprinkled plummy arpeggios into the night.

There would have been plenty of food from a caterer on Brant Street laid out on a table in the main room and spun around and upstairs on trays: apple and brie quiche, smoked salmon, and orzo pasta. That was Noah's indulged and self-indulgent crowd.

Cigarettes, cannabis, and ashtrays, Weiss thought sourly.

They weren't Noah's generation's ubiquitous crutch, but his was an addictive crowd. Not cigars, Weiss guessed. That was another type of crowd—the rich and successful, which Noah was, of course, but Noah wasn't a capitalist, just a beneficiary of the crazy burgeoning market for tech wonders. He wouldn't have been at home with business people.

He would have sought out and retained like-minded gamers and geeks who spoke a language of coding and game theory that outsiders couldn't penetrate. They would talk for hours without touching on anything real, extemporizing endlessly on cosplay, movies, and LARPS.

Then there were the drugs. Not just the usual buzz inducers, but mind-altering stuff that would turn the red tiles of the terrace into a waving blanket and make the lights dance pirouettes.

"Earth to Eilert," Joshi said sleepily, not really caring if Weiss left his reverie. He was just as mellow in the next chair.

The pool terrace spreading out beneath them glistened in the artificial light. The light standards, tall and swan-necked, and a couple of modern floods mounted on the pavilion, picked out large shallow puddles on the red tile of the pool deck. The puddles were like ponds of grey-blue glass reflecting the overcast. Inverted images of the lamp posts glowed up from the puddles as if they were arc lights in deep water.

Weiss and Joshi sat there, by unspoken mutual agreement, taking a break from the oppressive sadness of Moreland House, and aware of the gentle movement of the air. It felt natural to take in the beauty of the evening. The moon appeared through a flaw in the cloud cover and the red tiles around the pool leapt into even sharper relief.

Joshi smiled wistfully. "You never take me to nice places like this anymore."

"It's hard to keep the magic alive, Prem."

The pooled rainwater rippled briefly as a breath of wind carried a few raindrops from the trees. Then the puddles calmed and became still once again.

It would have been impossible for them to miss it.

The scene was stretched out before them like a tableau: the sheen of the wet tile barely touched by the breeze, the great sweep of the rainwater puddles, too round and sinuous to suggest shattered glass—it was more as if someone had laid rimless mirrors beneath the balcony. The rain had stopped, so there was nothing to mar the perfect surfaces of the puddles.

And then suddenly, a great disturbance—a heart-shaped puddle in the near distance instantly spread to the size of a table. A second later, the same thing happened to the puddle two feet away from the first.

For a beat, the two detectives just sat there unmoving.

"What the *shit* was that?" Joshi gasped.

Weiss continued to stare, but the shapes vanished, the displaced water rippling back to fill the momentary void. The closest puddle returned to its heart shape. The night seemed to contract around them in the same way, but everything remained still; it was as if the night had never been interrupted.

The moon slid behind the overcast again, dimming the post-card diorama of the terrace beneath them. Weiss turned to Joshi, his eyes trailing, reluctant to leave what he had just seen.

"What the fuck did we just see?"

Joshi looked at him, his eyes wide. "It looked like...foot-prints. Bare feet. *Big* bare feet. Toes...a heel..."

"Which it couldn't have been. There was no one there, and no one has feet that big, anyway. Come on, Prem. We're trained observers. How would you write it up?"

"Are you kidding me? *You're* the Hemingway of paperwork. What would *you* say?"

They looked at one another for a moment. At last, Weiss broke away, his eyes returning to the empty terrace. "I say we're not going to be able to tell anyone about what we saw. Not while we're sober. We'd wind up on disability leave."

Joshi nodded. "We could say—"

A sound came from beneath them, slow and steady, a grinding and a kind of distant sizzle. Plastic shrivelling in a fire? A puff of cool air wafted from the terrace as though inhaled by the balcony door behind them.

Joshi said, "What's happening?"

Weiss turned to the door. "There's someone downstairs."

They both stood and considered that, but the movement downstairs seemed massive, the sound drawn out like torsion in a leaf spring. They could feel a rumbling through the decking beneath their feet. There was a sudden lurch and crash that came from the terrace below. Weiss returned to the terrace, resting his hands on the rail of the balcony.

Looking down, he saw a wooden rectangle and broken glass. "It's one of the downstairs doors. It must have fallen right out of its frame."

Joshi moved beside him, looking over the rail. "Can you see any movement?"

"Nothing." Weiss jerked his head up. "The sounds have stopped."

Joshi pulled open his jacket. "Here's where we draw our firearms and proceed with caution. Remember that. You're going to have to write it up."

Weiss touched his holster. "Fine. If it comes to that, you do the shooting, I'll do the writing."

Joshi shook his head in pity. "I'll lead." He drew a police-issue pistol from his belt holster and held it at arm's length. "Let's go."

"What are you planning to shoot? Whatever it was, it sounded bigger than a rhino."

They moved slowly to the balcony door and started down the stairs, Joshi in the lead. There was an abrupt cracking sound behind him and Joshi spun around.

"What happened?"

Weiss gestured at the stairs beneath them. The handrail had broken in Weiss's hand, spilling grey dust down the steps. Weiss silently tested his footing. The stairs they had climbed minutes before had lost their spring and now felt spongey beneath their weight.

Joshi turned back towards the downstairs room, trailing a look of disbelief. In a few steps, they were on the landing. The downstairs lights still burned bright, revealing the empty games room. A couple of the games tables had collapsed into grey heaps and the debris was littered with dominoes and poker chips.

Joshi moved ahead slowly, pointing his weapon until they were in the main room. The missing door was a grey-blue void opening onto the terrace.

Weiss moved past Joshi, reaching the doorway. He blinked out at the night for a few moments, then turned with a mixture of surprise and relief.

"There's no one around."

Weiss stepped out and Joshi joined him outside, his gun sweeping the terrace. They had to step around the fallen door, crunching glass underfoot. While Joshi continued to squint into every shadow, Weiss squatted down to examine the door.

"It fell forward," he said. "The whole door frame just rotted away. And look at this stained glass. It's practically opaque."

Joshi put his gun away reluctantly and peered down. "Yeah. Pitted, abraded."

Weiss slipped out his phone and scrolled for a number.

"Who are you calling?"

Weiss didn't answer. "Hello, Merrit? This is Detective Weiss. I need to speak to Ruth. Could you put her on, please?"

CHAPTER TWENTY-TWO

While Merrit was making for the landline phone, Ruth was upstairs standing with Eric in the hallway near the library. Through the glass doors, they could hear Clemmie cooing to her patient.

Ruth shivered. "Hold me, Eric."

Eric gave a sharp tug to his lapels before putting his arm out for her. "I understand. The police nosing around—it's unsettling. Just remember you've done nothing wrong, Ruth. God knows what happened to that Krauss person, but it didn't have anything to do with us."

"But what was James doing out there in the woods?"

"What did that gang always do—drink, buy drugs, get high."

"But I did use him, Eric. We wouldn't have Noah's medicine without James."

"They can suspect all they want, Ruth. They can't prove a connection. They can't trace the money you gave him, and now, whatever happened to him, they can't question Krauss."

"Poor James. Noah did love him in his way."

"Noah loved people who shared his destructive addictions,

Ruth." He paused and then decided to chance it. "People like Merrit."

Ruth stepped away from him. "Merrit cares for Noah, too. It's a corrosive love, but I think they had some happiness together. I wouldn't tolerate her here if I didn't believe that."

"Christ almighty, Ruth. Merrit's an enabler. You know the kind. Even after Noah started to show symptoms, she watched him use his hallucinogens and God knows what else. Powerful dissociatives, Ruth. I don't know what did him the most harm—the mind-altering drugs or the sudden withdrawal when he could no longer forage for himself. It doesn't matter now. Noah's mind is lost in a chemical prison of his own making. You have nothing to blame yourself for. You did everything that money and influence could do. You still are."

"We're taking such an awful chance, Eric. Even you aren't sure what effect the therapy is having on him—on his mind."

"My conscience is clear. How can you harm a man who has no awareness, no right to a future? It's a roll of the dice, but faint hopes are what we're dealing with at this stage. The drug we're giving him may be experimental, but it's just the latest refinement of a benzodiazepine. If we waited for it to be approved, Noah would be brain dead. We've managed to spark some measurable brain activity. You did what you had to do—and sometimes..."

Ruth looked up at him. "What is it?"

"I don't want to give you false hope, Ruth, but Merrit's right about one thing. There are moments when I see something in his face. Rapid eye movements, the ghost of a frown, small movements of his head as though he were looking at something unseen."

"Then you think he *may* come back to us, that there's a chance?"

Eric shook his head. "If we could get even a few hours of lucidity—I know you don't care about Noah's patents or his money, but think of all that falling into the hands of his shiftless daughter and Merrit."

"I don't begrudge Merrit her annuity."

"Maybe you should. I can't prove it, but I think she's doing what she's always done, feeding him the poison that destroyed his mind in the first place. Merrit is an addict, and she thinks like an addict. She thinks giving him an opiate or a hallucinogen is a mercy. She doesn't know the first thing about drug interactions and probably doesn't care. Noah wouldn't—and she's just like him."

"My God." Ruth recoiled at the idea. "Have you confronted her?"

"Of course I have. She denies it, acts as if she's horrified at the accusation." Eric tugged at his tie. "But it would be easy for her. Noah's IV line is always vulnerable, and Clemmie can't be there all the time. I send blood samples to the lab regularly and there's nothing they can detect in Noah's blood beyond his medications, but our therapy could be masking whatever it is she's forcing on him."

"I can't keep Merrit away from Noah, Eric. Not on mere suspicion. She may be an addict, but she was the only one that Noah loved, except for Sammy."

"And what about Sammy? You know what she's like, Ruth. She's a lost soul, just like her father. She makes bad choices."

"Maybe they're not such bad choices if she can afford them. At least she's not an addict. She's living the kind of eccentric lifestyle that guaranteed wealth allows her, but she saw what drugs did to her father, and she's too afraid of that to make the same mistake he did."

"You have no idea what Noah's intellectual properties are worth. Can you really see them in the hands of that—"

"Be careful, Eric. She's my only niece."

Merrit came up the stairs from the hall with a cordless phone in her hand. "It's that detective—Weiss."

Ruth glanced at Eric, then came forward to take the phone. "Yes, Detective. The pavilion—yes, you had a look around then?" Her expression turned to alarm. "Damage? What damage?"

Ruth looked back at Eric, her face white. Speaking into the phone, she asked, "Had the doors been left open to the weather? We noticed damage to the carriage entrance last week. I assumed it was because the double doors there had been left open. They're wide. We seldom use that wing now. How bad is the damage down there?"

She listened, Eric hovering close. "I don't know what to say. I'm at a loss. A prowler, you think? Yes, of course. Just come back up on the cable car and we'll see you shortly. Yes, I'll make a formal statement, but God knows what I can say."

She pressed the end button on the phone and stared at Eric. He came close and held her shoulders as she lowered her forehead onto his chest. "Extensive damage, Weiss called it. What does that *mean*? He thinks perhaps a prowler, a vandal I suppose."

"All right, listen, Ruth. When they get here, keep his attention on the vandalism. Don't volunteer anything about Noah."

"What are you saying, Eric? It sounds as though you're saying Noah's linked to this somehow."

"No, of course not. But Noah's friends—you know perfectly well that they made the pavilion their place, where they congregated and partied. All those spoiled degenerates with nothing to do but indulge their senses. What if one of them—"

Eric abruptly stopped, remembering that Merrit was standing nearby.

Ruth gestured to Merrit. "Merrit, darling. Would you mind spelling Clemmie for a bit?" Ruth opened the door and called to Clemmie, who was sitting holding Noah's left hand.

"Clemmie? Clemmie, it's time for Noah's medication. Eric

will be right there. Merrit will stay with him for a bit. I'm going downstairs now."

Clemmie stood without a word. Her expression, which had been animated and playful, became neutral as she rose. She laid Noah's hand gently on his lap, nodded to the three, and walked directly out and towards her room.

No one noticed, but Noah's hand had risen slightly from his lap. While his eyes roamed about the room, his slender fingers closed until they resembled a fist, which subsided slowly until his hand was resting back on his leg.

CHAPTER TWENTY-THREE

They were at a sports bar, and Carly was trying to understand the pleasure of watching other people watch a TV screen and drink.

"Why cider?" Evan asked, placing the glass in front of her.

"Because I hate the taste of beer."

"I never noticed. You like white wine, so you're not a teetotaler."

"No, but I prefer it if my drink doesn't taste like nail polish remover."

Evan grinned and sipped his own beer. "We're not much alike. Maybe that's why everything about you seems fresh to me." He looked at his glass thoughtfully. "Or maybe it's the lust," he smiled. "I'm good either way."

"We're in a sports bar; you're supposed to be in a frenzy about some team, not stewing in lust."

He considered that. "Okay, the Blue Jays then."

"Oh, right. But isn't that a summer thing?"

He nodded at the closest screen. "It's a preseason game from Dunedin in Florida."

"That would explain all the nice green grass."

"It's AstroTurf. Man, I've got a lot of work to do, but you're going to be a fan before I'm finished with you."

"I like a man with a long-term plan. A *really* long-term plan. I've read a lot of W. P. Kinsella. Does that help?"

"Who's he?"

"You know, *Shoeless Joe?*"

Evan looked blank.

"*Field of Dreams?*"

He held up his glass in celebration. "All right! Yeah, that helps. I'd hoped all this hubbub might get you out of the doldrums. I haven't seen you this worried since your dad's illness."

"Am I the only woman in here not wearing jeans?" she griped, looking around.

Evan was wearing a long-sleeved, open-necked shirt because of the weather, but he had turned the sleeves up to mid-forearm —or had his wardrobe team turn them up. He slouched, happily at ease.

"You look fabulous in that blouse thingee," he said. "It shows off your shoulders, which would be a glory anywhere."

"I tend to shop at my advertisers. They're a bit too upscale for this place." Carly held on to her smile, but it was an effort. There was a noisy cheer from nearby and the pause allowed her to change the subject. She studied the amber depths of her cider, and then: "I don't think I want to be a writer."

Evan looked at her in astonishment. "But you're a great writer. You run a successful magazine."

"I mean a fiction writer." It was a painful admission for Carly. "I was always jealous of my father's gift for storytelling. For all his pretense of being a travel writer, I figure his work was half research and half imagination. Maybe sixty-five percent imagination." She sipped the cider. It tasted almost like unsweetened apple juice but she knew a tall glass of the stuff could scramble her head. "I've been trying to let my imagination run riot, but it scares the hell out of me."

"Your nightmares."

"And morning mares. Is that a thing?"

"Does writing it down help? You know, catharsis?"

Carly gave a little bow. "Catharsis. Good for you, Evan. You make me feel like I have to learn the name of a starting pitcher in return."

Evan sipped his beer. "Fair's fair." He watched her glance at the closest TV screen. Carly was doing her best, trying to look interested, but she was fidgeting with her glass way too much. "Is this still about Noah Goodwyn?" he asked.

She instantly forgot the screen and took to toying with her coaster. "When Weiss came to see me about Goodwyn, that really seemed to kick my imaginings into high gear, but there have been other times. Daydreams, sleepless nights. I'm beginning to think I'd be happier giving up my romantic dreams of writing novels. Maybe I'm going to have to be just A. L. Rouhl's daughter. I mean, look at me. I've been uneasy all day. I keep imagining…"

"Noah Goodwyn in pain?" he offered.

"Yeah, that. And other stuff."

"What other stuff?"

Carly looked at him, and then her eyes focussed on some invisible horizon. "Something that doesn't exist. Or something that can only exist by sucking all of the life and solidity out of the real world around it."

Evan took her hand. Her fingers were cold from the glass. "Well," he smiled, "you're a poet, anyway."

Momentarily, she was back, and she softened at his touch and gentle tone, but then, whatever nightmare existed out there between the tables, Maple Leaf sweaters, and paper plates soggy with pizza, it claimed her attention again.

Evan held onto her hand, willing her to return when she was ready.

"I'm sorry, Evan. I'll just be a minute. I have to make a phone call."

"The office? Who?"

"I'm not sure. I'll have to think…"

"Fine, but finish your apple juice."

"It's not apple juice. This stuff can make you drunker'n a skunk."

"I look forward to it."

She persisted. "Really. Stay right here. I'll be back in a minute."

With that, Carly stood and worked her way out past the cash desk. She stepped out onto the patio, the early evening air cool and damp on her face, the tables empty, the chairs turned up. It was still too chilly to sit out.

In the comparative quiet, with the odd car swishing by on the wet blacktop, she cradled her phone and punched up its number pad. Her finger hung indecisively above the screen for a moment, then she tapped three times. There was a voice on the line right away.

Carly answered, "I want to report an emergency."

CHAPTER TWENTY-FOUR

Joshi was the first one to arrive back at the terrace level platform of the cable car.

Weiss followed, still clutching his phone.

"Who are you calling now?"

"Just reporting in," Weiss said. "I'm going to tell the dispatcher we're investigating a break-in."

"I suppose tearing a heavy door off its hinges would be 'breaking in.' Not too subtle. Only, the doors were unlocked."

Weiss was now seated in the carriage on a bench, still talking on the phone, when Joshi closed the carriage's gate and raised the lever. The carriage lurched upward, showing its age, and then began to climb steadily towards the upper platform and the house on the ridge. Weiss stared out at the cliff face which was dark now and put his phone away.

"I've heard this used to be the shore of a massive lake in prehistoric times: Lake Algonquin. The escarpment is an ancient shoreline."

Joshi moved down the carriage to the high end and looked down at the terrace falling away below. "Must have been a pretty deep lake."

Weiss joined him and grinned. "You're right. I don't buy it either."

"What did Ruth say?"

"When I told her about the damage, she seemed genuinely surprised, like it was news to her."

"That's crap. It takes years to erode wood like that. The door must have been hanging on a flake of rust to just fall out."

"Who are you trying to convince, Prem? You opened the door yourself on the way in. It didn't so much as creak."

"We must have missed the damage somehow."

"And do you remember the state of the tapestry in the carriage house? Ruth made it sound like the damage to that wing was only discovered recently."

"What do we know? Maybe the tapestry has never been restored. Maybe she's treating the carriage house like a museum."

"Like that place in Charleston you were telling me about?"

"Yeah, exactly. I'll tell you, it was like being in a haunted house. The different layers of wallpaper were exposed, the furniture was threadbare. Creepy as hell."

"Speaking of creepy," Weiss said, "I had the sense in the pavilion that there was something big…heavy… moving around beneath us. Is that the way you remember it?"

"Yeah—your rhino."

"And all we know about the pavilion is that it was a haunt of Noah's friends."

Joshi winced. "Do me a favour. When you write the report, try to avoid the word 'haunt,' okay?"

The dampness in the air from the low overcast felt cool and clean. Once more, a light rain had started to fall, pattering on the carriage roof.

Joshi remained standing, agitated and sullen. There was a slight jarring as if the motor high on the ridge drawing them upward had begun to labour.

Weiss sat back on the wicker bench and it made a rustling sound as his weight shifted, while Joshi took hold of the vertical hand bar and wrenched at it moodily. Weiss watched the weak moon shadows moving across the seats of the carriage as it rose through the early evening mist. His thoughts were roiling and had now returned to Noah and the IV tube that would always be strung down to his vein.

The carriage shuddered slightly, then rolled smoothly on its rails up the rock face. The grinding of the wheels was so far below at the outer end of the carriage that it sounded muted, and the illusion of floating upward was pleasant. What sound there was came mostly from the inward end of the carriage where the wheels were tucked up close beneath the angular steel frame.

Weiss looked in the direction of the sound and an alarm went off in his mind.

At first, he wasn't sure why his chest was beginning to constrict. Maybe it was the realization that they were pulling into the dark hiatus between the lights of the terrace and the lights of the upper platform. They were committed, sent on their way by the pull of a lever and at the mercy of an electric winch far above that they couldn't see.

It could have been no more than that, but the carriage had a feel to it, just the sum of the forces lifting it and its weight. It was impossible, of course, but it felt as though the whole structure had become heavier, putting new pressure on the steel wheels. They were grinding up the rails, their movement vibrating steadily through the metal and wooden beams beneath them. Weiss's eyes kept probing the shadows, looking past Joshi at the moving rocks with their patina of moss and lichen. The relentless push of the wood strapping on his feet buoyed him up, and he sensed its power in his knees.

Joshi frowned. "What's the matter with this thing? Its speed is getting kind of irregular."

That was probably why Weiss had felt the movement. Steady pressure wouldn't have been noticeable. There was the merest hint of a sway from side to side caused by minute differences in the two rails, but that wasn't it. The speed was definitely varying and Weiss wondered why.

The small sensations taken together became vaguely worrisome. The faint moon shadows of the pine and maple saplings that here and there pushed from cracks in the rock moved along the length of the carriage against the steady shadows of the window frames. The tiny windows above, meant to suggest the design of Pullman coaches, were the only steady glow in the shifting gloom. All the other shadows rippled across the shape of the wicker seating and leapt from hand bar to armrest.

It was then that an impression began to build in Weiss's mind, an impression that seemed to develop like photographic paper in a dark room.

The thing he saw at the far end of the carriage, behind Joshi's swaying shape, was neither in full shadow nor in the moonlight but seemed to inhabit the spaces in between—the moving line within. It was as though the tenuous edge of the shadow were to sketch a shape in passing. As soon as he saw the shape emerge, it was gone—a creation of the moment—but each shifting shadow seemed to redraw its outline more firmly.

The shape appeared to crouch low against the rock face end of the carriage near the exit gate.

At first, he thought he was imagining the thing, and he rubbed his eyes. Then, he began to tense.

"Who's there?" Weiss called out.

Joshi looked down to stare at him. "What's up with you?" Then Joshi's eyes followed Weiss's, and he swung quickly to Weiss's side, staring at the far end of the carriage. "Eilert?"

Weiss did get the sense of a face there; there was no mistaking it now. An impossibly *big* face. It was a distortion, an exaggerated feature here and there, like something in a carnival mirror.

Somewhere in the confusion of leaf shadow and moon flicker, he glimpsed stupendous hands, too—as pale as the light itself, the long fingers splayed in imitation of some great grey spider clinging lightly to the window ledges and doorframe.

Weiss sensed Joshi standing over him, breathing rapidly, beginning to edge towards the high outer end of the carriage, but Weiss couldn't move his legs to get up. Some cool vestige of his mind was compelled to understand what he was seeing, and he kept straining to sift a recognizable shape out of the clutter of light and dark. Where he inferred its body should be, bent or kneeling low against the floorboards, there was nothing; only that damned face looming there, hanging in darkness. Less than a face really, just those vaguely familiar features emerging from nothing at all.

Weiss felt a stab of panic when it telegraphed its presence unmistakably for the first time to his feet as a moving weight on the ribs of the floor.

Such weight! How could it have such weight?

The carriage had slowed noticeably by now, and the moaning of the distant motor up above them began to drop in pitch as the drag on the carriage increased. The immense hands moved slowly through the flicker of blue light and blue gloom.

Somewhere below, a joint creaked and a vibration came and went.

Pressed back into a merciful shadow, Weiss was rigid, his mind beginning to jolt back and forth between seizure and cold panic. The lips on the thing were loathsome in a way he couldn't process. They seemed to drift in and out of clear definition, but he could make out a sort of grimace, a taut tug of the lip suggestive of revulsion at the fact of its own impossible being.

A dark brow, empurpled in the blue light—the shadowed

eyes were like a stain on a shroud. There was no emotion in the face beyond a vague anguish, an emptiness that you could fall into, numb and powerless.

Weiss felt utterly lost sitting there. Something in his heart short-circuited and he had to resist the urge to whimper and cover his eyes.

Joshi was cursing in a high pitched, sobbing way. He jammed himself into the corner behind Weiss and had one foot on the bench as though he were prepared to launch himself out the window. He began to scrabble at the window frame, like Weiss, unable to take his eyes off that thing that filled the other end of the carriage, pulsing with menace.

Weiss had no idea what he was seeing.

It fitted no ghostly or horrific image he'd ever imagined. It was the face of an impossible giant of a man, grossly Neanderthal and—so it seemed—graphically insane. Its mindlessness only made it more threatening; those gigantic fingers groping the woodwork, even straying to its own bloated features, fluttering like some hermit crab feeling its way out of a shell of darkness.

"Eilert," Joshi hissed, "Eilert! What do we do?"

Weiss managed a shaky glance at him. The carriage creaked throughout its whole length, the inexplicable weight of the thing groaning in every tortured strut and spar of the floor.

"We can climb," Weiss said stupidly, stealing a glance at the doorway behind them. "We can climb down."

Weiss had no real plan except a frantic urge to back away from the thing, all the while expecting it to either spring from its black lair—or to come slowly grinding towards them on haunches as impossibly large as its hands.

After all, that's what happened in the movies.

The thing planted its hands and shifted. It was trying to move, dragging its increasing weight and limbless mass. Weiss groped towards the doorway behind them, knowing that it opened to a narrow wrought-iron balcony. He gripped Joshi's coat with his free hand, compelling him to follow.

It made no sense. There was no escape from the high end of the carriage. Only a long fall to a deadly slope.

"We're practically stopped," Joshi gasped, risking a glance at the steep rock face below. "Listen to the fucking motor up there! It's going to burn out."

The squeal of rotor brushes wasn't close enough. Weiss shuddered, realizing they were still less than half the way up to the house level. The abomination in the carriage was no spirit; from the sound and feel of the carriage, its solid weight must have been staggering, and yet it had come to the carriage quietly as though settling out of the night air itself. Where did the thing get its substance?

They edged out onto the narrow vestibule with its cast-iron railing, and now there was nowhere to go.

Weiss could see right away that his talk of climbing down was nonsense. The night hung in a diorama around the terrace and the distant woods. He saw the rock face clearly, with the glint of the rails below them. It wasn't an impossible drop to the rock face, but the steep angle of the surface was so great that any leap from here would end in a deadly tumble all the way down to the terrace.

"Jesus, Eilert. What do we do?"

The carriage lurched and Weiss turned back to the black gap of the doorway, half expecting to see fingertips curling around the frame. The thing was still there in the gloom, and the sounds told him it was still twisting and bending the wood and metal frame around them—and that the distant motor had taken to slipping against the weight.

What would happen if the cable broke? Were there automatic brakes, or would they plummet down onto the terrace platform?

Joshi whispered in his ear. "I'm jumping, Eilert. I'm going over."

Weiss grabbed his arm. "The slope's too steep."

"Can't you hear it?" Joshi breathed. "It's coming towards us."

Weiss didn't know if Joshi had anything to go on—his imagination or his overloaded senses—but he peered back frantically into that black doorway, willing the shadows aside.

He saw nothing; there was the creak of shifting weight, a heart-stopping slump, and splintering wicker. The massive hands were finding purchase on the benches, the unreadable face, drawing towards the centre of the carriage.

Joshi was right. It was coming for them.

As if to encourage his lurid imaginings, the sounds of the wheels below began to change in pitch.

In a moment of despair, Weiss thought he might step out into the darkness. He went so far as to look down, but whatever primitive mechanism calculates our chances in moments of crisis, the alarms rang in his chest and he knew he was contemplating a spectacular suicide. He imagined hitting the slope, his broken ankles and wrists drawn into a blind tumble down to the rocks and beams below.

Weiss couldn't quite see the wheels, but the grinding of their bearings told him that the weight was shifting toward their end of the carriage. He leaned out far over the little platform, gripping the handrail. Nothing in the world would have made him turn again to the doorway.

Joshi swung past him, out over the railing, his feet on the very edge, his hands gripping the handrail. Another second and he would be gone, skidding down the rock.

"Wait!" Weiss shouted.

Joshi's answer sounded hoarse and ragged. "Look at the door frame! It's withering. Just like in the pavilion. It's crumbling. This whole platform will break away if we don't jump now. Look at the window glass!"

The only glass panes in the carriage were the two narrow rectangles on either side of the balcony door. They had been clear a moment ago. Now it was as if they had been sandblasted.

Weiss's mind wasn't on window glass. It was on the rails below, and he could see the narrow secondary rails inside the main track. He knew that since they were still moving, however slowly, the heavy counterweight must be just ahead of the carriage and descending towards them. In a minute, it would pass right beneath them.

"Listen, Prem, we're going to drop to the counterweight and hold on."

Weiss joined him, climbing backwards over the abyss. It looked like he had been right—and only barely in time. The squat flat block of creosoted beams, banded in studded iron, was rolling slowly down from under the front axle, its eight small wheels barely turning.

Whether he understood or not, Joshi lowered himself.

"There!" Weiss said, suppressing the urge to shout. "The counterweight will be under us in a second. Wait as long as you can, and try to hit the upper end of the block. You'll slip down a bit, but you can grab one of the iron bands."

Something fell away from the carriage floor, and it struck between the rails. It looked like a piece of planking, but it smashed to a pale smear on the rocks. The counterweight slipped over the stain and moved under their feet. Weiss tried to judge the right moment, but Joshi let go before him.

Joshi landed well, slumping to his belly and starting to slide. There was a desperate scramble, and it looked like he was going to go off the bottom of the block, but at the last moment, he found a handgrip on the iron band.

Weiss twisted to see, his tweed hat falling from his head. The hat bounced on the counterweight and tumbled right over Joshi onto the dark slope below, and Weiss suddenly realized if he was to jump now, he would surely dislodge Joshi and send him sliding down the rocks.

By the time Weiss thought it through, the counterweight was gone—too far down now to stop his fall. For a moment, he calculated his chances on the bare rock and gave up.

Weiss watched Joshi's struggling figure riding the counterweight down into the grey gloom. That meant that the carriage was still ascending. He switched his grip and turned back to the doorway.

There was a sudden lurch, and the note of the distant motor changed. He listened, waiting for the groaning of floorboards or the twisting of beams.

Something had changed.

The carriage seemed to pick up speed, lifting him up towards the upper platform. He searched the darkness of the carriage, but the doorway seemed empty. Weiss remained where he was, waiting, and after a few minutes he was startled to see the upper platform drop into place beside the carriage: he had reached the top.

The lights of the platform threw a new kind of light through the windows of the carriage, banishing the cold shadows, replacing them with harsh, angular shapes. No great face loomed there, just a ruined scene of bleached wood and dissolving wicker.

When he could make his legs move, Weiss hauled himself up over the end railing and crouched on the little vestibule staring inside the carriage.

He moved cautiously inside, but he didn't get far; the floorboards collapsed, leaving a fragile web of ash-coloured crossbeams. Moving his hands from one chrome handrail to the next, he swung along the edge of the carriage, working his way to the back. There was a sudden silence as the motor disengaged and the carriage settled to a stop, level with the lighted platform.

It took Weiss several minutes to work his way along the

tattered benches to the rear gate. He kicked it aside, unwilling to give up his hand grip. The gate buckled and fell away, allowing him to make the step out onto the platform. The broad platform felt reassuringly solid beneath his feet. Looking down, he noticed the streaks of rust and ash on his legs. His coat was torn, though he couldn't remember how it had happened.

Reaching inside his jacket, Weiss pulled out his cell phone, getting it all caught up in the silk of his pocket in his haste. At last, he got it clear and lit up the screen. But before he could enter a number, it rang. He looked at the caller I.D. and his eyes squeezed shut. He breathed a sigh of pure relief and answered.

CHAPTER TWENTY-FIVE

Minutes earlier, Joshi had been scrabbling with his bare hands, trying to find a grip on the great wooden blocks that made up the counterweight.

They were greasy to the touch, and damp with the fine rain. He kept slipping further down until his shoes were dangling off the lower edge. If he let go, he'd tumble, maybe all the way to the base of the rock face, beneath the lower platform—and if he survived that, the counterweight would keep descending, rolling down on top of him. He might find himself jammed into a space he couldn't escape from.

His terrified imagination made him reckless and his hands began to bleed. He managed to catch the corner of the wide metal band binding the beams together. It stuck out enough on the side so that he could get a firm grip. He drew one of his legs up and managed to dig his heel against a bolt head. It was precarious, but if he could just arrest his fall for a few more minutes, he would be at the bottom.

The seconds ground by with the squeak of the steel wheels, and then the lower platform rose up beside him. The big rectangle of heavy beams gave a mild jolt as it came to rest against a rubber barrier made of old car tires. It was enough to shake him loose, but it was a short tumble to the barrier, and he could at last rest his shoulder against something hard and stable.

Every part of his stocky body ached. Although he had managed two trips a week to his gym at the mall, he carried some superfluous weight. That wasn't helping; his age trumped his fitness. Now that he had the luxury of thinking, he recognized the most focussed pain; his left ankle was throbbing and probably sprained.

He slowly unfolded himself and tried to stand on the angled rubber surface, but had to support his weight with his ravaged hands. Edging to one side, he realized he could let go of the sloping beams and stand. It was too dark in the pit to see much of anything, but he recognized the footing that his toe had found—one of the horizontal sleepers that supported the rail bed.

Once he got the idea, he could slowly and painfully climb up to the level of the platform using the ends of the sleepers as a ladder. When he got high enough, he slumped forward onto the platform and dragged himself flat on his face.

He didn't have time to steady his breathing or his pounding heart. He rolled to his back, reaching into his jacket pocket for his phone, and called his partner. Weiss answered immediately, breathing hard. They started to talk at once, but Joshi spoke the loudest.

"I'm fine. I'm fine, Prem," Weiss assured him. "The thing just disappeared—as fast as it came. What about you?"

"Minor scrapes and a sprained ankle. What are we going to do?"

Joshi heard the regular crunch of gravel on the other end. "I'm headed for the house. I have to make sure Ruth and the others are safe. I'm working on the assumption that this—whatever it is—is not over. In the meantime, stay put where you are and wait for help to arrive. I've already called it in."

Joshi thought about disputing this, but he had no way up the cliff face and their car was parked by the main house portico.

When the phone call to Weiss ended, Joshi laid his hands by his sides, and, still flat on his back, breathing in the moist evening air seemed to calm him. The adrenaline was ebbing and his heart rate was approaching normal. He did a brief mental inventory of his aches and pains and began to think about what Weiss was going to tell the people up at the house.

He gazed up at the low overcast, feeling the fine drizzle on his face when a voice came from somewhere behind him.

"You all right, Detective?"

A uniformed paramedic carrying a folded canvas stretcher was looking down at him. Surprise and some vestige of dignity gave Joshi the strength to sit up. Nearby, at the edge of the red terrace tiles, he saw the flashing lights of an EMS van.

The paramedic studied his face for a moment. "I'm guessing you're Joshi. We got your name from your division."

Joshi blinked and his mouth hung open. Not more than two minutes had passed since he spoke to Weiss. Joshi rubbed the grime from his palms and tried to catch up.

"My…uh…ankle is shot," he said. "Just a sprain, I hope, but it's a bad one. At my age, that can become chronic."

The medic knelt beside him, laying the stretcher down on the planking of the platform. "What about these abrasions on your hands and knees?"

"Damn." Joshi looked at the torn knees of his trousers. "I think I have some slivers from the wood. I've got to get this cleaned or they'll get infected."

"Let's get you into the ambulance and I can help you with that. Can you walk?"

Joshi accepted the man's help getting to his one good foot. They began moving towards the flashing lights, Joshi using the medic's shoulder to keep weight off his sprained ankle. He had the feeling he had missed something.

"Ambulance...right. I appreciate you getting here so quickly."

The medic supporting him, a well-built young man not much taller than Joshi, gave a snort of amusement. "Quickly? Yeah, right. We got lost, missed the entrance, had to drive all the way up the escarpment to turn around. The instructions we got were pretty vague—no address, just the name 'Moreland House' and a description of the gardens."

Joshi tried to stare but found his nose inches from the medic's cheek. "What are you talking about?" he said. "I'm just barely picking myself up."

A second man, taller, with a closely shaved head, came up to them, looking around, trying to assess the situation. There was nothing to see but a dishevelled cop in a wet topcoat with torn trousers. The terrace and the cable car platform looked as utterly normal as such a structure could be.

Joshi looked from one man to the other. "Detective Weiss called you guys, right?"

From under Joshi's arm, the medic said, "Weiss? He's the other detective, right? No, it was some woman. Said a pair of detectives were in distress. We checked that out with your division, of course, and they confirmed they had a couple of guys at Moreland House. That's where we got your names and descriptions. Hal, what was the woman's name—the one who called 911?"

Hal opened the double doors at the back of the van and was starting to pull out some steps. "Cassandra something, I think."

Joshi frowned. "Cassandra? Who's she?"

The first medic, still supporting Joshi with his arm around his back, raised his eyes to the overcast heavens. "Okay, here we go. She's the woman who called 911. Hal, check his head for a concussion."

"The point is, I don't know anyone named Cassandra."

"Fortunately, she seemed to know about you."

"The 911 dispatcher made it sound like it was some kind of an accident. Is that what this was?" Hal asked.

Joshi looked back. It had become too dark to make out the ruined carriage at the upper platform, but he pointed anyway. "The damn carriage gave way. Yeah, let's call it an accident. I'll have to consult with my partner."

"Let's *call* it an accident, you say? Okay. And your partner, where is he?"

"He made it up to the top before the whole damn thing collapsed. I just spoke to him on the phone. He's okay, but he may be in some kind of…difficulty up there."

The medic glanced up at the shadowy slope. "More 'difficulty?' What, is he accident-prone?"

Joshi thought about calling the incident a fire—something they might understand, but his instinct was to say as little as possible until he and Weiss could get their stories straight. Anything he said now could come back at him.

"We have a situation at the house," he said at last. "I can't talk about it right now."

The medic began to repeat the word 'situation,' but caught himself. "You say he's not injured, this Weiss person?"

"Sounds like he's in better shape than me. We'll have to compare wounds—it'll be fun. He's very competitive."

"I have to know, though," the medic persisted. "You're saying he's all right? We don't have to hurry?"

"I didn't say that. Do you think you can find the upper grounds?"

"Are you being sarcastic?"

"No, sorry. But I have to get up there. The ankle can wait."

"This isn't a shuttle service. If Weiss isn't hurt—"

"What's with the attitude?"

"Oh, I don't know. We do get testy when our clients are evasive."

Joshi fumbled for his I.D. "Look, you just got commandeered, okay? I'm sorry, but I think the people up there at the house may be in danger."

"People? What people? Danger from what?"

Joshi's eyes darted in confusion. "From… Look at me. I'm getting in your ambulance. We can talk there. Can you just drive?"

"You've got a damn phone. Call your partner again. See how he is."

"Yeah, he'd be in the house by now. I'll call again from the ambulance."

Joshi limped up the steps and sat on a wheeled gurney secured by clamps to the floor while Hal went to get the unused canvas stretcher. He tapped in Weiss's number again. After a second or two of purring, Weiss picked up.

"Eilert. Tell me you're still okay."

"Yes, and Eric, Ruth, and Merrit are safe so far. Clemmie, the nurse? I haven't seen her yet."

"Christ. Eilert. What's going on?"

There was a pause and the sound of Weiss's phone shifting. "Is anybody monitoring this call?"

"I'm in the back of an ambulance getting my knees wiped. I'm not on speakerphone, but I can't talk freely."

The medic looked up from his swab and frowned. "You guys spies or something?"

Weiss sounded confused. "You're in an ambulance already?"

"Yeah, about that…"

"Look, never mind. As long as you're safe, Prem. I think that thing may be back—the homunculus."

"The who? What did you call it?"

There was a moment—Weiss breathing close to the phone, a brief tut of exasperation…

"I think I understand what's going on, Prem—at least some of it. Call it a working theory. I think that this is all about Noah. There's no short way of explaining this, but that thing we saw— if I'm right, it could be up here in the house now. When you get here, you've got to keep people outside until I can think what to do."

Joshi closed his eyes, trying to visualize the layout of the house: the central stairway, the two great front rooms, the upstairs bedrooms and library.

"Where are you?"

"I just got to the library. They're all here Merrit, Ruth, Eric— in Noah's room. I'm going to keep us all together for now. Look, I'm going to call the fire department. Maybe they can get one of those inflatable things to the back of the house, under the back balcony. You know, so we can jump if we need to. There's a steep roof and a long drop from the eves, so it would be a desperation move, but I want a way out if that thing shows up again. None of us are really up to it, and it would be as risky as hell. I'd only consider it as a last resort."

"You think the thing is downstairs?"

"I don't know, but the lights are out down there, and… You know that smell, Prem? The smell of *age* we talked about? It hit me as soon as I stepped inside. Anyway, I'm circling the wagons up here until we get some help."

"What about a ladder?"

"This could all happen in a hurry. I don't know if there will be time for a ladder rescue of four people—five counting Noah."

"You think that thing could get upstairs?"

"I think it's already *been* up here, Prem, and I think it will come again. From what we saw on the carriage, it seems to congeal out of the air wherever it needs to be. Look, I haven't figured everything out, but you need to know we're not dealing with a rational mind. I don't know if it thinks at all. Maybe it's just a projection of raw emotions. After all, you don't think real clear when you're being tortured to death."

"Whoa, slow down. You're scaring the piss out of me. Just give me something I can actually *tell* everybody."

"Fuck if I know. Make something up. Gas maybe. How about a natural gas fire ignited by an electrical spark?"

"Gas. Right. Good. Sounds…not entirely insane. Keep me up to date and I'll try and manage things on the ground. I'll call you when I know what the situation is outside the house."

Joshi held his phone in both hands and spoke to the medic. "My partner says… He says there's been a gas leak up at the house, and a fire. A flash fire. More than one. Get some backup. More ambulances for up to five injured people. The people in the house may be forced to jump from an upper story balcony. My partner's calling the fire department."

The medic named Hal was back, and he slid the stretcher along the floor. He'd heard the comment about a fire.

"Is that why *you* had to jump? A fire on that trolley thing?"

Joshi's mind raced. There was no natural gas on a rail carriage. He felt like a crook desperately trying to hold his alibi together.

"Look, I'm not an electrical engineer, but the power in the house has shorted out—the power in the winch housing, too. Maybe lightning struck? Maybe the overload ran from the winch cable to the carriage. All I know is that the carriage was starting to collapse from the damage."

The two medics exchanged glances but Joshi pressed on.

"Somehow, my partner was able to hold on until the carriage reached the top. Me? I decided to take my chances on the slope. So, let's step on it. That house is a death trap and they're going to need our help."

Hal thought for a second, surrounded by the gentle whisper of the night, then began to close the rear doors.

CHAPTER TWENTY-SIX

When Weiss arrived at the doors of Moreland House, Ruth Moreland was standing in the front hall holding an LED flashlight in her hand.

"My God, Weiss, what happened to you?" Ruth took in Weiss's torn coat and dusty shoes with a single appraising glance.

"Why are there no lights?" Weiss said, looking about.

The rooms to either side of the front hall were a labyrinth of tall shadows thrown by the windows. The splendid high ceilings and the luxurious panelling seemed cavernous in the dark. He sniffed the air.

"One of the breakers must have gone," Ruth was saying, her manner that of affronted dignity. "In a house this old, they may even be fuses," she added dismissively. "I'm sure I don't know. At least it's just the main floor. I can't get an electrician until morning."

Weiss nodded his understanding, but the cold chill in his chest was back. "My partner is down at the terrace. Safe, thank God. I spoke to him on the phone."

Eric crowded Ruth aside. "What happened to you?"

"The cable car...part of it...disintegrated. It's no longer useable."

Ruth held Eric's arm. "But that's impossible. We keep it in perfect repair. It has to be or the elevator inspection people would shut us down." She frowned. "I suppose you're going to sue me."

"What?" It wasn't the reaction Weiss was expecting. "No, that never even occurred to me." He had to remind himself that Ruth couldn't possibly understand the near panic he was feeling at that moment. He had to take this in careful steps, and he had to maintain his authority. "What I want is—"

He had to think...

Weiss's first thought was to get Ruth and Eric out of the house, but Merrit, Clemmie, and Noah were up in the library, and Noah was in his wheelchair. He was going to have to assess the situation upstairs, and he might need Eric as Noah's doctor to understand what was happening. For that matter, he might need Ruth for permission to move Noah to safety.

He summoned his air of command and spoke. "I want to see Noah."

Eric was instantly defensive. "Noah? Shouldn't we be talking about vandals? A break-in, you said."

"There was damage, and you did say the pavilion was a favourite gathering place for Noah's friends."

"Yes, but you've seen Noah and Noah's not going to tell you anything. You know that."

Weiss knew Eric was right, but he also sensed that the thing on the carriage had something to do with the desiccated little man upstairs.

"I assume Merrit or Clemmie is with him right now since you're both down here."

"Yes, Merrit is with him. I believe Clemmie is resting. Her room is right beside the library."

Eric held his ground, but Weiss was firm, gesturing towards the stairs.

"If you'd lead the way."

It took a light touch from Ruth, but Eric eventually pivoted on the decorative carving that formed the bottom end of the bannister, and with bad grace, stepped up onto the staircase. Weiss let Ruth go next, noticing the carving as he followed behind. He recognized the incised oval as a stylized pineapple, and he had the sensation of being in one of those dreams where you can't wake up.

The corridor at the top of the stairs that led to the library was really an extended balcony because its left side was, in fact, an elaborately carved wooden bannister overlooking the great room downstairs. They passed a closed door to their right, Clemmie's room presumably, and Ruth gently knocked. She listened at the door briefly, before she walked on, arriving at the double entranceway of the library. Eric swung the nearest glass-panelled door aside, letting Ruth go in ahead of him, and left the door wide for Weiss.

Merrit, who was sitting with Noah, stood as they came in. She noticed the state of Weiss's coat and the dusty smudges on his knee. There was a murmur of questions and sympathy as Ruth tried to explain about the carriage collapsing, but Weiss wasn't listening. He was taking Joshi's call from the ambulance.

When that call ended, he called the fire department, arranging, so he hoped, a second way out of the house.

"Tell the fire people to come to the back of the house," he told the dispatcher. "I don't want anybody going in the front. It's not... It might not be safe."

He knew when this was over he was going to have to talk his way out of a mess. The last thing he wanted to do was waste time right now trying to explain something that no one would believe, anyway.

Pocketing his phone, he edged towards the shrivelled figure

seated in his wheelchair by the fireplace. The IV stand was beside him. Someone had lit a wood fire behind the large andirons, and the logs flickered on Noah's wild unshorn eyebrows and emotionless pout.

Weiss stopped in front of Noah and shut out their questions for a long moment, and then he inclined his head in a small nod of greeting and said, "Noah?" as though casually saying hello.

It was such an incongruous, tasteless thing to do that it stunned them all to silence. Of course, Noah went on looking at nothing at all, the only life in his face the dancing warmth of the fire. There was a tremble to his lips that Weiss hadn't noticed before, and the pale hairless hand fluttered more than ever.

"Merrit," Weiss said, still watching Noah's micro-movements. "In your opinion, what was it that really *drove* Noah? Was it just his addictive personality?"

Merrit glanced down at Noah as though wondering what Weiss was seeing there. "No, that wasn't it," she said. "Noah always seemed such a large-scale personality. Loud, brash, a trickster, but I knew it was an act. A backup personality, you might call it. The truth is, he was self-conscious and awkward." Weiss looked at her, urging her on.

"I think deep down he hated himself," she said at last. "He was bitter about his height, his features, his gait. He'd call himself the elephant man, a gross exaggeration, but I think that self-loathing was at the root of everything. I couldn't snap him out of it."

"So the drugs were a...distraction?"

"And a kind of therapy, maybe—at least at the beginning. Noah favoured the drugs that would take him out of himself: Special K, angel dust..."

"Dissociatives," Eric groused. "I thought so."

Merrit turned to Eric, defending Noah. "He wanted out, you see. Out of his body. Psychedelics did that for him. He could float out there—said he could see his own body."

"Is that why he liked to hack into other people's software?" Weiss asked. "To get out of himself?"

"Well, yes. It's the same, isn't it? He loved that. 'Easter egging,' he called it. We'd have a laugh over that. Some of the crazy places he popped up: charities, government sites. He even got his image into correctional facilities. There were so many, but it was all just gaming to him."

Weiss looked up, searching the great empty arch over their heads. "What about here? Is there any way Noah could escape from *here* without being seen?"

Noah was so obviously incapacitated this felt like a non sequitur. He had lost Merrit.

She looked stunned. "But that's an absurd question. Look at him."

"What about out there?"

Weiss took a few steps towards the balcony doors. Weiss knew that he was just casting about, trying to make sense of what was happening at the house.

Merrit shook her head, adamant. "It's a sort of widow's walk. It stretches across the back of the house. But there's no way down from it." Then she caught herself buying into Weiss's crazy premise. "What am I saying? Noah can't walk a yard on his own. He can barely stay on his feet."

Suddenly, the library lights—two large fixtures hung by chains from the vault—went out, and only the moving light of the fireplace illuminated the room.

There was a surprised silence for a few moments, then soft curses and the attention was back on Weiss. Maybe they all thought he had lost his mind, because Eric moved in and looked him straight in the eye. He was a couple of inches taller than Weiss, and with his shoulders hunched forward, broad and powerful looking.

How many times had he put the fear of God in his congregation through his sheer physical presence, Weiss wondered. Even the black-framed glasses worked for him, giving his eyes an owl-like intensity.

"Detective Weiss," he said with an edge of suspicion in his voice, "Where is Detective Joshi? You went down to the terrace together, I believe." This was Eric's idea of a counter-attack.

Weiss had become vaguely aware of the condition of his clothes. Somehow in the solemn splendour of the Moreland library, his appearance now was an affront. He ran his fingers down the ragged tear in his coat—something had apparently caught on his pocket. Every part of him was streaked with the unique grey residue he'd picked up from the carriage; he looked like he had been in a fight. Weiss realized that his anger at Eric was building, and he took his time answering.

"I told you, I spoke to Prem on the phone and he'll be fine. Sprained ankle, some bruises."

It must have irritated Eric that Weiss kept peering down at Noah with impertinent interest. It was like mocking the afflicted, and it wasn't nice, but, though he wasn't ready to explain why, Weiss couldn't help it. He knew the answer was right there in those aimlessly roaming eyes.

Losing patience, Eric grabbed Weiss's arm firmly as though he were dealing with a drunk or a man in shock, and managed to turn him away from Noah.

"Christ, man. What happened to you?"

"Prem fell from the carriage," Weiss said.

"What? How could that possibly happen?"

"Where's Clemmie?" Weiss asked, ignoring Eric's agenda.

Foremost in his own mind was the thought that some kind of unfathomable danger was lurking nearby.

Eric looked around in amazement, knowing perfectly well that Clemmie wasn't there, perhaps wondering why all the commotion hadn't drawn her into the library. When he turned to Weiss again, he was shaking his head in pity. But Weiss was losing patience; he tore Eric's hand aside, wanting to lash back at Eric's petty indignation. Ruth, frightened by what she saw as imminent violence, stepped forward.

"Clemmie was in her room next door," and she indicated in the direction of the wall of books behind her. "I knocked as we passed her room. I thought I had roused her."

Something caught Weiss's eye as Ruth gestured, and he walked over to the bookshelves. Clemmie's room would be on the other side of that wall. He drew a book from the shelf and slowly opened it.

The pages ran out onto the floor like snow, the paper dissolving in a cloud of dust at his feet. He felt a chill and the hair on his neck prickled.

Weiss stood still for a moment and then he elbowed past Eric, strode from the room, and the others followed, Eric in a barely suppressed fury now. "Show me Clemmie's room," Weiss barked, any pretence of civility gone.

Eric growled over his shoulder. "I'm going downstairs to call your superiors, Weiss. You can tell me what's going on, or I can say you refused to say more."

"I don't think you should go down there," Weiss said, still walking. "You may find the landline is down, anyway."

"Why should it be?" Eric said, sounding puzzled.

They were in the long hallway which formed a balcony over the downstairs rooms. Weiss peered down from the bannister. In the gloom where the front entranceway threw a patch of feeble light across the front hall, he could just make out a subtle stain about four feet wide across the wooden floor.

"Look around you, Eric. Half the circuit breakers in the house have tripped. They do that when the wiring degenerates."

Eric leaned over the railing and looked down into the rooms below. The downstairs level was a swimming darkness.

From behind them down the hall, Ruth's voice was trembling with fear. "It's true, Eric. Noah's bedroom is dark, too."

Eric brushed past Weiss, heading for the darkened stairs, but

Weiss caught his elbow forcefully. "I think you'll find the whole house is dark. You'll be safer here with us."

"Safer? Safe from what?"

Weiss almost spat the words: "From the one who's been destroying this house," but then he took a breath. "I'll tell you what I can, but first we need to find out if Clemmie's all right."

Merrit's slender shape was outlined by the firelight coming through the library doors. "I have to stay with Noah," she said.

"Merrit. Where's Clemmie? Why hasn't she come out?" Ruth asked from the darkness.

"It's all right. She's still in her room. I heard her moving about earlier," Merrit said, turning back to the warmth of the library.

CHAPTER TWENTY-SEVEN

Ruth had caught up, groping her way in the dark.

"This is Clemmie's room," she said. "I don't understand why she hasn't come out. I heard a bump on the floor when I knocked earlier. I thought she was moving about."

Weiss waited while Ruth knocked again, waited some more, and as she prepared to knock again, Weiss moved past her, gripping the door handle. There was something about the muffled sound of Ruth's knock and the way the door handle rotated uselessly in his hand that made a sick feeling come over him.

He gave the door panel a firm push, and the door swung inward almost normally.

"Clemmie?" Weiss said to the shadows.

Inside the room, the drapes were drawn wide to the night, backlighting the shape of the bed and dresser.

On the floor at his feet, the inside door handle lay in a dusty heap.

"Clemmie?" Ruth's voice came from the darkness behind him. "Are you here? Wake up."

An arm reached past Weiss, and he heard the light switch's antique snap.

"This light isn't working either," Eric grumbled.

Behind him in the corridor, Ruth didn't understand why Weiss was frozen near the doorway. She placed her hand on his shoulder and felt him shiver at her touch. He peered into the darkness of Clemmie's room, half expecting to see that awful face with its caricature of desperation and pain emerging from the darkness.

Finally, speaking Clemmie's name again with a pitying softness, Weiss edged forward. Ruth tried to force past him, but he put out his arm and held her back.

"Weiss, don't. What's the matter?"

"Wait," he said, his voice tight and unnatural.

Eric rumbled with annoyance from behind them, filling the doorway with his bulk, but by then Weiss knew. His eyes had adjusted to the darkness and the bleached pallor of the room seemed to scream at him.

"Is there a flashlight nearby?" he asked. "The walls in here are eaten away. The wiring probably went with it."

"What's the point of—"

Eric began to protest noisily, but Ruth had picked up the terror in Weiss's voice and she almost pushed Eric from the doorway.

"Eric, please, we must have light. There's one in your valise."

Deciding there wasn't much point in making a scene in the hallway, Eric stopped abruptly and felt his way back into the library.

Weiss stood there in Clemmie's room, breathing audibly, afraid to touch anything.

"Ruth," Weiss said quietly. "I saw something on the carriage. I've been turning it over in my mind, and I've tried to make myself understand why it was so...familiar."

Weiss expected her to ask questions, but when he glanced back, she was just staring at the furniture with her palms on her ribs in that peculiar posture people take when they are disgusted by what they are seeing.

"The windows, Weiss," she whispered. "Like in the carriage house—roughened as though they'd been engraved."

Through the eyeless panes, the ambient light of the night sky, lit by that occasionally moonlit overcast, allowed in a dull glow that was grainy and marbled with shadows. It daubed the room with grey. Weiss was afraid that if he touched the windows, he would find the impossible; he would find the *inside* worn.

"There's something else," Weiss said to Ruth. "A picture I saw in a book once. I've seen something and I have to explain."

Ruth wasn't listening. "Clemmie had her room done like a child's," she said. "So much colour and life. But now it all looks…"

The furnishings and even the disordered bed covers, topped with a thick duvet, might have been sculpted out of pumice, or, if such a thing were possible, out of ash. A soft grey blighted everything, the colours gone—from the heaped bed covers to the gathered fabric around the vanity.

Ruth left Weiss's side and moved to the foot of Clemmie's bed.

"Watch your step," Weiss said, remembering the pavilion floorboards, and he noticed how muted his voice was in the small untidy space, as though the walls were made of egg cartons, drinking up the sound.

Ruth looked up at him. "My God, Weiss. What's happening? What's doing this?"

"A picture in a book…" Weiss began.

Suddenly, Eric's voice loud and full of irritation could be heard in the hallway and light pooled in along the floor of the bedroom in a narrow beam.

Eric came in and stood defiantly tall in the centre of the room.

"What in the name of…"

His indignant strut made the ashen room seem a mere imposition. He shone the light around his feet where it fell through a low stratum of dust. The carpet was awash, having dissolved where they'd stepped. He shot the flashlight around quickly, making sharp shadows on the bed and the dresser.

"What you're seeing is age," Weiss said.

"What are you talking about?"

Eric's flashlight shone on the vanity with its pitted mirror, the silvering bubbled, and on the dull hardwood of the jewelry case. Weiss struggled to make sense of the blight that seemed to have touched everything in the room.

"What we're seeing is the way this room might look if it had been abandoned for decades."

"You're making no sense," Eric said with a dismissive wave of his hand.

Weiss picked up the jewelry box where it glowed in the light of Eric's flashlight. The bottom of the box immediately gave way, spilling necklaces and hair clips into the surrounding dust. Even in the narrow beam of Eric's light, the paste diamonds had lost their lustre.

"No, I'm wrong," Weiss said, his brow furrowed in concentration. "Not even age does this to wood. It's like Styrofoam—its structure broken down from within. Something incredible has happened here and around the house, and it's a process I don't really understand, a process that takes all the solidity and substance out of things. It leaves an effect *like* ageing, but different."

And then, in the way these things happen, the answer came to Weiss unbidden and he knew why the apparition in the carriage had seemed so impossibly familiar.

Eric sniffed at the dry air. "Ruth, dear. Perhaps you should find Clemmie and warn her away from this. She's a simple woman and she's apt to take it personally as some kind of judgement. She must be prepared for this."

Weiss stared at Eric. *My God,* he thought, *Eric doesn't know. And poor Ruth. Maybe she hadn't seen it yet. Someone has to tell them.*

"It was personal, Eric. Clemmie was in more danger than any of us because she was the one sitting with him while that poison worked through Noah's veins. You would inject him, and then leave."

Eric shook his head in exasperation and tried to ignore Weiss. "Just find her, Ruth."

"For Christ's sake, Eric." Weiss wanted to make it easy on Ruth, but Eric made that impossible. "I knew where Clemmie was the second I came in the room."

A loathing came over Weiss as he reached across Clemmie's bed. Before he touched the mound of bedding, Ruth knew, too, and she began making a tiny whining noise behind her hands. She and Eric watched Weiss lift aside a ragged square of the duvet in a stream of white dust, and the sheets below now bore the unmistakable outline of what lay beneath them, as pale and desiccated as everything else in this room.

Driven by a determination that froze his blood, Weiss peeled the sheet back.

Clemmie had died with her eyes screwed shut and her shoulders drawn up in child-like terror. Against the darkness, she looked as she had in life except that even in the half-light, you could see that all the colour was gone from her skin. All of it.

The one who had come to Clemmie had taken everything from her—had absorbed her personality, life, and even her solidity.

Weiss let his breath go with a sound that might have been a sob, realizing that a small part of Clemmie's shoulder had come away with the sheet he held in his hand.

CHAPTER TWENTY-EIGHT

The EMS van bumped and swayed away from the lower gardens until they were out the gate and on the highway. Hal was driving, accelerating up the escarpment. Hal took the steep grade at speed, plastic boxes and racks shifting and clattering all around them in back. Joshi held onto the gurney he was seated on, and the other first responder steadied himself, waiting for a chance to work some more on Joshi's knee.

After an interminable climb, the EMS van turned onto the Moreland house road and Joshi saw the stone gateway slide past the rear window.

When the van stopped, Joshi ignored the medic dabbing at his torn knee and opened the rear doors himself. He jumped down and, wincing with the pain, started hobbling until he had a clear view of the front of the house.

It looked absolutely normal. There was no evidence of a threat inside. No smoke, no smell of burning…

The windows were dark, but the solemn face of Moreland House gaped placidly out at the sprinkle of city lights below. The dignity of the facade made Joshi feel suddenly foolish. He had no idea what he was dealing with, but Weiss had said the group upstairs might have to jump.

Joshi hobbled to one of the great windows fronting the hall and looked in. The interior was dark and empty. He moved to another window that afforded him an angle on the great living room to the left.

The flashing lights of the EMS truck shot unhelpful flickers through the windows and around the interior of the house. Joshi's eyes darted until they were stopped by a sudden movement caught in a blue flash. Were there huge eyes looking back at him? Could they see Joshi's head and shoulders backlit by the evening gloom? He wasn't sure, but he had a nasty replay of his last moments on the carriage.

Then a red flash—and the shape inside moved.

He couldn't make out any details in the scattered light, but the scale of the movement made it seem as if a whole wall had shifted. It convinced him that blundering into the dark hallway would be a monumentally bad idea. Joshi jerked away from the window, almost falling as his ankle gave way, and turned to see the two medics watching him with exaggerated patience.

Joshi half hopped his way back to the EMS truck where the two had now taken to frowning up at the quiet sleep of the stately home.

"We've got to go around back," Joshi said.

"Look, Detective, we're not the fire department, but that door looks safe to me, and you say there are people inside in trouble. There's no fire, no nothing. We can see that from here. Maybe Hal and I can make our way upstairs."

Joshi had a fleeting sense of panic, realizing they might act on their own initiative. And for all he knew, they would be right. But Joshi had seen the thing on the carriage and the thought of something like that looming in the darkened downstairs rooms made his flesh crawl.

His responsibility to those two yahoos weighed heavily on

him. He knew more than they did. He stood his ground as well as he could on one good ankle, drawing himself straight, his shoulders back.

"Look at me," he said in his coldest voice. "I'm the fucking police, and I'm trying to save your sorry asses. Now, Detective Weiss told me the group upstairs might have to get out by the back balcony. If they jump, you're going to look damn silly knocking at the front door while they roll around with broken legs and elbows in back."

The shorter medic watched Joshi's face and read the intensity there. He hesitated, then made a twirling motion with his index finger that Hal seemed to enjoy, and Joshi wanted to run them both in on a charge of...obstructive gesturing with intent...or something.

But, the paramedics turned away. "Fine. Hal, follow the driveway to the back of the house."

Joshi crawled in the back of the EMS truck without the use of the steps and pulled his feet in. The medic swung the door shut, pointedly offering Joshi no assistance, and the ambulance began to move again, its lights still radiating blue and red flashes against the house front.

After a couple of minutes of swaying and grinding gravel, the truck stopped and the medics climbed out. Joshi swivelled on his behind and slid down to his good foot. The space in the back of the main house was a wide-open patio with flagstone pathways radiating out into the trees. Recreational trails, probably.

Joshi looked up at the back of the house. The architecture seemed unnecessarily complicated, with an elegantly scalloped two-tiered roofline. The balcony, a long affair that jutted to create two outside seating areas, was prominent. The lower floor, which was at least twice as high as in a conventional house, extended out under a sharply sloping roof so that anyone leaping from the balcony would find himself tumbling down to the eaves. After that, a ten-foot drop to solid pavement.

Joshi could make out the double doors letting into the back of the library. A faint warm light flickered from within, but no more than you'd expect from a fireplace. His mind raced, but he knew instinctively what his role was. He was going to have to stage-manage the scene that was evolving around him.

He didn't want the fire department roaring up to the front door and forcing entry. He had to make this grand rear patio the focus, in case Weiss and the others upstairs were presented with the same awful choice that he and Weiss had faced—confronting the beast or jumping.

By the time he limped his way beside the medics, he could hear the distant blatting of a second EMS truck out on Appleby Line.

"Get on your phone and make sure that truck meets us here. I'm going to get in touch with the fire department. Weiss probably told them the same thing, but I'm not taking any chances."

The medic pulled a cowboy pose with his thumbs in his belt. "I hope you're going to have something to tell them when they get here." He gave a disapproving look at the lovely patio with its topiary and symmetrical beds of decorative ground cover. "Me'n Hal got things pretty much covered so far."

CHAPTER TWENTY-NINE

Weiss leaned over the bannister of the upstairs corridor and listened to the silence of the main floor rooms.

"Eric, give me your flashlight."

Eric moved beside him, using the slender penlight himself to sweep the front hall and the rooms to each side. The light it gave was only slightly better than nothing.

"This damn thing is no good. It's just for eye and ear examinations."

Weiss took the flashlight from Eric and moved to the stairs. In the narrow beam, he could make out a flat, ashen swathe from the front hallway all the way upstairs to the corridor where they stood. It hadn't been there minutes before when they mounted the stairs.

He had a bad feeling, imagining the thing following them up in the dark. The bleaching effect faded on the upper landing, but the flashlight picked up traces of discolouration all the way to Clemmie's room. Weiss was reminded of the pathway of destruction through the pavilion games room.

Weiss felt like he was faced with a mad scenario—the thing could be anywhere, or nowhere. They were no safer here than they were downstairs. The only way out, untainted by the grey blight, was that sloping roof at the back of the library. If he could gather everyone on that back balcony, there was always hope of outside rescue.

And what then? Could the nightmare exist outside in the night, in the open air surrounded by emergency personnel?

The only answer that presented itself to him came in the form of a recollection: two great footprints on the puddles of the terrace—footprints made by something unseen even under the light posts. Something huge, invisible and lurking, waiting to solidify and loom anew.

Weiss handed the flashlight back to Eric and walked back to the library. He returned a minute later, dragging an armchair made of heavy oak. The noise it made seemed a provocation in the silent house. He lifted the chair with great effort and then heaved it down the stairs. There should have been an unholy clatter as the chair tumbled end over end down to the front hall, but instead, the chair appeared to imbed itself into the upper stairs with a muffled thump, sinking in a cloud of dust.

Eric recoiled. "What in God's name…"

Weiss clung to the bannister, trying to quell his fear, trying to think strategically. "I thought so. The stairs are no longer usable."

Eric played the light on the white dust cloud rising from the chair. "That means if anyone's down there, they can't get up here."

"It doesn't work like that," Weiss said and stared at the darkness below.

"You've told the police and the fire department about the intruder, Detective. Why not just wait until they get here?"

"There's no intruder. At least not—"

Weiss couldn't help jerking away from the balcony railing when he saw something move downstairs. Something big. Eric's flashlight did nothing, but the pale light from the double entranceway caught a glistening shape. At first, Weiss didn't know what he was seeing; the shape drew back and disappeared quickly, but not before he registered the wetness of a tongue and the merest hint of enormous lips. Then it moved again, and Eric too saw it partially emerge from the profound blackness of the dining room.

"Good God in heaven, Weiss! What is it? Why does it have no body?"

The thing turned its enormous eyes upward. The pale orbs, each as big as a waning moon, caught a highlight from Eric's flashlight. Weiss felt the gaze as a killing frost in his chest. He grabbed Eric's arm.

"Let's get back into the library. I'm going to try and explain what I think is going on, and I don't have time to repeat myself."

"Just tell me one thing, Weiss; what *is* that thing? Who killed Clemmie?"

"It's Noah."

"Oh, for Christ's sake, Weiss," Eric cried, his voice wavering. "Is that all you can say? You're blaming a mindless man confined to a wheelchair?"

CHAPTER THIRTY

Visibly shaken, Eric allowed himself to be pulled into the library by Weiss where Merrit and Ruth were standing near the fireplace.

Ruth caught on right away. "Eric, your face—you've lost all your colour."

Weiss turned and secured the big dolphin handles on the double doors behind him. He took off his necktie and knotted it around the two handles so that entry to the library was blocked.

He came back from the doors, unfastening his top shirt button, and then he knelt down in front of Noah's chair, trying to read the vacancy there. Noah's odd pinched features, so reminiscent of a fairy tale imp, gave away nothing. Weiss, whose apartment was filled with golden age illustrations, thought of Arthur Rackham, the English illustrator: the signature visage was there in Noah's large hooked nose and his lidded eyes.

"My partner and I," Weiss began, "were confronted by something on the cable car. I believe it's the same thing Eric and I just saw downstairs."

Eric grasped Ruth's arms. "A giant face—no legs, no back— just lips and fingers..." His eyes were wide and fixed. He was shaking so badly that he had to release Ruth's arm, fumbling one hand onto Noah's chair to support himself.

Ruth turned to Weiss. "What is it, Detective?"

"I think it's Noah, Ruth."

She blanched, uncomprehending.

Weiss got up slowly. "Merrit, Noah spent his life trying to escape his shrivelled shoulders, his distinctive features. I'm thinking that his computer mischief wasn't just a lark. All the pranks, all the psychedelics; he was trying to escape, to transcend what he saw as his own inadequate body. He wanted to project himself—out there somewhere. Now Eric tells us he's treating Noah with a dissociative drug; I have reason to believe it's something experimental and untried. Something James Krauss got from MorwynBIO."

Eric said nothing, but he flashed a look of warning to Ruth.

Weiss kept looking at Merrit, her beauty scarcely marred by tattooed images of coiling vines that peeked from her sleeves and neckline. "And Merrit—what have *you* been giving him?"

It was pure guesswork on Weiss's part, but he got the reaction he hoped for.

Merrit held her head high. There was no guilt, no uncertainty. She was simply a drug user, speaking her mantra.

"The withdrawal—that's what's killing him. Even Eric said so. I was just helping Noah. I'm his *wife*, but no one listens to me." She went on, her hands clenched into fists.

"No one is seeing this from Noah's point of view." She singled out Eric with her stare. "I think you've been reaching into that dark place where his consciousness has withdrawn, and you've been tormenting him. You..." She pointed at Eric. "His doctor." Her words were filled with all the disgust she'd felt over years of withdrawal and rehabilitation. "I don't know if there's a lucid corner left in Noah's brain, but he understands pain, and he understands desperation."

Eric rubbed his grey hair in frustration. "What has all this useless speculation got to do with that thing out there?"

Weiss realized he still had his damp coat on. In the steady heat of the library, it seemed natural to take it off and drape the coat on a chair.

"I began to understand," he said, "when I remembered an illustration in an old Carl Sagan book. Illustrations tend to stick in my mind; so much more memorable than pages of text. Sagan called the drawing a 'sensory homunculus.' The drawing was just simple lines, but it was an attempt to show a human being from the point of view of his senses alone. We're aware of our fingers, we're aware of our lips, our tongue—because that's where most of our sensory apparatus is. And that's what Noah is projecting. We aren't aware, from moment to moment, of our back or our scalp." Weiss held his fingertips near his face.

The others had drawn closer, Noah immobile at their centre with his hands twitching slightly on his blanket.

"But what Noah's projecting, it doesn't have any substance of its own, you see. It's more like an extension of his senses driven by pain."

Eric's whole body appeared clenched in his effort to understand. "But the damage...what he did to Clemmie, to the house...the stairs?"

"I don't know how it works, but this part my partner and I have seen up close. That thing, in order to materialize, leeches all the solidity out of its surroundings—the wood, the metal, the glass—all of it. You've seen the damage around the house, Ruth. I know you have. I don't know how many times Noah has been driven out of his body like some wraith by Eric's drug...but wherever this homunculus materialized, it's been at the expense of the floor, the tapestries, the grass. Everything aged, turned to ash. That's where the homunculus is getting its substance."

There was a dull thud from outside the library doors and they all looked. The two leaded glass panels disclosed no shape, but they visibly misted over as if being abraded by a silent dust storm.

Weiss pointed at the door. "I don't know if Noah's senses are wandering aimlessly or lashing out in his confusion, but that thing has to get its solidity, its weight from somewhere, and he's drawing it from your house, Ruth—from the pavilion—from Clemmie's room. He's been leeching the life and the solidity out of everything he touches."

Ruth stared into Eric's eyes. "Eric, what if Noah came after Clemmie because she was the one who was always there, sitting beside him?"

Weiss finished the thought. "He must have sensed Clemmie was the one hurting him. But he was wrong, wasn't he, Eric?"

Eric's eyes were wild. "And then me..." he said. "He'll come for me now, won't he?!"

Eric tore his eyes from the door and stared down at the little man with the blanket over his bare legs. The wheelchair shook and Eric saw the way Noah was now gripping the armrests. If any doubts remained in Eric's mind, they must have gone then.

Weiss couldn't take his eyes off the necktie he'd knotted around the door handles. The tartan had been chosen because his mother's brother had served in the Black Watch regiment of the British Army. It was mostly a cool dark green woven with grey, but the grey...

It seemed to be spreading, the fibres unravelling before his eyes. The tie sagged slightly and a few of the threads parted, leaving a ragged edge. It seemed inevitable that the material would part and the tight little loop fall away.

But before that could happen, there was another dull bump and once more, they were all riveted on the door. It took a moment for Weiss to register what had happened because it was so patently impossible. And yet there it was: one of the dolphin handles had fallen, leaving a dusty heap on the floor. Weiss's tie hung from the remaining handle, swinging gently, its green tartan now drained of colour.

The same thing was happening to the wooden framing of the door as though the atrophied handle had infected the grain of the polished oak. It was losing its shine. It was like watching the effects of exposure to wind and rain speeded up with a stop motion camera. The silent horror of it took Weiss's breath away.

With an effort of will, Weiss forced himself to move closer to the door where the glass inserts were fast becoming opaque. His instinct was to turn and run, but rationally, he knew he had to make sure there was some place to run—some place to escape— some way down to the ground below the balcony. He pulled out his phone, tapped, and Joshi answered immediately.

"Prem, what's the situation out there?"

Outside, the darkness surrounding the house had started to take on a carnival air.

At the back of the house, a fire truck had just arrived with its lights blatting away at the dark trees and bushes. Joshi's EMS truck was off to one side and its lights were still blinking red and blue. The second EMS vehicle was tight up behind the first. Joshi had been shouting directions to the gathering group of yellow coats and helmets, pointing up to the balcony.

He had his phone in his hand already when Weiss called. "I've got one fire truck deploying and two EMS units so far. The fire people tell me the chief will be here soon. I don't like the evil eye I'm getting when they say stuff like that."

"Prem, is that inflatable in place yet? "

"They don't have one of those, Eilert, but they have a tarp they can stretch out to catch people if you have to jump."

"Okay, that'll have to do. Listen, Prem, I'm going to get everyone out onto the back balcony. We may have to drop to the roof. Then it will be a fall from the eaves, got that? I'm thinking I'll have to carry Noah. We've no choice. Just tell the medics we're coming. Tell them to do what they can."

———

In the library, the great vaulted ceiling hung over everything like a starless sky. The second door handle fell into a soft heap at Weiss's feet. He was still facing the door and away from the others. Behind him, he heard Merrit's voice.

"Eric, what are you doing?"

Weiss was about to turn around to see what was going on when the door began to open. Weiss wanted to shout at the others—to get them out onto the balcony, tell them they had to jump—but the door swung aside, and...

Nothing.

The hallway outside the library was empty. Even in the darkness, he saw that there was no looming shape, no bulbous eyes. Weiss backed up, prepared for the thing to materialize in front of him. He knew from experience it could happen fast— the homunculus settling out of thin air, sucking the molecules out of the floorboards and the carpet. But the seconds passed, and the silence seemed to hiss steadily in his ears.

He looked about, wary, at last casting a glance behind him.

By then, Eric was removing a needle from the soft rubber valve spliced into Noah's IV tube—the long tube that ended in a needle in Noah's vein.

At first, Weiss didn't understand what he was seeing. When Weiss had moved to the door, he'd left Eric terrified—rooted to the spot; now Eric was placing a hypodermic into the small black case on the table. Weiss stared.

"What have you done?"

Eric's paralysis was gone and some of his aloofness was back. "I've released Noah. It was self-defence, Weiss—you *know* it was. He would have killed me...all of us."

Weiss gaped. It was difficult to process. He had come upon the consequences of violence plenty of times in his career, but he'd never seen a murder actually happen. Extreme violence should be noisier, showier. And yet here it was: Noah's head sagged back and his eyes were fixed on the blackness above them.

Merrit began to weep and dropped to her knees. Her brow sank onto Noah's lap. Ruth was wide-eyed with horror—a horror that was directed not at Noah, but at Eric.

"Eric, what have you done?" she whispered.

"How did you do it?" Weiss said.

Eric straightened as though he were attempting to gather his affronted dignity around him like a judge's robes. "More of the same," he said cooly, "—but enough of the drug to kill him. It would have been quick: brain death. It's over. This whole nightmare is…" His eyes found Ruth, and his composure weakened. "I'm so sorry, Ruth. I had to save us all. I had no choice."

Weiss tried to think; he ran his hand inside his open shirt collar and stared at Noah's lifeless body. It was as if an impending train wreck had just gone into slow motion. And what was he left with? Another impossible judgement.

He remembered the empty corridor and spun around to stare at the emptiness. This is what he'd been doing while Eric was quietly and efficiently murdering Noah Goodwyn. Staring at nothing. Was he responsible for Noah's death, too? Had his preoccupation with his own bizarre and unprovable theory let it happen?

There was the guilt—and then there was the relief: the torture was over and Noah had finally slipped free of his unsatisfactory body. But Noah was a man with a daughter and a wife, and now all that ever mattered about him was gone.

Merrit collapsed even further towards the rug. Ruth backed away from Eric's touch. The mourning had begun.

CHAPTER THIRTY-ONE

By the time Carly got back to the booth, the sports bar had gotten louder and the gaiety more kaleidoscopic. Servers wove in a complex dance between tables and men and women came and went in a steady buzz from the deserted tables outside on chilly Brant Street. But the joyous partisan cheers and serial toasts only made Carly feel more hemmed in and alone.

Evan was still there, and a young couple who knew him from the TV had somehow talked their way into the four-place booth. With the overcrowding, it would have been churlish to deny an open seat. At least Evan had someone to talk to.

Evan looked concerned as Carly slid in under his arm. The seating was so closely packed that voices from other tables would intrude if you weren't focussing. Carly still felt vaguely preoccupied as a free-for-all conversation surged this way and that.

"I got you another apple juice," Evan grinned.

Apple juice, Carly thought, peering into her new glass of Strongbow cider. The glass was large and beaded with condensation. "There must be some apple juice in there somewhere," she murmured, her words already beginning to slur. "How do you turn apple juice into fire water?" She sipped, then took a cheek-plumping gulp. "I can't even taste it anymore, but I'm drinking it like water."

Her mind wandered, the people around her moving in and out of focus. *Wait a minute,* she thought. *Who are these people? Do I know them?*

She hadn't actually spoken the words, but here was someone answering her. "Are you having a good time? These are my friends. This is James and his wife, Candace. Don't call her Candy—she hates that. This is Merrit. That's Gordo over there. Cassie and Ben. Best forget about Gordo, though. He's off in a world of his own, lucky sod."

Somebody said something about the Bluejays, but it sounded far away, then, up close in her ear the other voice: "These were my happy days, my laughing days, you see. I did have a few, you know. People I like who like the sort of stuff I like, sitting around the pool when the heat of the day is being radiated back into the night sky."

"Carly," Evan said, patting her hand, "I think you'd better eat something if you're going to drink that stuff."

Carly strained to follow what was being said around her but kept tuning in to another table, maybe even another place.

"Watch your head," someone said. "Some of those silver trays come in low. I'd probably been eating junk food all day in front of my laptop." The voice was sad, intimate. "We'd call it brain food as a joke, but it'd be salt and sugar tarted up and over-packaged. But the canapés on the terrace, now—ah, that was actual food—bruschetta and prosciutto e melone, and it went down well with the appletinis."

The speaker was charming, just as he had been in her living room months ago.

"I don't think I'm actually dead," he said thoughtfully, "but it's been days, months maybe, since I felt I was part of the real world, and it won't be long now."

It was Noah's voice as she remembered it from their interview, and it felt as distant and unreal as a memory.

"Don't think I was never happy. I was—sometimes, 'even as larks in cages sing.' It's hardly surprising that I would come here at the end. After all, it's where I was most at ease and the closest I ever came to having a regular home. Oh, sometimes we'd get into good games and the time would fly, and I'd be content.

"But those were battles, after all," the voice she remembered from her living room sighed. "Here on the balcony, looking down on the terrace, you can forget about conflict and winning and rules and dice. Here, it's the glow of remembered sunshine on your skin, the touch of a lovely woman, her scent. Real food that looks like a magazine spread but tastes like tiny morsels of home cooking.

"Not that I ever had any real home cooking in my life. Even lunch was a chunky chicken salad on a croissant prepared by a professional. None of my friends had croissants for lunch, but I can bring them all here to sit and laugh, and finally, my money makes sense. Look around you—I can make my friends happy."

The disconnect didn't bother Carly—a disembodied voice that seemed to float in and out of the racket around her, now like a whisper in her ear, and then like an echo. And it was talking about chicken salad.

"Listen to the music in the background," the voice droned on. "Do you hear it?"

Carly listened obediently and there it was, melodious and sweet, but you could only discern it by ignoring the foreground hubbub. It was James Taylor and Linda Ronstadt as though glimpsed through a blaring picket fence of techno sampling.

The music went on, seeping through to the foreground. They listened together, effortlessly now, until the voice finally said, "I have to go now, don't I? We're getting to the end. I'm not afraid. Fear was never my problem. Anger, maybe. Indignation. That's what kept me on the roller coaster, popping pills and snorting thrills. So this? Well, this is just another trip.

"A downer, this time—in fact, I can feel the pace slowing and everyone is laughing in slow motion. It's getting harder to sustain a thought. I'm just hopping from memory to memory, taking stepping stones across spacetime, only there's no far bank, see? I guess you just take the last hop and then…nothing."

Carly reached out and touched a hand nearby. "I'm sorry they were hurting you."

"Yeah, they were, weren't they? I was in a fog of pain; I had all the memories, but for a while there, I had to just watch from a distance and suffer. Do you know what it's like to see your friends laughing and drinking and you're out in the cold, excluded? I read somewhere that the old clerics defined hell as being aware of heaven and being cut off from it. I'd see myself and Merrit, but I had to hang back in the dark and drown in longing.

"Well, that's over now. Everything is shutting down. The chairs are up on the tables. I wish I could die here on the terrace, but I think I have to go where the pineapples are. Not such a bad place, I guess, but this is where I'll leave my heart—under the summer sky with the pool reflecting the night—with these people, in this place.

"Damn. There go the lights—and I thought it was dark before. And here it comes—the end, like a freight train running up through my veins. I always liked trains, but this one's going to run me down.

"Thanks for looking in, by the way. It's just a hunch, but I think your dad and I would've gotten along. I bet you're just like him."

———

Carly couldn't remember the conversation ending, or, for that matter, much of the walk home along Lakeshore Road. The onshore night wind didn't help dispel the wooliness in her mind, and she kept colliding with Evan's shoulder which seemed to be the only steady object in the vicinity. He didn't mind, looping his arm around her shoulders until she strayed off a few steps, only to dock her hand in his elbow again. Another collision.

"You're a cad, getting me drunk," she moaned.

"A cad? Like the kind that forecloses the damsel's mortgage?"

"I don't have a mortgage. Not anymore, thank God. But I bet you'd tie me onto the railroad tracks."

"Not the railroad tracks."

"Aha! See? You've thought about it. Cad. You probably spiked my drinks."

"What do you spike cider with? Cinnamon?"

"I love cinnamon. That'd do it. I told you, I'm not a drinker, and you got me drunk."

"I guess I did. You seemed so uptight, worried about nothing. I read that women are less tolerant of alcohol."

"A drowsy numbness pains my senses, as though of hemlock I had drunk."

A strand of her chestnut hair blew into her mouth and she sputtered.

"You're quoting. Cut that out. You know it's wasted on me."

Carly gave a boozy groan of exasperation. "This is *so* beneath me. I'm a Rouhl, for God's sake."

"You told me your dad always had a bottle nearby when he wrote all that great stuff."

"Yeah, funny. He never seemed drunk exactly, not falling down like I am right now. But he had a kind of boozy languor going while he wrote. A lot of his generation worked like that. I always thought it was a risky way to write—you know, with your judgement... With your judgement... What were we talking about?"

Evan laughed. "Someone told me that the ancient Persians used to make important decisions twice—once sober and once drunk. When you sober up, you can compare notes with yourself."

"Crazy. Crazy way to live. I believe in maintaining control. I'm not the type to let go and dance with ghosts."

"Who said anything about ghosts? You were dancing with a ghost?"

Carly stopped and swayed, looking at him. "What? Did I say that?"

"You said you danced with a ghost. Are you being metaphorical again? I skipped the liberal arts, remember. I'm a scientist. Sort of. We frown on metaphor."

Carly sniffed in derision at the very idea of skipping the arts but took his steady arm again anyway, and they continued to walk along the lakefront parkland towards her father's house. Her house.

They had been colliding and redocking for several minutes before Carly spoke again. "We didn't dance," she murmured. She took Evan's arm in both hands. "Did we?"

CHAPTER THIRTY-TWO

Several minutes had gone by since Noah's death, and it was as if everyone in the room had withdrawn into themselves. No one made eye contact. Even Weiss was making small pacing movements, trying to think things through.

In a simpler world, he would be obliged to place Dr. Eric Hudson under arrest. The man was a physician who had just violated his oath—a murderer. It seemed obvious, and yet it wasn't. Nothing was obvious about the situation Weiss found himself in.

Even Noah's death. Weiss stopped in his tracks, facing the shrivelled little man in the wheelchair.

"Noah's chest—it's moving. He's still alive!"

Eric shook his head. "I said it was brain death. His body might continue to function for a few hours, but there's no activity in his cortex."

"How can you be sure?"

"I can't be one hundred percent sure without an EEG, but there's no movement of the iris in response to my light. I know the signs."

"Can he be resuscitated?"

"Brain death is final and irreversible. His body will shut down very soon. His heartbeat is already weak."

"So you're just declaring him dead." Weiss stared at Eric. "You cold bastard."

Eric's eyes flared. He decided to take the insult stoically and turned away. "I'm a physician. I'm qualified to make that determination."

Weiss stared at Eric's back in disbelief and then—wide-eyed, his own brain seized up with indecision—he looked down at the carpet. It felt like he had a few precious seconds, standing there, waiting for the real world to come crashing down on him like a giant wave, and then he would be underwater.

Weiss thought of the audience of emergency response people standing below the balcony. Everything was in play here: two dead souls demanding justice, a bereaved sister who had risked everything for her brother, an arrogant physician who thought he could make moral judgements to suit himself, and a wife who loved her tragic husband the best way she knew how.

And then the career of his partner, Prem Joshi, hung in the balance. His own, too, of course, small thing though it might be, but Prem—he had a family, a pension, and a reputation for honesty.

As for him? The last few years, Weiss had been holding onto his job and sense of self by his fingernails. He'd stared into the abyss five years ago when his wife committed suicide, and as Nietzsche had once said, when you stare into the abyss long enough, it begins to stare back at you.

He felt its stare now, and an anger building in him. He wanted to be honest, and an agent of…not just the law, but of justice. But here he was with no way out. The truth wouldn't make him free; it would plunge everyone left standing into an impossible quagmire of denial and recrimination.

He followed the pattern of the carpet, a symmetry of lines

connecting…pineapples. Pineapples for the hospitality of the wealthy.

His mind unhappily made up, he faced the others.

Weiss reached down and gently helped Merrit to her feet. When she was composed, her right hand on her left elbow, he fixed Eric with a stare, addressing him, knowing that Eric's ego was the biggest threat to them all.

"Listen to me. We're all going to go out on the balcony. There are fire and ambulance people down below. I'm going to shout down to them. There's no time for me to negotiate or explain any of this, so you're going to have to come out and listen to what I say and decide for yourself if you're going to back me up. If you don't, you're on your own."

He gave one last glance at Ruth and Merrit and began to walk to the outdoor balcony doors. The others made a half-hearted move to follow, so Weiss turned and spoke with the vestiges of his authority: "I said, come with me."

They fell in behind him; Eric straightening his lapels, Ruth raising her chin.

They filed out onto the narrow concrete platform. The rain hadn't let up, but it was as fine as mist and seemed to float rather than fall. Weiss heard the low rumble of distant thunder. He waited for a flash, but if there was one, it was lost in the glow of the vehicles; the overcast was a palette of pastel colours with the two EMS trucks and the fire engine adding their red and blue flashers to the twilight. It was a wonder that Prem had managed to ride herd on all these people. Thinking of his partner down in the middle of all that, Weiss was filled with a sense of gratitude and admiration.

It felt ridiculously theatrical for Weiss to be standing at the railing while the other three arranged themselves silently and warily behind him.

He waited until they were all at the railing, and then, "It's all right!" Weiss shouted down to a dozen upturned faces. "We're safe now. The fire…the fires have burned themselves out. There are two casualties."

A take-charge fire chief stepped out of his newly arrived red SUV and strode forward. Weiss recognized the broad-shouldered, deep-chested figure from the church fire.

"I'm McCullough," the man shouted, his voice booming from the driveway. "Are you Weiss? What the hell are we doing back here? Why can't we come in the goddam front door?"

Weiss shouted back, "We're safe up here, McCullough. There's a lot of damage to the downstairs area. I think it may be safe to come in the front door now, too, but watch your step down there; the flooring is badly damaged and the main stairs are unusable."

The fire chief looked ready to shoot some recriminations up at Weiss, but he was acutely aware of his audience waiting for direction.

"We're coming up," he said at last. McCullough gestured at the firetruck, and its extension ladder began to swivel towards the four people standing against the balcony railing.

McCullough said something to one of the firefighters, and then there were hurried gestures and a half-dozen men and women in yellow slickers carrying lamps and a portable ladder started to jog around to the front of the house.

Weiss glanced at the others standing beside him on the balcony, but there was no commitment or support in their faces. Finally, Ruth, Eric, and Merrit turned away and went back inside where they pulled chairs out from the walls. Weiss stood in the doorway for a minute, watching the squads organize and mount the fire truck, then went in to take up a place by the hearth.

After that, there was a period of waiting. A succession of medics and firefighters made the tricky swing from the ladder over the balcony railing, their heavy boots clattering. They walked in, crossing the library with suspicion written on their faces and visible in the slouch of their shoulders. Led by Chief McCullough, they walked warily, looking up at the high arch of the ceiling, and at the undamaged panelling.

They quickly took in the group of sullen residents, reading not indignation or relief on their faces, but collective guilt. McCullough paused near Weiss. This was a time for Weiss to say something, but he remained silent, returning McCullough's stare. McCullough was probably good at recognizing reluctant witnesses.

"Second casualty?" he said, indignant at having to ask.

"First room to the left," Weiss said without expression.

The firemen went through the glass doors to the corridor, pausing to examine the abraded glass on the outside of the door panels. At last, McCullough followed them, deciding to let the scene tell the story.

"Be careful near the stairs," Weiss called after them.

The two medics who had accompanied the fire department personnel laid their packs beside Noah, and before they even acknowledged Eric, they knelt to examine the sagging body in the wheelchair. Weiss heard one say, "He's alive," and they deployed a small respirator.

Eric looked like he was going to say something, but then he looked at Weiss and shrugged. One of the medics, a young man with a shock of yellow hair, got to his feet and noticed the way that Eric stood nearby with his arms crossed.

"You the doctor?"

"Yes."

"We're going to bring in a backboard, immobilize him, and strap him flat—let him down from the balcony. You all right with that?"

"Yes."

Weiss listened to Eric's curt answers in disbelief. And yet he understood the tactic. He'd seen it used by white collar criminals and lawyers: say as little as possible. Don't get involved. Later there would be attorneys and formal statements. As far as this physician was concerned, Noah was already dead.

Eventually, Toni Beal and Tom Krosnow were in the library, too, recovering their dignity after an awkward and unpracticed crawl up the fire ladder. At the top, the clamber onto the balcony hadn't been pretty. Toni took the time to take off her coat, throw it on a chair, and wipe her brow.

"You all right, Eilert?"

Weiss tried to remember what a professional officer of the law would do and say in this situation. The trouble was, he was a desperate man about to lie to one of his only friends. In practical terms, that meant his mind was racing, trying to limit the falsehoods to what was absolutely necessary.

"I'm fine. How is Prem?"

"I've sent him off to a hospital so they can check out his ankle and clean his abrasions. He wasn't happy about it. He would have climbed that damn ladder if I'd let him."

Weiss felt his chest swell with gratitude. "Thanks for playing the grown-up again, Toni."

Toni nodded slowly, then looked around at the quiet room full of tidy undamaged furniture and subdued people. If there was any scent in the room, it was disinfectant. Merrit had remained in a chair and Ruth was staring at the embers in the fireplace from hers. Only Eric looked wary, glancing repeatedly at Weiss, waiting to hear what he would say.

"So," Toni said, waiting. "Two casualties, you said?"

Weiss indicated Noah in his wheelchair. His head was back, his mouth agape, but he might have been sleeping.

"This is Noah Goodwyn." Weiss indicated Eric, who was listening carefully. "His physician tells me Noah's now brain dead. Dr. Hudson here will tell you…the rest."

Toni gave a slight nod to Tom, who immediately went to Noah's side and began whispering to the young medic.

"Dr. Hudson?" Toni said, remembering him from her earlier interview.

Eric could have been a showman. He stepped forward, his medical arrogance fully in place. Without being asked, he said, "I have a fully dated set of EEG printouts that will show that Mr. Goodwyn was catatonic and in a pattern of precarious and wildly fluctuating neural events. He could have flatlined at any time."

Toni frowned. "But now? Was Noah even aware of what was happening to the house?"

"I would say, no, but…" He turned to Weiss and fixed him with a look that said, 'I dare you.' "Detective Weiss will affirm that Noah was gripping his chair and showing signs of distress right before his collapse. Have I got that right, Detective?"

Damn him, Weiss was thinking. But, he said, "Yes."

In that moment, he felt he was no better than Eric. And yet, every time he tried to think of something else to say, it seemed to lead towards a slippery slope.

Toni waited, expecting more from Weiss. "I believe Dr. Hudson administered a drug to Noah while I was here," Weiss said in a flat tone.

"Correct," Eric countered. "In an effort to stabilize Noah's condition. I judged he was in imminent danger of seizure. Unfortunately, it was too late to do anything for him."

Weiss said nothing, the silence corroding him from within. Ruth looked up from the fireplace but her expression was unreadable.

"He's still alive, all right," Tom Krosnow said, returning to Toni's side. "His breathing's shallow and his heartbeat is faint."

Toni turned to Eric. "Can he be moved, doctor?"

"He's clinically dead, Detective."

Toni's eyes were wide with disbelief. "And the other casualty?"

Weiss took a slow breath. "Come on, Toni."

He led the way out into the corridor and towards the stairs, stopping at Clemmie's door. It was open and the interior was ablaze with light from the fire response team. The yellow slickers of chief McCullough and a fireman glowed in the small space. The fireman had a compressed air mask hanging loosely from his neck.

"Brace yourself, Toni," Weiss said quietly.

Seeing Toni in the doorway, the two firemen stepped aside to reveal Clemmie's body on the bed. Sheets had been peeled back like puff pastry, exposing a barely recognizable body that could have been shaped out of pressed charcoal.

Chief McCullough gave a gentle kick to a pitted and dissolving box on the wall. "Vented natural gas space heater. That's my first thought." He was speaking directly to Toni, his voice tightly controlled, and he was ignoring Weiss. "I've never seen anything like this, though. If it was a gas fire, why isn't there evidence of an explosion? And there isn't even residual heat in the remains." His eyes shifted briefly to Weiss. "What are those people telling you?"

Toni turned back to Weiss. "What *are* they telling me, Eilert?"

"They're telling you they can't explain any of this."

"And *you*, Eilert?"

This was the worst part: looking in Toni's eyes, knowing that any attempt at the truth would get them all into a morass of psychiatric evaluations and deflected blame. Even Toni would suffer because she cared about him. And so Weiss clung to the narrow raft of ignorance he was on and said, "How *could* I possibly explain something like this?"

Toni wasn't buying it, but Weiss was saved by another fireman who had come up from downstairs on a portable extension ladder. His yellow pants with their reflective bands were coated in ash and there was a slight tremolo of fear in his voice.

"There's damage in several parts of the house," he said. "It's like somebody went crazy with a flamethrower, 'cept there's no chemical smell. There are other places where it looks more like a century of neglect. Damage, but no evidence of burning. Damnedest thing."

Toni and Weiss turned and went back to the library in silence, and Weiss knew what she and Tom would have to do: write something down and sign it. He'd have to do that, too—and Prem.

Mercifully, Tom and Toni went over to talk to the others, taking down notes independently. Weiss had no idea what Ruth and Merrit were telling the detectives, but if either of the women were talking about giant backless beasts, it wasn't evident in their solemn body language. Weiss had the odd feeling that the truth was the one thing that posed no threat to him. The women hadn't seen the monstrous thing, and Eric wasn't about to blow his credibility just when he really needed it. Only Merrit glanced at Weiss, quickly turning away when he caught her eye.

Left to his own devices, Weiss wandered over to the large table beside Noah. The medics already had him on a long blue board with his head and neck stabilized. They were busy strapping his body down, the blanket still mercifully over his waist and legs, so they paid no attention when Weiss opened the black case that Eric had left on the table.

Joshi had said that there were two vials inside. Now there was one, and it was clearly labelled benzodiazepine, followed by numerals and letters that distinguished this variation of the common schedule IV drug. Weiss put the little case down, and, moving away from the table, he looked at Eric's back as he was speaking to Toni. Eric's arms were crossed in indignation. He wasn't used to being cross-examined. Weiss noted the lines of the physician's suit. The pockets were visible but they looked flat, and the contours of his jacket were perfect.

For her part, Toni concentrated on Eric's face. She was a pro and had no doubt recognized the hostility and evasiveness of her witness.

Continuing to pace slowly about the room, Weiss let his mind and his eyes range over the furnishings and walls. The missing vial didn't appear to be on him, so Eric would have had to hide the small glass bottle somewhere in this room. Weiss imagined Eric, not so many minutes ago, probably when Weiss and Toni had been in Clemmie's room—imagined him moving about, not wishing to attract attention. Eric would choose a spot somewhere out of sight, beneath or above eye level. If he had bent down, someone would have wondered what he was doing, Merrit or Ruth probably.

On the shelves, behind the books, perhaps? But the bookshelves were hard to get at because of the displaced furniture. There were two drawers in a sideboard within easy reach, but they were also easy to search.

Above, then? Weiss glanced up as Eric would have done, and once more, the arching hammered beams led his eyes down to their supporting pilasters. Each was topped with a carved capital, but because of the furniture, there was only one of these carved capitals within easy reach—the one he'd pointed out to Prem. Of course, it bore the familiar sculptural trope, a pineapple, a carved wooden pineapple with criss-crossed oval carving imitating the structure of the fruit. The prominent leaf shape on top with its characteristic overlapping spears jutted up, offering a narrow wedge of space hidden from the room.

Weiss gave a quick look at the others, then reached up. In the space behind the spiky leaves, his fingertips brushed a small bottle. He dropped his hand immediately, leaving the bottle in place.

Here it was—another crisis of conscience: the clear suppression of evidence. Weiss had no illusions about it; this was the evidence that could potentially link Eric to MorwynBIO: the barcoded vial. And then what?

It could be a link to James Krauss, too, but Weiss didn't believe for a moment Eric had murdered Krauss. He knew who had done that—or rather, *what* had done that. It was as plain as the trail of bleached grass crossing the lawn and delving into the woodlands.

Had James been running from the thing? Or was he just hiding in the woods when the homunculus settled out of the air, draining Krauss's skin and bones just like it had Clemmie's?

CHAPTER THIRTY-THREE

That morning, Carly was working from her living room table in the house on Lakeshore Road. It made no sense to keep her condo on Maple when this lovely old house was closer to her work and mortgage-free. Still, it was an act of faith to move here—faith that she would come to terms with that little office down the hall. She believed that she would find some peace with it in time, but for now, the dining room table was an adequate desk. It's not as though she entertained much company.

Of course, Evan was another matter. He'd stayed over again last night and she could hear him clattering around in the kitchen as she worked. His own career, which alternated between consulting and flaunting his good looks on television, allowed him frequent free time, which he used to seek out and lay siege to Carly.

Last night had been nice—not just because of Evan's attention, but because she had slept well afterwards; no bad dreams or morning anxieties had come out of the darkness of her bedroom.

Carly smiled at the thought of Evan padding around her kitchen in his socks when her phone played a little tune.

She looked at the screen and answered. "Hello, Detective."

Weiss's voice sounded tired. "Hello, Carly. I may be on the clock, but this call is informal and off the record, so to speak. The fact is, I'd very much like to call on you. Would that be all right?"

"Of course you can. I hope we haven't got too much history, Eilert. You can be charming when you're relaxed."

She could hear the quick breath that told her he was smiling. "Do you mind my asking where you are?" he asked.

"I'm at the Lakeshore house. Are you all right?"

"Yes, but my partner is at home on short-term disability, and I could use a sympathetic ear. I've lost touch with most of my old friends. My wife managed to alienate a lot of them."

"I'm sorry to hear that. Maybe you could tell me about that sometime."

"Perhaps. I could try if you like...but this is about Noah Goodwyn."

"Yes, I pieced together what happened with the help of my staff and that article on the CBC website."

"Y-es. That stuff about gas mains and flash fires—none of that matters; what matters is that Noah Goodwyn and his care-giver are both dead, and once again, I find myself tasked with writing their story. Well, assisting anyway."

"And you need my help?"

"As a sounding board, at least."

Carly realized she was in an awkward position. "Actually, Evan Favaro is here at the moment."

"I see." Weiss didn't sound flustered. "I only need around an hour of your time. Do you remember the park where we...ah... discussed your father's passing?"

"Yes, I get it. We talked about *his* final story there, didn't we?"

"There—in say, a half an hour?"

"O-kay…"

There was a silence, and then the call ended.

Evan walked in and put a coffee mug down beside her. On the mug was written, "Hyphenated. Non-hyphenated. Now, that's Irony."

"Love that coffee machine," Evan smiled. "It's idiot-proof." He waited for her to say something clever. "Hey, I just gave you an opening for a snide reply and you're letting it lie there. What's wrong?"

"Oh, sorry. How about: 'Don't worry. You'll find a way.' Kidding. It seems I have to go out for an hour or so. I have to meet Detective Weiss."

Evan slid into the chair beside her. "Weiss again? He's not done with us, is he?"

"It's just a little talk in the park. It's a nice day. Well, at least it's stopped raining and it's not so cold."

"Not the park again. Are you serious?" He struck a pose for a moment, but when she didn't react, he said, "Fine, I'll get dressed."

She reached across the table and squeezed his hand. "Weiss sounds like he needs to unload. I think I need to go alone. The park is our cone of silence, you see."

"I know what you're saying. After the Marcella Cole business, Weiss used the park as a way of working out a viable story with you in private. We were both up against a wall after Cole got shot. But Weiss is still a cop and he deals with mayhem and death. Are you sure you want to let that stuff into your life? He's got nothing hanging over you this time. You don't have to go."

"I'm no A.L. Rouhl—but I'm a reporter and, God help me, I'm a writer."

"You're also a soft touch, kid. I don't really understand what you think you owe that policeman. He's not…pressuring you, is he?" He had almost said 'blackmailing,' and Carly could tell.

She bristled and started to say something, but Evan stopped

her. "Look, I'm sorry. Go on and talk to the lonely soul. Just remember, I'm waiting back here—and, what did you call it? Stewing in lust?"

The cloud passed, Carly laughed and kissed his hand.

———

Carly was sitting on one of the park swings when Weiss arrived on foot. Everything was wet and she'd had to wipe the seat with a tissue. Weiss was wearing his jacket without a topcoat and it was open to reveal his buttoned vest. His tie was different—not the green Black Watch tartan he favoured.

"No children?" Weiss said, looking at the water beaded slide and climbing bars. "I suppose our recent spate of bad weather has been keeping everyone indoors." Carly thought Weiss looked worn out. "There's something lonely about a playground with no children."

"Let me turn it around on you, Eilert. Are *you* still lonely? Is that what this is about?"

Weiss grinned, and raised an eyebrow, determined to make light of her question. "Well, there's been talk at the station. You wouldn't think police personnel would be matchmaking types."

Carly laughed. "Good for them. I look forward to updates on that. There will be updates, won't there? I mean, I'd like to hear from you."

Weiss nodded, "So far, there's barely even been a date, never mind an update."

"Well, get on with it, Eilert."

He gave a little laugh and looked out at the lake. He gripped the chain of the next swing with his gloved hand. "Do you remember I told you how much writing a police incident report is like storytelling?"

"Ah, yes. You're faced with telling a story again, and I'm the daughter of A.L. Rouhl, the great storyteller. But why here again, in the park? There's a nice Panne Fresco down the road."

"Well now, I'm not sure. I think I may be turning into a superstitious person. This park worked for me once before when I was in an impossible position. So, here I am. I'm hoping the mindset will work again. Besides, it's quite a pleasant spot in the spring, isn't it; nice view of the lake, custom seating?"

As if to demonstrate, Carly stuck out her legs and gave a creditable swing back and forth, smiling.

"Mind you," Weiss said, "last time we were negotiating. This time, I think what I need is a confessor. You see…Noah Goodwyn died because I allowed myself to be distracted. I took a phone call from my partner, and while my back was turned, Dr. Eric Hudson gave Noah Goodwyn a fatal overdose."

Carly searched his eyes, her own suffused with sympathy. Weiss pivoted on the chain and took the swing beside her.

"You'll get all wet," Carly said. His moustache seemed somehow funnier when he was holding onto a child's swing.

"I'm telling you things that no policeman should be telling a journalist. That's one of the reasons we're here, of course. I've got no business telling you this stuff and we both need to know it's between us and off the record."

"Deniability. I see. We worked out that protocol last time, didn't we? That bit about Noah being given an overdose wasn't in the news report. But you aren't seriously taking that on yourself. Eric Hudson did what he did. It's not your fault. You couldn't have stopped him."

Weiss turned to watch her eyes, grateful for the absolution, but then his gaze drifted to the cold lake. "The thing is, maybe if Eric hadn't killed Noah…"

In Carly's mind, a dark shape with exaggerated lips seemed to form. She twisted to look at him. "*You* might have had to?"

Weiss held onto the chains and hung his head.

The magical isolation of the lakefront playground made

Carly bold. "I understand more than you know. The thing you were afraid of—the big face, the fingers?"

He glanced up to stare at her. "How in God's name could you know about that?"

Carly felt a slight spark of fear at his reaction, but her trust in this oddly miscast policeman held. "I told you, I've been writing. It's in my story."

"But how could you possibly—"

"Look, Eilert, why don't we just keep this little understanding between us?"

"I don't think 'understanding' is the right word."

"Arrangement then. You tell me what you can, and I'll be your literary critic. So, where are you in all this?"

"Well, it all started with someone called James Krauss—for me, anyway. Krauss was, and remains, an unsolved death."

"But now you know how your James Krauss must have died?"

Weiss frowned, bewildered by her quick grasp. "Yes, I think so."

"But you can't write it up. So, you're going to write the report *around* what really happened?"

"Is that what I did with the death of Marcella Cole?"

"In the process, you got me out from under a lot of wrongful suspicion."

Weiss closed his eyes. "At the time, my superiors were suspicious of me, too, you know. The internal review people weren't sure I had gotten over my wife's suicide. But in the end, my report on Marcella Cole satisfied the evidence, and so it satisfied the superintendent."

"Can you do that with James Krauss? Satisfy the superintendent?"

"I'm not sure. I'm fond of saying that when you eliminate the impossible, what remains—however improbable—must be the truth."

"Sir Arthur Conan Doyle. Sherlock Holmes, if you prefer."

"Yes, I suppose that's where that comes from. The thing is, Noah Goodwyn's suffering and his tortured revenge on Krauss are the impossible here. And if you eliminate that…then you've got to cobble together something that passes for the truth."

"But isn't," Carly said.

Weiss gave her a baleful look but didn't say anything.

"Then Noah *was* being tortured?" Carly went on, looking shaken at this confirmation of her fears.

"You could call it that. He was being given a powerful drug. Hudson called it a dissociative. I don't know enough about the brain to explain this to you, but I've got this idea in my head that the drug was tormenting Noah's poor damaged personality, forcing him to lash out in the only way he could."

"At his tormentors."

"At his nurse. The poor woman who was with him most of the time while he suffered; at James Krauss, the friend who started it all by bringing the drug to the house; and Eric Hudson, the one who would show up regularly to stick a needle in Noah's IV. You see, that's it—Hudson knew he was going to be the next victim. That's why he killed Noah. In a crazy way, it really *was* self-defence on Eric's part. I can't say for sure, but he may have saved the lives of everyone in that room, including me."

"But you still have to account for Krauss's death."

"It's even more complicated than that. Technically, James Krauss's murder wasn't my case. I'm going to have to sit down with my friend Toni—it's her file—and advise her. What in God's name am I going to tell her?"

"I see. Here you are again, needing an ending for your story. One that will fit the evidence."

"And satisfy some idea of justice—don't forget that."

"What did we do last time, faced with the death of Marcella Cole?"

Weiss considered that for a moment. "We gave a kind of closure to the families of the people Marcella murdered, and we spared the innocent."

"Well, there you are then. Go and help your friend Toni do that: spare the innocent."

He squeezed his eyes shut at that idea, looking pained. "Hard to believe, but it was easier last time. You really *were* innocent. This time, I think they all have something to answer for."

Carly waited. When Weiss didn't explain, she said, "It's nice of you to debrief me like this. That's what this is, isn't it?"

Weiss got up and looked down at Carly. "Yes, but I'm also here to thank you."

"Ah, because I tipped you off that Noah was a tortured soul?"

"Well, yes, that. But, I also wanted to thank you for helping out Prem."

Carly broke eye contact and leaned back as though waiting for hands on her shoulder to push her into a high, arcing swing.

"Prem? Your partner? How did I help him?"

"He got pretty banged up in his fall, and it could have been a lot worse. After he phoned to tell me he was safe, I called in his location and asked dispatch to send him an ambulance. But, there was one on the scene minutes after he reached the lower terrace. I spoke to the 911 operator this morning. She sent that first ambulance out to Moreland House at 8:03. That's earlier than my request for help by about twenty minutes."

Carly held her pose, looking strangely glamorous with her hair blowing gently back over her shoulders.

Weiss allowed his gaze to drift from her to the indistinct horizon over the lake. "In fact, the first request for assistance is actually earlier than Prem's fall. Imagine my surprise."

Carly stared straight ahead. "Sounds crazy."

Weiss's voice seemed as far away as the horizon. "What I'm

saying is, the ambulance was dispatched before Prem and I needed help."

"You must have that wrong."

Weiss gave a gentle laugh. "In my business, cases often hinge on time discrepancies. I was able to find out that somebody named Cassandra phoned in that first distress call."

"A neighbour of the Morelands?"

Carly fought to maintain her charade of mild curiosity, but Weiss sensed she was troubled. "Prem's not much of a reader, Carly—not literature anyway, so the Cassandra reference was lost on him. But I'm sure a literary type like you would know the name. Cassandra was the prophetess, wasn't she? Greek mythology, right?"

Carly let the swing hang naturally and rubbed the wetness off her fingers. "Cassandra's curse was that her prophecies would never be believed. I mean, who *would* believe such a thing? If Cassandra was smart, she should have shut up."

Carly got up, Weiss taking her elbow to help.

"May I walk you back to your house?" he said.

Carly smiled her acceptance, and they made their way back across the damp grass towards the house where Evan still, presumably, stewed. They walked in an easy silence, as though leaving one another with unresolved questions was part of their arrangement. Arrangement, not understanding, she had said.

Weiss knew Antonia Beal wouldn't be so forgiving.

CHAPTER THIRTY-FOUR

Eilert Weiss drove a boring car, and it was getting old. He didn't use his own car much and he hadn't needed to impress anybody, so he hadn't gotten around to buying something more up to date. It got him to Prem Joshi's house in the Tyendaga neighbourhood in relative comfort, but it looked out of place with the late-model Hondas and Buicks of Joshi's neighbours.

Weiss hadn't been here before, but he knew Joshi's wife, Liana, was a prosperous optician, so the tasteful landscaping and elegant entranceway weren't a surprise.

A pretty teenager with bright, dark eyes and an asymmetrical bob let him in. He'd met Joshi's daughter and wife before. Joshi was proud of them both and showed them off at social gatherings. Weiss found Joshi lounging in an armchair by the front bay window, staking out his neighbours. His tension-wrapped ankle was elevated and his hands were lightly bandaged. He had a lidded water bottle that could have been a prop in a sci-fi movie.

"Have a seat, Eilert. You can watch the birds stealing me blind. I bought some Spanish moss to stuff those hanging baskets out there and the birds just help themselves for building their nests."

Weiss looked around. "You've built a nice nest for yourself, too." He accepted a chair that would have been Liana's. "Liana at work?"

"Saturday's her busiest day. Farah's been waiting on me hand and foot—her mother's orders, she says. She could probably make us tea if I explain the whole bag and string thing to her."

"No thanks. I have a feeling you've been over-caffeinating sitting here." Weiss admired the decor in envy, thinking of his small apartment. "You have a brass elephant," he said.

Joshi blinked. "So what? You doing an inventory of cultural clichés?"

"What I mean is that the elephant is *all* you've got. The rest of the house looks like something out of HGTV: tasteful and fashionable. What about all that stuff you said about pride in your cultural heritage?"

"Liana does all the decorating. Besides, I just laid that culture stuff on you because you were razzing me about never having been to Islamabad. So what's *your* place like? Edinburgh Castle, I suppose? Bagpipes over the mantle?"

"At least my hat was Harris Tweed."

Joshi frowned. "I thought that was English."

Weiss winced. "Oh, God, Prem. Give me strength."

"I knew a guy called Harris. *He* was English."

"Harris is a Scottish Island. Just don't, okay?"

"So, you came to make me feel better about my ankle?" Joshi shifted his leg on a soft hassock. "Big fail."

Weiss unbuttoned his coat and settled comfortably into Liana's chair. "I'm distracting you from thinking about your pain."

"My ankle only hurts when I try to pick up the elephant. Why are you really here?"

"Oh, I don't know. How about post traumatic stress?"

"Yours or mine?"

"I'm not sure. You're the one who dropped ten feet onto a moving platform."

"And you're the one who stayed and stared that bloody thing down." Joshi looked out at the tidy street and the greening lawns, but he didn't seem to be focussing on anything. "Why did it disappear anyway?"

Weiss rubbed his cheek. "Maybe Noah sensed we weren't the ones hurting him. We'll never know." He watched Joshi's face, aware of his partner's ability to mask concern.

"I've been thinking about the Moreland house and the terrace down below," Weiss said. "All the damage. That thing must have been showing up here and there for days, maybe weeks, sucking the life out of anything nearby to make itself real." He paused, hooking his thumbs in his vest pockets. "And I think it went out into the woods after James Krauss."

Joshi looked around quickly. "Krauss died the way Clemmie did—like a desiccated mummy in a museum?"

"And probably only a few weeks ago. Only, maybe poor James was *running* when he died."

They looked at one another for a long moment. Joshi grabbed his water bottle and took a gulp.

Finally, Weiss asked, "How are you processing it all? Nightmares?"

Joshi's mask of indifference was back. "Strangely enough, no. You?"

"Not about the homunculus, no. After what I went through with my wife's suicide, I'm not all that enthusiastic about staying alive."

Joshi frowned at him. "So, what are *your* nightmares about?"

Toying with the brass elephant, Weiss appeared to choose his words carefully. "It's the future that really scares me. After the Marcella Cole case...and Noah's death...I don't think I'm a detective anymore. Detectives disclose the truth—I seem to be in the business of disguising it."

"And you don't think what you're doing is important?" Joshi pushed himself higher in his chair. "Let me tell you something, Eilert. I've moved around a bit more than you have. I was up in Orillia for five years and Gravenhurst before that. There was a guy in Orillia; Macklin was his name—Mac. Big lumbering cop, but smart. Introverted. I never got to know him well. Maybe nobody did, but it was generally known that he earned his keep.

"There wasn't any policy or anything written down, but Mac seemed to get most of the unsolvable cases, the ones we all knew weren't going anywhere, and he kept this box of files that we all joked about—the dead files. When his shift was over, you'd sometimes see Mac with that box open on his desk, laying out folders, and moving them around as though he was looking for a pattern that no one else could see."

Weiss grunted. "I bet the poor son of a bitch was miserable."

"No. It wasn't like that. Mac was a shy, kind man with a wife and kids, and one way or another, he gave some of the victims' families a sense of comfort and even closure—when none of the rest of us could."

As he remembered this, Joshi's gaze rose to the white popcorn ceiling. "And then there was Clendenning in Peterborough. I never knew him personally, but we'd hear his name sometimes because he was always consulting with the smaller regional divisions."

"What did he consult on?"

"Well, not to put too fine a point on it, weird shit. Sound familiar?"

"I'm...not sure what you're telling me."

Joshi shook his head like an impatient lecturer. "I'm saying that even the most boring cops—I'm thinking of the superintendent—know there's a lot of dark stuff out there that never gets written up. He knows that somebody who's really clever with paperwork finds a way of tidying up the record, protecting the innocent, and comforting the families. Now, isn't that better than just shrugging it all off and moving on?"

Weiss thought for a moment. "But isn't that what we'll be doing? Shrugging it off? I'm not sure I see the distinction."

"I'll give you a small example," Joshi said. "My wife wanted to know how I got hurt, so I told her I jumped from a carriage that was falling to bits around us. Now Liana keeps saying I should sue Ruth Moreland for failing to maintain her property."

Weiss nodded. "Ruth Moreland has lots of money and no reasonable explanation for the damage. She'd be an easy mark."

"But we *don't* sue her, do we? We see the reality no one else sees. Okay, maybe she's responsible for what happened to us, to Clemmie, to Krauss. Or maybe she was just a sister taking desperate steps to save her brother, stealing from herself in the process. We get to sit in judgement because—"

"Because we're the weird squad?"

"Dammit, Eilert," Joshi sighed. "I'm trying to make you feel better."

"Big fail." But then Weiss gave him one of those unlocalized smiles that suffused his whole face. "But thanks for trying."

CHAPTER THIRTY-FIVE

It was dark, and the parking lot at the District Three station was shiny with melting sleet. Eilert Weiss's car wasn't a classic model or a carefully restored vintage chassis—it was just tired. It didn't have much rust, but the finish was dull and even the most broad-minded car enthusiast wouldn't have palpated over the humped rear fuselage and grinning chrome grill. Inside, it was somehow tidy and neglected at the same time. It was on its way to becoming the car that died of indifference.

Detective Toni Beal sat on the passenger side, her long legs and black suede flats folded to one side as she turned and sighed. "This is a new one, even for us Eilert. What are we doing meeting in this old heap of yours?"

Weiss looked out at the windswept parking lot. The rain had turned to wispy snow that would swirl with the air currents, melting as soon as it touched the blacktop.

"I learned this on the job," he said. "Sometimes you need to be able to hash things out quietly when you know no one in authority is listening in." He gestured at the dash. "Look. No microphone, no police band radio. Hell, I can't even get the FM to work anymore."

"Fine. I get it. This is just between you and me. So, is this where you tell me what the fuck really happened in that house? I'm the sorry so-and-so who's got to write the report this time."

"Yeah, I know, and I thought you might need some help with that."

"No shit. So, what happened to Noah Goodwyn? The paramedics strapped him to a backboard and let him down off the balcony, but they said his heart gave out before they even got him to the hospital."

Weiss nodded solemnly. "Dr. Hudson's given you his account of Noah's brain death. Did it sound plausible?"

"Who am I to argue with a doctor?" Toni sounded bitter. "I didn't understand half of the jargon Eric Hudson used on me; stuff about the antagonism of the glutamate receptors. It all comes down to this: Noah was in precarious health, and he passed away last night from complications from his drug use over the years. Hudson says Noah's EEG printouts show a pattern of declining brain function." Toni closed her eyes, trying to remember Eric's callous words. "...generalized delta slowing."

"Okay. Hudson's the only one who can testify to Noah's condition, and he's got abnormal EEGs to back him up."

"Do I order an autopsy on Noah's body?"

Weiss didn't answer directly. "Who stands to gain from Noah's death, Toni?"

"His daughter, Alicia."

"She goes by Sammy."

"Yeah, we met her. Kind of weird, but a nice enough kid—if all that money doesn't drive her nuts. She'll hire a business management team and sit back and try to come up with something to do with her life."

Weiss nodded agreement. "So far, she's making a name for herself as an artist. It will be interesting to see how much of her father's creativity she's inherited."

Toni went on. "Merrit Simpson gets a comfortable annuity for life, and a woman living in Las Vegas gets some money."

"That's Sammy's birth mother. What about Eric? Eric's motive for hastening Noah's death would be what?"

"Well, nothing. He's alienated Ruth, so now he's out in the cold. No more retainers as a medical advisor, no more spiritual advice."

"Sounds to me like you just talked yourself out of an autopsy."

"Jesus, Eilert, is *that* how you work? What about that Clemmie woman, the nurse?"

"What's the fire department telling you about Clemmie?"

"The best McCullough can come up with is she was killed by a flash fire. That's what you told them, and nobody's disagreeing with you—yet. Some kind of chemical fire. There was no smoke damage or smell, so it must have been incredibly hot and fast. All they've got to work with is ash."

"Did they say what kind of chemical was to blame?"

"The house is old and it still has natural gas space heaters throughout. Their best guess so far is localized leaks of natural gas, enough to sustain a flame but not enough for an explosion. That could explain damage in other parts of the house and grounds, too. The house is a mess. The terrace, the cable car— all of it.

"Frankly, I don't give a damn about any of that. Ruth More- land has money and she can afford to rebuild. Chief McCul- lough says the ignition source had to be electrical, but he thinks the whole scenario stinks."

Toni looked like she was about to say more, but she was silenced by Weiss's hand on her arm.

"Look, the fire investigators are going to put together the best guess they can. That's their job. Stay out of it, Toni. Keep your head down and let McCullough make his report. It's his problem, not yours."

"God, you were nearly killed. Don't you want to know for sure what caused this?"

Weiss didn't say anything so she kept searching his eyes until it dawned on her. "Wait a minute. You *don't* want to know, do you? What aren't you telling me?"

Weiss made a 'what the hell' gesture with his hand. "What *am* I going to tell you? That Prem and I were attacked by a monster that materialized out of thin air?"

"Don't you fucking dare tell me anything like that. You know how hard I worked to keep you on the force."

Toni's hand was draped on the seatback; Weiss reached up and touched it.

"Thanks, Toni. Thanks for making this easier. You know I love you, right?"

Toni's face flushed with annoyance and something else, and she drew her hand away. "Of course I do. And I love you, too, but don't tell my husband I said that."

"Look, Toni, you have no real motive for foul play here. The nurse's death is tragic, but unless the fire department finds an accelerant in the ashes of her room, you've got no case there either." He was silent for a moment and decided to take a risk because it was Toni he was talking to. "They won't find one."

She stared at him. "How the hell do you know *that*?"

"Fine, I couldn't know that. Just wait until the fire department gives its final report."

"What about James Krauss? Tom and I are investigating his death, remember."

Weiss looked out at the parking lot and the flags pulsing in the breeze. "I believe Krauss was stealing actual drug samples from MorwynBIO. And I believe Eric Hudson was using them on Noah."

Toni nodded. "Tom and I followed up with the drug company, too. We went over the list of drugs that Krauss might potentially have had access to. There's only one—a new derivation of benzodiazepine that might have relevance to Noah's condition. It hasn't even finished clinical trials yet, but it's a whole lot like the drug Eric *says* he was using. The whole case is a fog like that."

Weiss said, "Eric Hudson is doing a pretty good job of keeping it that way."

Toni glanced down at her door. "Jesus, Eilert. This is a manual window opener. You do *know* these no longer exist in the civilized world?" She turned the handle and the window squeaked down. "I hope you didn't take Heddy out in this." The wind wafted cold, damp air into the stuffy interior. A few wet snowflakes melted on the arm of Toni's coat. "You're suggesting I call Noah's death natural causes?"

Weiss shook his head wearily. "I don't know how natural it could be with all the stuff in Noah's veins from Hudson's therapy—and maybe even Merrit's tampering. Eric thinks he can call it 'complications' brought about by the medication and Noah's years of substance abuse."

"Then what about Clemmie? When they tried to move her, all they got was ash and carbonized bones. There will be a few fragments left to examine—and to bury."

"Just like James Krauss."

Toni was wide-eyed, ready to open her mouth, but Weiss looked away and she hesitated.

Weiss asked, "So, Clemmie's relatives and loved ones will have questions?"

"No children or living parents. The husband who left her after her aneurysm lives on the west coast and doesn't seem all that interested. He sounds like a real piece of work." Toni lowered her lashes. "But what about justice? Doesn't somebody have to pay for all this?"

Weiss rested his hands on the steering wheel. "And who would that be? Eric, because he was treating Noah with an experimental drug? Noah was already brain damaged and his sister was encouraging Eric to try desperate measures. Merrit? Whatever she was giving Noah, she did it in a misguided attempt to give her husband some release. The Noah that Merrit knew was an escape artist who spent a lifetime trying to transcend his body."

For a moment, Toni looked out at the wet snow swirling around a light standard like fireflies. "So, we're back to James Krauss."

"A cold case," Weiss answered. "Everybody figured James was a fugitive. Well, congratulations, Toni. You found him."

Toni sighed and looked out at the fine snow turning to beads of water on the hood. "Honestly, Eilert, if you're going to take women out, you need a new ride. And consult with me before you buy a car. I'll give you a few tips on what a woman wants to see." She looked about. "Hint: this isn't it."

"Always watching out for me. Thanks, Toni."

CHAPTER THIRTY-SIX

Carly had left the living room TV on while she made breakfast with Evan. The sound of a morning news show was droning away, but off in the kitchen, neither of them was paying attention. Indy, however, enjoying the fireside rug, raised an indifferent eye, drawn by the creeping text that moved across the bottom of the screen, so he was the only one who saw the news anchor.

"Our reporter, Valerie Bruner, is in Halton this morning with a report on a local landmark. Val, there's a lot of disappointment in North Burlington."

Indy blinked at the change of scene.

"Yes, Casey. I'm here with Burlington Fire Chief, Mark McCullough, and behind me, you can see the beautiful old rural railway station called Ridgeway Heights. Local preservationist groups had high hopes of saving this abandoned and disused station by moving it to the site of the Halton County Radial Railway Museum. As you may know, that wonderful attraction in nearby Milton has been used in several film shoots and the public is welcomed there each spring. Chief McCullough, the fundraising plans to move the railway station are being abandoned. Could you tell us why?"

"Yes, uh, the Ontario Fire Marshall has ruled that the building would no longer be safe to transport, and I have had to inform the group of local railway enthusiasts that their plans are no longer viable."

"And why this change, Chief?"

"Well, our most recent examination of the station interior shows evidence of significant damage. Our best assessment is deliberate arson. It appears that large sections of the floor and benches in the old waiting room area of the station have collapsed. It's not clear how the damage was inflicted, although some kind of controlled burning is most likely."

"Controlled?"

"Yes, the damage to the structure of the building is substantial but seems to have been limited to specific parts of the interior. Clean, focussed carbonizing of this sort is consistent with the use of a device such as a propane torch."

"Thank you, Chief. As our viewers can see, much of the exterior of the old station appears saveable and preservationists say they still have hopes of removing some vignettes of early railway travel such as the ticket booth and this classic track signal beside us. Chief McCullough, what is the historical significance of the site?"

"It was, uh, built in the early nineteen-twenties to service a mansion here on the escarpment: Moreland House. The abandoned station is a pleasant walk from the house, which is still in private hands. Of course, only members of the family and their guests have been able to walk to the site, and it was hoped that the new location would allow the public to experience the nostalgic charm of Ridgeway Heights."

"Think of that, Casey. This classic wooden structure on an old spur line made the building of the nearby mansion possible and allowed its wealthy family easy access to the glamorous social life of Toronto and Guelph. Here's hoping that some vestige of that romantic era can live again in a new location. This is Valerie Bruner reporting live from Ridgeway Heights in North Burlington. Back to you, Casey."

To Indy, the voices on the television held no interest. He was used to the babble—it was such a *noisy* house. Most of the shouts and murmurs came, at all hours of the day and night, from the old man's office at the end of the hall. Sometimes, it was the old man himself.

Indy had no difficulty shutting out the sweet talk and occasional chuckle from the kitchen either, but in the middle of that, he recognized his name, so he got up dutifully and padded off, hoping there might be snacks there.

The End

ABOUT THE AUTHOR

Doug Cockell was born in Edinburgh, Scotland and did graduate work in Literature with acclaimed novelist and playwright Robertson Davies at the University of Toronto. Doug has taught Literature, Art, and Media Studies in Oakville and Burlington and was awarded the McLuhan Distinguished Teacher Medal for showing the common visual language shared by illustration, the movies and computers. He has offered courses through The University of Toronto, Brock University, and The Art Gallery of Burlington. In addition to being an author, Doug is an accomplished artist who came to art through his love of the great Twentieth Century illustrators, delighted by their charm and whimsy as well as their skill.

Requiem For Noah is the second novel in the Requiem Series. Remember to add this author to your watch list so you don't miss future mysteries.

Doug enjoys hearing from his readers and he'd love to know what you thought of Book 2 in the Requiem Series. You can reach him via email at douglascockell@gmail.com